IN A FLASH

IN A FLASH

a lesbian romance novel

Kris Rugg

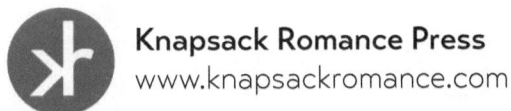

Knapsack Romance Press
www.knapsackromance.com

ISBN-13: 979-8-9861534-0-7 (e-book edition)
ISBN-13: 979-8-9861534-1-4 (paperback edition)

Cover design by: Kris Rugg
Printed in the United States of America

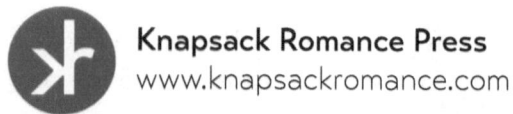

Knapsack Romance Press
www.knapsackromance.com

To all the tenderhearted ones who love sappy tears and beautiful connections: this is for you.

Chapter 1

Fifteen minutes early and twenty minutes late, that was always the difference between Mae and Cabot. Mae arrived early at the cafe to study the menu, so she wouldn't be caught off-guard when she needed to order. She hated the anxious feeling that built in her chest as soon as the barista asked what she wanted. It felt like she was immediately inconveniencing the staff as she attempted to decipher the differences between a macchiato, latte, and Americano (wasn't it all just coffee?). Mae settled on a vanilla latte; it was simple enough that she didn't feel like a burden to the overworked, high-octane barista who cupped her hand around her ear to hear Mae's soft voice over the din. Feeling awkward and unsure of where to stand while she waited for her drink, Mae surveyed the crowded room in search of a quiet place to sit. Of course, it needed to be close enough to the door that Cabot would see her when he came in but far enough away that the bitterly cold grip of winter's icy fingers wouldn't reach her every time the door opened. Drink in hand, she navigated through the throngs until she found two comfy, recently vacated chairs. Bundled up, Mae crawled into one of the overstuffed armchairs, slipped off her wet and muddy boots, tucked her legs underneath her, and took out her drawing pad.

On her walk over to Slate Cafe, she'd spotted a migrating hawk and wanted to get down a sketch while the image was fresh in her mind. It had soared overhead without a sound, graceful and light. It astounded her how these small aviators traveled across the entire continent each year, visiting places she only dreamed of going.

Mae took out her colored pencils and bent forward until her face was within inches of her drawing pad. The curling pages rustled as she furiously scribbled across the page. Long elegant wings, gray-blue head, reddish back and wingtips, and distinctive markings around the eyes took shape and breathed life on the page. Engrossed in hues of rust, inky black, cream, and blue, she tuned out everything: the grinding, whistling, and screeching of the espresso machine, names being called, and the door chiming as caffeine-addicted pedestrians collected their drug of choice and braved the bitter winds again. All of it faded away. She imagined her bird gliding on warm winds, soaring over the quaking aspens of Colorado, down through the arches of Utah, and maybe even into the stunning desert landscapes of Arizona. Out where the sun touched every inch of land, where blue skies held endless possibilities, and where a magnificent raptor could soar without bounds. Where one could stretch out and feel rejuvenated by the brilliant sunlight, warmth, and endless possibilities and adventures. She sighed as she looked up at the only stoplight in town, its blinking light encased in the usual gray morning fog that weighed heavily and made this sleepy town feel even dozier. Equally gray slush clung to the sidewalk in sloppy piles mirroring the drab sky as winter refused to relinquish its cold hold on the town.

Southwest Harbor was a small town located off the coast of Maine whose inhabitants survived each year as salt-encrusted lobstermen or caretakers for the small mansions owned by the ridiculously wealthy summer folk. In the winter, for the few brief hours that the sun was above the horizon, the sky and ground both took on a muddled gray color she could only describe as blah. The transition from night to day and back into night again was so gradual that by and large it was anyone's guess what time it was. Instead, around here people moved with the tides, having long been accustomed to bowing to the bitter and unforgiving sea that was the lifeblood and livelihood for most. After having spent her entire life within 200 miles of this exact location, she'd grown used to the seasonal shifts, the ebbing and flowing of boats in the harbor, the rush of visitors who flocked to the coastal town during the long summer days, the temperamental seas, and the crusty (sometimes crustacean) locals.

A warmth radiated nearby, taking her mind off her wild daydreams. Joy filled her heart as she looked up into a pair of warm brown eyes twinkling down at her. Cabot. His huge hand engulfed her shoulder, and happiness filled his soul as he tilted his head back and laughed. Mae leaped to her feet and into Cabot's arms, letting her drawing pad and colored pencils tumble to the floor with a clatter. His towering height and cuddly teddy bear figure completely swallowed her whole as he picked her up and held her tight. He was warmth personified; the kind of person who saw you for exactly who you were within a moment of meeting you, and embraced you wholly. After a few long minutes, Cabot set Mae down and the two of them stood holding hands and looking each other over. It had been a long month since they'd last seen each other.

"Coffee," Cabot said and spun on his heel, taking long strides toward the counter to procure additional hot beverages for what would likely be a long catch-up conversation. He moved deftly through the throngs with a confidence and ease Mae envied. Looking back over his shoulder to where Mae sat, Cabot chuckled to himself, again remembering the sight of his friend as he entered. As usual, she was lost in her world, one colored pencil held sideways between her front teeth, three others in her left hand for easy access to rotate in as she worked methodically across the page. A smudge of graphite smeared along the side of her nose, her short, curly auburn mop unruly and askew, hazel-green eyes equally focused and glazed over, and that impossibly deep dimple peeking out when she smiled at whatever thoughts were coursing through her mind.

Cabot returned to the table with two, nearly overflowing lattes, never spilling a precious drop. "You look amazing, Mae. Or, should I say a-Mae-zing?" He held his mouth wide open and looked at her expectantly as if to say "You see what I did there? Aren't you proud of me?" It wasn't his first pun, his worst, or his last, but it was his goofy face that always got her. He was like an expectant child waiting for praise or recognition. Mae rolled her eyes but grinned at her best friend. She had missed his easy, positive energy and the sunshine that followed him around wherever he went.

"No, really," he continued, his joy not dimmed by her lack of laughter. "You look more like you. More centered. Stronger. And happier. It's good to have you back." Cabot never held back on compliments nor on showing his true feelings for his friends, and he had no better friend than Mae. She smiled meekly and blushed. It had been a long time since she felt this good. It felt tentative, but with every passing day, she felt a bit more like herself. Of course, Cabot would notice; he was keenly aware of the emotions and struggles Mae had wrestled with over the years.

"So, how was your trip? What did you see? Where did you go? What did you do?" Mae questioned. Uncomfortable in the limelight, she returned the focus to Cabot.

For the last month, Cabot had traveled up and down the west coast, visiting friends, checking out the sights, and experiencing some amazing cuisine. During the spring every year, when winter in Maine lingered on and the gray sameness ate away at one's soul and sanity, Cabot escaped the dreariness, traveling across the country, living out of a suitcase and rental car, and experiencing something other than rural life. Mae longed to tag along but had never been free to join. Instead, she lived for these moments when he wove wonderful tales about his hilarious and beautiful adventures.

"Did you meet anyone? Go on any dates? Fall in love with any sweet and sexy men?" Mae asked hopefully, ever the romantic.

Cabot laughed wholeheartedly again, filling Mae's whole body with joy. There was something about Cabot that made you feel happiness and sunshine bubble up from every part inside you; as if he were wrapping you in a warm hug with every chuckle. For years she'd watched as hopeless visitors, typically older ladies and young men, fell in love with Cabot's charm and easy joy, though he never seemed to notice the effect he had on those around him. She could count the number of gay people who lived on the island on a hand and a half, and Cabot was the only one she wanted to have anything to do with anymore. Of course, there were the tourists who swung through for lobster and a "Main-ah" experience, but even then, the rainbow population was limited.

She'd met Cabot fifteen years earlier, when they were freshmen in college, both away from home for the first time. Though looking back, Bangor didn't count as "away from home," considering she could get from her dorm room to her childhood bedroom in about an hour. Mae felt completely out of her depth on campus, away from everything she knew. Even as an awkward scrawny teen, still somewhere halfway through puberty, Cabot stuck out at orientation, his positive energy palpable. When they were paired together for an icebreaker activity, his warmth completely welcomed Mae in, and they quickly bonded. One night, while finding solace in Mae's room while Cabot's roommate partied with his frat brothers, Cabot became uncharacteristically serious and quiet. For a few minutes, they sat in silence, Mae sensing he needed a moment. Finally, in a voice barely above a whisper, Cabot confessed he was gay. The concern that furrowed his brow, the pleading look on his face, and his struggle to meet her eyes nearly broke her heart. Without hesitation, she took his hands in hers and simply said: "me too." Her voice was so quiet she wasn't sure if she had actually said it aloud, having never spoken those words to anyone else before. Looking into Cabot's warm eyes, she felt the acceptance she'd been longing for, and the heavy weight of secrecy was lifted from her shoulders. She let out a deep sigh as Cabot leaned forward and pulled her into a warm hug, the tears rolling down his face matching those streaming out of her own eyes. From that point on, they were inseparable.

"So? Did you?" Mae prompted her friend again.

"Gentlemen don't kiss and tell," he said, with a twinkle of mischief in his eyes.

"Good thing you're no gentleman," Mae said, a wry smile teasing at the corner of her mouth.

Cabot laughed again, knowing Mae spoke the truth.

Mae lived vicariously through Cabot's tales of the dashing men he'd met over the years: the very flexible yoga instructor who practiced aerial silks and slacklining along the beaches of California, the rugged rancher who wore leather chaps for something other than pride parades and slept most nights under the open Montana skies, or the marine biologist who spent his days scuba diving and studying the wondrous sea life of the Hawaiian reefs. If she didn't know better, she would have sworn he ripped them right from erotic novels with hunky, ripped, barely dressed men on the covers. His dating life was vibrant, exciting, and alive; a stark comparison to her own. She had only really dated one person and it hadn't ended well. It's not like there were many options. Growing up, she thought the island was teeming with queer ladies and regularly had crushes on the beautiful and strong women she saw in town. Of course, she never realized she had crushes on women; she figured she just really liked them and looked up to them. Unfortunately, it turns out many straight Maine women have similar characteristics to lesbians (in Mae's limited experience): self-sufficient, short, no-fuss haircuts, and a deep abiding love of flannel. It was confusing at times (does she like me, or is she just friendly but to the next level). She and Cabot often played "lesbian or Mainer" whenever a new person came into town, and almost always, the answer was straight Mainer, much to Mae's disappointment.

She envied the way Cabot did exactly what he wanted. He didn't want to be in Maine in the winter, so he left. He didn't want to hide who he was, so he was 100% himself at all times. He didn't put up fronts, he was never false, and he embraced and loved himself for exactly who he was. Mae wanted that too. She was inspired by his joy and his authenticity.

When they first met, Mae was more open, like Cabot; easily joyful, truly herself, strong, powerful, determined, and courageous. They had grand plans to move out West. She was going to write and illustrate books and have adventures in the wildest places she could find. She'd discover new bird species, get lost in the wilderness, survive the very worst nature could throw at her, and live to tell incredible tales.

Cabot, on the other hand, was going to fall in love with

a tall, handsome cowboy and run a shelter for lost animals. He always had an acute fondness for lost animals, Mae included. They had that in common. She remembered the time she snuck a baby porcupine, a porcupette, wearing a pair of oven mitts for protection (Mae, not the porcupette) into Cabot's dorm room after she found it crying on the side of the road. The two of them cooed over "Sporty Spike," her name courtesy of Cabot and his love affair with the British pop icons, the Spice Girls. They kept her hidden for a solid week before the resident assistant found out and they were forced to take her to a rescue center.

Cabot's dreams of falling for a handsome cowboy never seemed out of the realm of possibilities. Plus, he looked damn handsome in a cowboy hat. Even his name screamed boot-wearing, horse-riding, dusty western cowboy—Ryder Cabot Wheaton, a family name that sounded more well-suited to the wild plains than the rocky coast of Maine. Whenever she teased him by using his full name, he'd lay on a deep drawl and say "Well, yes pretty lil lady," tipping his imaginary cowboy hat. He was surprisingly good at a southern drawl for a Maine boy. (It wasn't until years later after his brief fling with the aforementioned rancher that Cabot wore a cowboy hat for the first time, and he was even more handsome than either of them would have predicted.)

Together Cabot and Mae were unstoppable on campus. A little queer island in a sea of sameness, they supported each other, and together, they soared in school. As co-founders of the Rainbow Adventure Club, and as its only members, they spent every spare minute between classes in the forests surrounding Bangor birdwatching, avoiding the occasion-

al moose, kayaking the Penobscot River, and searching for
beavers (the animal kind, get your mind out of the gutter),
exploring and discovering. They were free, able to fully be
themselves for the first time, and felt loved and supported,
even if it was only ever the two of them.

One winter break, unwilling to hide who they were
able to be every day on campus, they promised each other they would come out to their respective families. That
night, when Mae arrived on his doorstep at 2 am with tears
streaming down her face and a duffel bag in hand, Cabot
didn't ask any questions. He simply held the door open,
made up a bed for her, tucked her in after a long hug, and
laid down next to her while she cried herself to sleep. The
next morning, her head pounding from all the tears spent,
Mae walked into the kitchen and directly into the arms
of Cabot's sweet mom, who pulled her in for a tight hug,
kissed her forehead, and told her she'd always be welcome
in their house. Since then, Cabot and his mom had been her
only family and she was so grateful to have them.

But the courageous version of Mae—the one who had
started the adventure club dragging Cabot along, saved a
porcupine, and once threatened bodily harm on a Bangor
townie twice her size when he'd had the gall to call Cabot
a particularly derogatory term in front of her—that version
of "Mae Ass-Kicking West," as Cabot liked to call her, had
dimmed and dwindled over the last six years. In the last
year alone, that light was nearly extinguished completely.

It had been a tough year and one that she was certain she
would not have survived had it not been for the ever-amaz-
ing Cabot. Every time she thought she was at the end of her

rope, or the tears cropped up again, he was right there by her side, loving, accepting, and protective. Feeling the joy spread across her face, she beamed at him as he recounted tales of surfing with some adorable blond-haired man, and she reached across and touched his hand. Without question, he wrapped his hand around hers and squeezed it.

She listened intently as he described the landscape he saw along the coast, the way the ocean felt so much different than the one just outside their doors here, welcoming and beautiful, instead of inhospitable and bitterly cold. He talked about the incredible food he ate, and she laughed at his descriptions of trying real sushi for the first time. She could almost taste the buttery salmon as it melted in his mouth and mixed with the fresh sweetness of the mango. She teared up when he talked about lying on the hood of his rental, dwarfed by the high canyon walls of Yosemite National Park, looking up at the night sky in awe; the same night sky she saw every night, although worlds apart. She could imagine every part of his trip in such intricate detail; it sparked the wanderlust within which she often tamped down.

Her mind drifted off to the daydream adventure she often returned to. She imagined herself out West, somewhere in a national park, backpack strapped on, sketch pad in hand, a huge smile on her face, looking out over the wilderness. She felt the excitement rise in her chest, excited with the teeming possibilities and longing for adventure. She felt the twinkle of adventure glimmering in her mind, even bigger than it did those days tramping through the Maine woods.

"Mae?" she heard a familiar voice call somewhere behind her. She was pulled suddenly from her daydreams, where joy and excitement warmed her very soul, and thrown into the icy cold, as violently as if someone had thrown her into the frigid sea lapping a few blocks away. The world dropped out from underneath her. She paled and she saw Cabot's usually peaceful demeanor switch suddenly to one of a protective bear. He tensed and clenched his fist at his side, knuckles turning white. A scowl crossed his face and he stared death daggers over Mae's shoulder. Never one to be violent, Cabot looked about ready to leap out of his seat with the intent to maim or at least seriously injure. The air felt colder and Mae's stomach twisted into a knot. She felt the tension rise up her spine and through her shoulders. The overwhelming urge to run filled every sense of her being.

"Dammit," Mae whispered as she turned to look behind her at her past. Terese McCaster stood in the doorway of the cafe and smiled coldly at the pair.

Terese-fucking-McCaster.

The Devil Incarnate.

Mae's ex-girlfriend.

Chapter 2

Toxic Mc-Ass-ter. Ass-hat McGee. Jerky McJerkface (to be fair, that one was not Cabot's best work).

Terese McCaster. The narcissistic, emotionally abusive, manipulative demon that had nearly killed Mae's spirit and erased her identity. Slick black hair, emotionless dark eyes, and makeup highlighting her angular features, she wore a well-fitted dark suit and tall heels (who wears heels in Maine?! Um hello, snow and ice, it's nice to meet you with my face). Terese was a cold, dominating figure in the doorway and her eyes were locked on her prey, Mae. She reminded Mae a lot of a coiled viper; smooth, sly, dead eyes, still, but ready to strike with a force and a poison that Mae wasn't sure she could survive again. The icy blast that streamed in with her seemed only fitting as if even on the hottest August day an air of bitterness clung to her and followed her wherever she went. She could suck all the joy and light out of Mae's world. Mae had once thought Terese was the most beautiful person she'd ever met. But now that she'd been able to see under the false, polished veneer,

Mae couldn't see Terese without recognizing the evilness beneath the surface.

Terese strolled up as if the previous year hadn't happened. As if she hadn't fallen off the face of the earth and disappeared without explanation or apology. As if she hadn't left Mae brokenhearted, confused, and lost.

She moved as though she didn't touch the ground, slithering closer and closer. Mae felt her chest restrict and all of the blood drain from her face, waiting for the bite that always came. The world seemed to drop away and the self-worth and joy she felt moments before flew out the door as fear and doubt flooded her system. Instinctively, Mae stayed seated and curled her legs into her chest, rolling her shoulders forward to protect herself. She retreated somewhere deep inside and she felt a familiar blank, emotionless wall rise. Her old protections that had laid dormant for months rose effortlessly. She feared the fall again and begged for this to simply be another one of her frequent nightmares. But she didn't wake up and Terese moved closer still.

Mae didn't dare look away from Terese's eyes out of fear, and she felt tunnel vision set in. The world went black around her, and all she saw were those two dark orbs boring into her soul. She felt the nothingness that lay behind Terese's eyes, the black hole that sucked in all of Mae's warmth and left her feeling lost and frozen in their dark glare.

She felt cold and lost until a warm sensation radiated across Mae's back. She knew it was Cabot's hand squeezing her shoulder; familiar, loving, and strong. She looked over to see Cabot standing next to her, his warm eyes melting the ice and fog in her brain. He looked concerned and ready for battle if needed as he clenched his jaw repeatedly. He gave her a nod and without words reminded her she wasn't alone. She would be okay.

Terese reached the pair and leaned down to hug Mae without any genuine feeling behind it. She was ever putting on airs. She might as well have assumed a posh accent and said "Daaarling, it's so lovely to see you," while kissing the air next to Mae's cheek. Mae sat perfectly still, treating Terese like the wild predator she was, hoping to fade into the fabric of her chair. As Terese moved away, Mae could smell the scent of Terese's perfume. Where once she had found it intoxicating, it now turned her stomach. She clenched her jaw, holding her breath until the air cleared to save herself from the worst of it.

Terese, unfazed by Mae's reaction, moved to hug Cabot, only to be met with a look of utter hatred as he hissed a firm but soft "hell no" and stepped away from her. He had no love for Terese and had no problem making that known.

Without missing a beat, Terese ran her hand along the sides of her hair, as if any strand would dare to move out of place, and turned to face Mae again, ignoring Cabot completely. She shot Mae a grin, one that never quite reached her dark eyes. It was the same grin Mae had fallen in love with six years earlier when she was first bewitched by the Wicked Bitch of the North, Cabot's favorite nickname for Terese. Back then, naive Mae didn't know the dark, cold, and calculating master manipulator that lingered in the background. Nor did she know the depth of pain she would suffer at Terese's hands. If only she could have seen the ugliness back then.

Terese's parents owned Current Tides, the local newspaper where Mae worked as an editor. Her parents were "from away," which just meant they were not born and raised on the island. Like many other wealthy residents, they were "summer people," stepping off their private planes looking as though they'd just emerged from a Vineyard Vines catalog, only staying for a short time during peak season each year to bask in the warm, long, summer days filled with blueberries, sunshine, salty ocean air, and fresh lobsters pulled from the harbor traps each morning. Like all of the rest of the immensely wealthy summer people, the McCaster's cottage, named Cliffside, was located on the other side of the sound in Northeast Harbor.

"Cottage" made Cliffside sound quaint, but that was far from the truth. No matter how much Terese protested and claimed it to be small and modest, it was palatial. It had two grand pianos—though no one in the family was even remotely musical—a wrap-around deck overlooking the harbor, two kitchens, a grand staircase, a second, much smaller servants' staircase, and too many bedrooms to count.

It killed Mae that the McCasters owned Cliffside but only occupied it for a month each year while local families struggled to survive during the dark winters when tourist dollars were long gone and hauling lobster traps took lobstermen farther and farther asea. In addition to being lavish and vacant most of the year, it was only one of the four homes the McCasters owned, which included a pretentious penthouse in upper Manhattan, a ski chalet in the Alps, and an equally massive mansion on a private island in the Caribbean.

Though Terese had grown up coming to the island every summer, Mae had never met the younger McCaster, unsurprisingly. Mae didn't run in the same social circles as the McCasters, having been born on the wrong side of the sound, as it were. So it wasn't until Mae started working at Current Tides that the two crossed paths. Terese, as the daughter of the owners, was working at the newspaper during the summer, though "working" might be a generous term for what she actually did. Truth be told, no one quite knew what Terese's role was, but she had her own office, executive assistant, and a packed schedule consisting of brunches, lunches, and drinks with other summer people.

Back then, the younger and more inexperienced Mae thought Terese was a striking figure. Terese easily commanded every room she entered. She was beautiful, intimidating, undeniably charming, and she had a way of making Mae feel like she was the only person in the room. Terese was incredibly different from anyone Mae regularly interacted with, and that was appealing. She was sophisticated, well-educated, powerful, rich, stunning, direct, and she openly flirted with Mae, which was a new and exciting experience. Never before had anyone shown any interest in Mae, and it was thrilling and addicting to feel wanted. Mae looked forward to every interaction and often found herself making up reasons to stop by Terese's office. She wanted to learn more about this mysterious woman, to be the reason Terese smiled, to be noticed. From time to time, Terese would swing by Mae's desk for a quick chat, which left Mae's heart pounding and her mood soaring well past the end of the day.

After a few weeks, Mae was surprised and even honored when Terese asked her out, and, beaming from ear to ear, she quickly said yes. After work, she dashed home, threw all of her nice clothes in a bag, and rushed over to Cabot's apartment to ask for his help in selecting an outfit. She twittered with anticipation, nervous energy filling every core of her being. Mae's excitement was contagious, and Cabot couldn't help but smile as he ushered her out the door a little while later, dressed to the nines, even by coastal Maine standards.

That night, Terese took Mae out to the nicest restaurant on the island, The Oyster, a place Mae had never visited. It was packed with tourists of a certain tax bracket. It was not a place that catered to locals, as the average dinner price far exceeded what most people earned in a day. The maitre d' ushered Terese and Mae to a secluded table close to the window looking out over the setting sun. It was stunning, the view, the restaurant, and the beautiful woman sitting across from her. Terese took the liberty of ordering for Mae, which was altogether a new experience for Mae. She wasn't sure how she felt about it, but the stunning woman across the table from her had chosen her, and that, in and of itself, was enough to keep Mae's heart aflutter. Terese picked out the most expensive items on the menu, accompanied by a bottle of champagne. Not one for alcohol, Mae only took a sip or two of the overwhelmingly fizzy drink. Terese didn't seem to notice and downed the rest of the bottle, promptly ordering another. The dinner went on for hours, and Mae clung to Terese's every word, more intoxicated by her companion than by the few cautious sips of champagne. Mae didn't say more than a handful of words the whole night. Terese was fully capable of carrying the entire conversation herself, but Mae didn't mind. Mae was enthralled with tales of Terese's life in Manhattan, her travels all over the world, and her plans for her next vacation. Terese's life was beyond anything Mae had ever experienced, and she was dumbstruck by the nonchalant way Terese spoke about her life as if it wasn't completely incredible. Mae wanted to explore like that, to travel the world, to experience sunrise and sunset somewhere other than this sleepy town. She wanted to wander and learn, though maybe not in a private jet nor in crowded cities. She was always more drawn to nature, rather than the large cities that featured prominently in Terese's tales. But Mae wanted to enjoy everything the world had to offer, and that was something Terese had plenty of experience with.

Terese's charms were out in full force that night. She pulled out Mae's chair when they arrived at their table, offered her arm after dinner as they walked, and even opened the passenger door of her car when the valet pulled it up. Mae was floating on air as Terese drove her home, whipping around the curvy island lanes with reckless abandon. Mae's head spun out of joy, or perhaps it was the excessive speeds. She clung to the handle on the door to keep her in place as Terese took the corners sharply as if she was running from the law.

When Terese slammed on the brakes in front of Mae's modest apartment, Mae felt her heart leap up in her throat. She wasn't sure what to expect, having not been on a date before. All night she'd been thinking about this moment. Well, overthinking it. She didn't want to admit she'd never been kissed. It was just another way in which she felt her experience in life paled in comparison to the woman following her up to her doorway. After Mae unlocked the door, she turned to Terese, who didn't hesitate to lean in and kiss Mae. Mae held her breath. She had always dreamt of her first kiss and read enough lesfic to imagine it time and time again. In her dreams, her heart raced and the world faded away.

But at that moment, Mae didn't feel anything of the sort. Overwhelmed and overanalyzing everything, Mae worried about what Terese would think. Was this what it was supposed to feel like? Where should she put her hands? Should she open her mouth more? Or less? Or not at all?

It was pleasant enough, but it didn't thrill Mae. Something felt hollow about the kiss and, having built up Terese in her mind, Mae assumed it was just her, and for not the first time that night, she felt that her ignorance of the greater world and her inexperience were blatantly obvious. As they pulled apart, Mae blushed under the intense gaze of Terese's dark eyes. Terese said in a voice barely above a whisper, "Well, that was nice." Terese didn't seem to notice the questioning look in Mae's eyes and quickly bid her good night before climbing back into her car and speeding off.

At the beginning of their relationship, Terese was incredibly sweet and giving. Mae could never remember the exact details of the first few months of their budding relationship, just that it was a blur of excitement and newness. Terese regularly treated Mae to fancy meals, bought her a charm bracelet—not Mae's style, but it was nice—and other expensive gifts, and always initiated their dates. Mae was flying high and was regularly with Terese to the point that Cabot called to confirm she was still alive after not hearing from his bestie for a couple of days.

One Friday evening after a few months of countless dates, Mae made the mistake of calling Terese her "girlfriend" in front of friends. A switch was flipped. An icy cold glare sent chills through Mae's heart as Terese stood up abruptly and walked away. Mae was left confused and worried. She quickly excused herself and followed Terese until she caught up with her at the bar. When she placed a hand on Terese's arm, Terese spun around and shot her a look that cut her down in an instant. "Girlfriend? Why are you trying to control me? I am free. I can do whatever and whoever I want. Grow up. Why do you have to be so needy?" Terese berated and belittled.

Mae dropped her hand and cowered slightly as Terese turned and walked off. Unsure what to do or what she'd done to receive such a response, Mae stood there in complete shock. Her face flushed with embarrassment as if Terese's words had been accompanied by a literal slap across the face. After a few moments, she returned to her friends, and slowly took sips of her drink, begging the tears that burned at the back of her eyes to not fall. After an hour, Terese had still not returned to the group. Mae walked outside only to find Terese's car gone, leaving Mae to find her own way home. Mae's tears fell freely, streaming endlessly down her face as she made a blurry and muddled path home. She was confused and wasn't sure what had happened, but believed whatever it was, she was to blame. Crawling into bed, she debated reaching out that night. She wanted to make things right and she spent the next hour drafting a long apology text only to rewrite it over and over again. She hit send, sent up a wish, and climbed into bed. She didn't sleep well, waking up ever so often to check her phone, only to be disappointed to see there were no new messages. When dawn came and still there was no response, the fear that had been lingering in the background filled her completely.

The weekend dragged on and she walked around in a daze, wanting to reach out again but not wanting to encroach on Terese's space. Each night she fell asleep clasping her phone, wishing the screen would illuminate her dark room. Monday morning at work, Terese acted like the whole episode never happened and didn't even acknowledge the message Mae had sent. For a few days, work kept Mae busy and life went on as usual. She carefully picked her words the few times they crossed paths. She stopped inventing reasons to pop by Terese's office in an effort to avoid setting her off again, unsure what would trigger another outburst. Instead, she just stole glances every time Terese wafted through her workspace, hoping to catch some sort of message that would make things right. On Friday, Terese swung by her desk, put on her most dazzling smile, and said "I'm taking you to The Oyster, babe. I'll pick you up at 6 pm." It was the first time Terese said anything directly to Mae all week, and the familiar "babe" endearment gave Mae hope.

That night, it felt like things finally went back to normal, and Mae could feel herself letting out the breath she'd been holding in. Terese pulled out her chair, offered her arm, ordered for her, and was her vivacious and charming self. All through the night, Mae studied Terese as she dominated the conversation, looking for signs, trying to read her emotions. Outwardly, nothing seemed different. Terese still reached for her hand, smiled brilliantly, and pulled Mae into a deep kiss at the end of the night. But as the days passed, Mae noticed some subtle changes. Though most of the time Terese was the affectionate, giving, sweet version of herself, there were moments when Mae didn't recognize her. It started small; a disapproving glance when Mae ordered a cupcake with her coffee, a dismissive laugh in her face when Mae suggested they go on a sunrise hike with a specially planned picnic Mae had spent hours preparing, a sneer when Mae talked about wanting to travel. "Like you'd actually leave Maine."

In the beginning, these darker moments were few and far between, and Mae could easily dismiss and forgive Terese's unkind words. She knew Terese was stressed and, although she lived a life of luxury, Mae knew it wasn't always roses and joy. During the particularly rough times, when the sweet words she cherished were few and far between, Mae read back through old text messages, promising herself the sweeter version was the real Terese. If only she loved a little harder, showed Terese she was safe and wouldn't go anywhere, maybe Terese wouldn't get mad at her.

And for a while, it would get better. There would be days when Terese opened up and would say the sweetest things Mae had ever heard. In those moments, Mae felt utterly seen and loved. She lived for those words, and it was those moments that carried Mae through the tough times.

But the cycle continued; moments of sheer joy followed by increasingly more frequent and longer periods of wondering what she did wrong, constantly trying to make the relationship work, and feeling like she wasn't good or worthy enough. Terese often got jealous and poured on the guilt anytime Mae chose to spend time with anyone else, including Cabot. She started canceling plans with friends and abandoned her adventures into the woods to make sure she was always available when Terese needed her. To compensate and gain approval, Mae changed the way she dressed and spent more time worrying about what Terese was feeling rather than her own emotions. She gave up her favorite hobbies in favor of Terese's interests and needs. Over the years, Mae's world shrank and her wild spirit evaporated until she was a mere shadow of who she had been.

And then, one day about a year ago, Terese was gone. After five years together, Mae came home to their shared apartment to find all signs of Terese removed. It wasn't unusual for Terese to disappear for a couple of days without a word, but she'd always come back home, never acknowledging her disappearance.

But this time was different; Terese didn't come back. Not after a couple of days, not after a couple of weeks, not even after a couple of months. There was no call, no text, no email, no carrier pigeon, nothing. No explanation for where she'd gone or what had happened.

As the days turned into weeks, Mae's hope faded, and fear and doubt consumed her. She completely fell apart. For five years she defined herself as belonging with Terese. Her schedule had revolved around Terese's, her friends had been replaced by Terese and her needs. She'd long been cut off from just about anyone she knew before Terese. And suddenly she was utterly alone, completely isolated from her friends, having never shared with them the dark person Terese could be. She was at a loss for where everything went wrong and felt adrift in her own life. Even at work, Terese's office sat vacant. No one was quite sure where she'd gone. Every night, Mae came home to their empty apartment and felt the vast emptiness that filled every part of her. She spent months analyzing what happened, trying to figure out what she could have done to keep Terese, where she had messed up.

After a few months, she finally accepted that Terese wasn't coming back. She tentatively began reaching out to old friends and rejoined social media, unsure how to explain what happened. They welcomed her back, and she slowly started exploring all of those parts of herself that had been killed off over the years. Cabot bought her a new drawing pad and showed up every Saturday morning to drag her on another adventure in the Maine woods. When she told him everything that happened with Terese, Cabot pulled her close and held her as she finally let all of the pain she was feeling flow freely. While she cried, Cabot came up with a long list of nasty nicknames for Terese: Count Bitchula, Vampire Diarrheas, Shit for Brains (most of the names involved swear words, feces, and / or plays on the word ass). That made Mae laugh for what felt like the first time in forever. She worked hard to rebuild herself and let go of the pain she felt.

After a long year, she was finally at a place where she felt joy again, where she didn't feel ashamed to pursue her interests, to have that cupcake with her coffee, to dream about and believe deeply in all of the possibilities the future held for her. She was coming back, however timid and cautious she still felt at times.

She never thought she'd see Terese again, or at least she'd fooled herself into thinking she wouldn't. The Mc-Casters always came back to Maine.

And now the evil apparition was standing before her.

"It's so good to see you, Mae! You look good! Just don't let those lattes catch up to you," Terese said. There it was again; that bitter bite that accompanied every perceived compliment. For the first time, Mae could see the manipulation and abuse as it was happening, and as much as the past year had helped Mae learn how to step out of the direct line of fire, it didn't stop the vitriol from singeing her as it grazed past.

"I was hoping to run into you while I was in town! It's weird to be back here. I forgot how dumpy this place is," Terese said with a sneer on her lips.

"My parents finally turned the newspaper over to me. I don't see the point of print when we live in a digital world. I've got a few competing offers from major news outlets who are dying to buy me out. They might actually be able to turn this rag into a halfway respectable publication. Of course, they'll need significantly better writers and editors, so in the next few months I'll be shutting down the office," Terese continued. Her speech was pointed and rambling, directed at no one in particular. She never cared who her audience was, or how what she was saying might impact them. It only mattered that she commanded the stage she lived on at all times. She should be the center of attention; there was no reason for anyone else to have a say.

Terese never seemed to draw breath when she went on one of her excited monologues, and Mae was too dumb-struck to say anything anyway. The newspaper was closing and until it did, her toxic ex-girlfriend was her boss? Fuck. Mae could feel the darkness beckoning her. It was too much to process. All of the progress she'd made over the last year threatened to abandon ship. Mae bit the inside of her lip, willing her stomach contents to remain inside her body and her threatening tears not to fall. She couldn't let Terese see her upset. Not again. Mae wouldn't give her ex the satisfaction of seeing her in pain.

"Baby, over here!" Terese's voice pierced through the fog surrounding Mae's mind. Terese looked across the coffee shop as a stunning woman walked in.

Terese reached for the woman's hand and said: "Mae, I'd like for you to meet Lara, my wife."

Chapter 3

Kes exhaled heavily into her mask, feeling her warm breath condense within the confines, making her feel even sweatier than she already did. Her blue eyes remained intensely focused behind her safety glasses while her long fingers worked deftly. The muscles in her forearms rippled as she firmly and purposefully turned her chisel. Around her wood shavings flew every which way. As she carefully guided the tool tip she could feel every fiber of the wood. She moved with the ease and familiarity of a master carver at work. The tactile experience was one of Kes's favorite parts of woodworking, and in her hands the rough estimate of a bowl emerged out of the wood blank spinning on the lathe. The well-oiled and loved antique machine whirred loudly, its motor drowning out the thoughts whirling through Kes's mind. In this practiced pose, she was able to lose herself in the moment and exist somewhere between the sawdust, sweat, and creation. It was a delicious place to be; not weighed down by the noise and demands of the world outside, not stuck with only your own thoughts for company, free of the pains and fears that lurked in the corners of her mind lately. Here she had a task, one that demanded only her passion and, in turn, produced something useful, meaningful, and altogether beautiful.

Taking a step back to look at the forming shape, Kes ran her hand over the smooth curve of the bowl. She still felt the vibration buzzing through her hands from the rhythm of the ancient lathe. She was so focused on inspecting her work that she barely noticed when the lights overhead began to flicker on and off. Cutting the machine's power, Kes pulled off her safety glasses and plucked out her earplug with a satisfying "pop." As she uncorked her ear, you might say, the sounds of the outside world came rushing back in. Hearing a noise behind her, Kes turned around and was met with the familiar sight of her friend standing in the garage doorway.

"Well, aren't you a sight!" said Tim, chuckling. Her face, hands, and forearms were purple, covered in a mixture of sweat and padauk sawdust from the piece she was working on. As she pulled down her mask, Tim noticed the only portion of exposed skin free from the purple tint was the now bright white ring around Kes's mouth, making it look like she was wearing a second, cleaner, mask under the original. Ribbons of wood clung to Kes's dark fauxhawk, and there were two noticeable indentations from the taut elastics of the mask. Sweat soaked every inch of her loose tank top, her shorts hung low on her hips, being a size or two too big now, and her once bright white Converse shoes were covered in paint splatters, unidentified oil spots, and a fine layer of sawdust. Kes flashed one of her signature crooked smiles at Tim, completely oblivious to the sheer disaster she appeared to be.

"Having fun?" he asked.

Removing the rest of her protective gear, Kes walked over to hug her friend, until she saw the look of absolute terror in his eyes. She glanced down at his uniform and then at herself, and for the first time saw herself the way she imagined Tim saw her now. Something akin to Pigpen combined with a Labrador retriever puppy let loose in a mud puddle. She thought better of smearing purple sawdust sweat all over his pristine shirt and stopped. He grinned as she backed away and put her hands up in apology. His hands rested easily on his hips, just above his duty belt. He looked relaxed but aware and prepared. It was a posture she knew all too well, as she often assumed the same position. Or at least she had until a few months ago. It wasn't a position taken out of power or to look formidable. It was simply the most comfortable way to stand when there were several pounds of gear strapped around your middle making you significantly wider than usual. What else were you supposed to do with your hands? She remembered when she first wore her duty belt. She kept hitting door frames as she walked through and knocked items placed too close to the edge of tables and counters, completely unfamiliar with her newly acquired girth. It took a few days to adjust, but she still hadn't figured out a more comfortable or natural way to stand.

"Chief is looking for you," Tim said, breaking her out of her thoughts. "Want a ride in?" Tim asked.

"Uh, yeah, sure that would be great," Kes responded

hesitantly, looking away from Tim. All of the thoughts she'd kept at bay under the cover of sawdust started to reemerge, and she felt unsure. She wasn't ready to be pulled back into the world. She kept her practiced face neutral so as not to worry those around her, but she wasn't sure she had the energy to maintain the facade in front of the Chief.

"Do you want to maybe rinse off first?" Tim asked with a worried look creasing the wrinkles on his forehead. For a moment, Kes thought perhaps he saw right through to her fears. She felt her walls rising even higher. As much as she trusted Tim, she wasn't ready to let anyone in.

Returning her gaze to Tim, she noticed his hand had moved from its usual position and was generally pointing down at her clothing. Looking down she chuckled and realized he was terrified by the thought of her sawdust-covered form entering his squeaky clean patrol vehicle. It was his idea of an absolute nightmare. How any park ranger could keep a vehicle immaculate in the desert, Kes had no idea. Between that, his pristine, spit-shined, never dusty boots, and his perfectly pressed green and gray uniform, Tim looked like the epitome of a ranger, quite her opposite at the moment.

"Why? Do you think I need to?" Kes asked, with a glimmer of mischief in her eyes. Tim was well known for his particular cleanliness and, seeing her friend pale even further, she chuckled. To relieve the fear she could see mounting in his face, she quickly added "Give me five and I'll be ready to go."

In the early July temps in Arizona, the garage had been sweltering, and Kes was grateful for a moment to escape the heat. As cool water trickled down her toned form leaving long canyon trails carved through the dust, she took a moment to close her eyes and take a deep breath. The water felt glorious, its cooling kisses caressing the sore and tense muscles of her neck and shoulders. She could melt right into the basin and let it wash over her, taking with it the aches she felt deep within her core. She turned her face toward the water to wash away her thoughts, grateful for the few minutes she had to gather herself before seeing the chief ranger.

After stepping out of the shower and drying off the last droplets of cool water, she slipped into her green slacks and noticed she had to cinch the belt down a couple of extra notches. Although her uniform was never snug, now it hung loosely on her frame, and she felt she could retreat fully and hide within it. She took a deep breath and looked at the bathroom door, knowing she had to step out. It had been a long three months since she last donned her National Park Service uniform, duty belt, and secured her "Ranger K. Wylde" nameplate to her shirt. Although she was always filled with pride and a sense of awe each time she pushed the sharp pin of her badge through the gray fabric of her shirt and secured it in place, she wasn't quite sure she was ready. But, having made enough wooden bowls, utensils, and various other knickknacks to last the entire Grand Canyon Village a lifetime, she supposed it was likely time.

On the drive over, neither Tim nor Kes said anything. Kes out of anticipation and Tim out of respect. He knew this was a big step for her, and tried not to make it obvious that he was studying her out of the corner of his eye. Professionally, she looked ready, alert, and aware. Tim couldn't read Kes past that. Her face was quiet, composed, still; but he guessed a lot was happening he wasn't privy to. *Rightly so, perhaps*, he thought. But still, his heart went out to her.

The radio traffic was enough to fill the silence: elks causing jams on the roads (*it's not the elks' fault*, thought Tim); someone needing medical attention after spending too much time in the sun at 7,000 feet in elevation, a near-daily occurrence; a visitor locked out of their rental car. *If this doesn't work out, I could always become a car thief*, thought Kes, having successfully gained access to cars from every make and model over the years. The dispatchers and rangers were always calm and direct on the radio in a way that felt clear and familiar to Kes. Even during her time off, Kes had kept the radio on at all times, needing something to fill the silence. Otherwise, she felt a terrible void in her home. It was something to remind her that life continued, business as usual, and it gave her something to hold onto when the world dropped out.

Arriving at Station One, the main base for all protection, search and rescue, and backcountry patrol operations at the park, Kes felt the familiar anxiety build within her chest. She was somewhere between extremely uncomfortable and utterly overwhelmed. She gripped the door handle, unable to will her hand to pull it and eject herself from the safety of the vehicle. It felt like too much to see everyone, to play the part, and fall back into the trivial conversations she'd once tolerated reasonably well. She didn't know if she had the energy to don the mask of "everything's fine, yes it was hard, but I'm okay." Feeling a warm hand on her shoulder, she turned to see Tim grinning as he playfully shoved her and said "Now, out of my car." She returned his smile, though her grin didn't quite meet her eyes as she exited the vehicle. Tim shooed her with his hands when she looked back at him, and she smiled a little deeper this time as she walked toward the office door.

"Chief?" Kes said while knocking lightly on the frame of the door. Kes's voice was strong and full even though she felt anything but confident.

From behind his desk, Chief Miller slowly unfolded himself, standing and rising to his full height. He was an impressive figure, with the kind of build that could likely bench press a small horse, but the kindness in his eyes reminded you he'd never put a horse in that kind of distress. His height made Kes appear "fun-sized." She'd always looked up to him, both physically and emotionally, and now was no different.

"It's good to see you, Kes," Chief Miller said, his arms opening to embrace her. She fit easily within his warm and welcoming hug. If he had a tagline, it would be, "built like Superman with the heart of a puppy." Typically, he would have never hugged an employee, especially not at work, but Kes was not just an employee. He'd known Kes since her dark mop barely reached his duty belt.

Back then, he usually saw her as a blur of energy and color. Her wild hair flew out behind her as she ran past him on the trail, both uphill and downhill, which was something of a feat considering one of his long strides required at least eight of her tiny, rapid-fire steps. Her freckles had been more defined then, covering the bridge of her nose, cheeks, and arms. She was an energetic kid, a little shy, but deeply inquisitive with an incredible memory for everything she learned. He remembered the first time he saw her heading into the canyon to camp with her grandmother. She was five and proudly wore her backpack. When he asked what she had in her pack, she showed him her notebook, crayons, teddy bear, snacks, and water. Her gap-toothed grin and twinkling blue eyes melted his heart and endeared her to him forever.

He'd seen her grow up through the years. He was there when she marched into his office at age six with a piece of paper covered with her hard-to-read crayon handwriting. When he'd asked her what it was, she'd said "Imma be a ranger, chief. It's my apple vacation." He'd barely kept in a hearty guffaw when she'd saluted him and marched out of his office, certain her application was in the right hands. He still had it tucked away in a drawer for safekeeping.

He was there when as a moody 14-year-old she set off on her first solo backpacking trip. A bit young perhaps, but tenacious, and at that point, she'd already hiked every trail in the park and was more well-versed than most of his staff.

He stood beside her grandmother on the day she stood on the edge of the canyon with her high school graduating class of five students (it was a big group that year), as she beamed, holding her diploma in hand, braces still on her teeth, never dimming the light that emanated deep within her. He was there for her first day in uniform the summer after high school and helped her tie the complicated knot on her hatband. And when she moved away to pursue degrees in environmental science and law enforcement, he felt the loss personally. He hadn't realized how much he'd grown used to seeing her every day at the office. But he was overwhelmingly proud when he watched her graduate from the Federal Law Enforcement Training Center and was able to offer her a full-time position at the park.

He was very protective of his people, and none more than Kes. She may have found ways to tame her wild hair and boundless energy, but he couldn't help but see the wide-eyed kid who captured his heart all those years ago. Unfortunately, the impish grin and spark in her eyes had faded lately. It broke his heart to see the fall Kes had endured, but he hoped his request would brighten her spirits.

"Kes, I'm going to need you on the next tour at Phantom," Chief said, in a voice that was warm and deep. It wasn't a question, though he never gave orders, per se. If anyone disagreed with him or had a concern, he listened intently, considered the options, and sometimes changed direction. Still, as a stand-in father figure for most of the staff, no one wanted to disappoint him, and he never made requests he wasn't 100% confident his rangers could handle.

Kes stood silent for a moment. Phantom Ranch was her true home. She'd been a backcountry patrol park ranger at Grand Canyon for the last ten years and spent more days below the rim than she did above it. Located at the very bottom of the canyon, at the confluence of the mighty Colorado River and Bright Angel Creek, Phantom Ranch was paradise. It was an oasis in the heart of the canyon, a refuge after a long hike. It was the place she'd always felt most at home and most like herself. It was where almost all of her happiest moments lived. Everything about the inner canyon called to her. But everything about it also reminded her of Sara and she wasn't sure she could handle dealing with those memories just yet.

"Trudy will be stationed there too. Kes," he paused, waiting for Kes to meet his eyes. It wasn't typical to have two rangers at Phantom for an entire tour, but the chief wanted to ease Kes back into her duties without throwing too much at her at once. "You have to get back down there and I think you're ready." His voice was soft, warm, and open. His eyes filled with kindness, without a trace of pity. Kes was grateful. Her protective mask was thin, and she didn't think she could handle it cracking right now.

"Yes sir. Thank you," Kes said quietly. She didn't trust herself to say more than a few words, worried her voice would betray the fear that still teemed below the surface. She almost believed his words. Almost. Could she do it? "I'll hike in on Tuesday?" Kes asked. It wasn't really a question as they always hiked in on Tuesdays, but she needed confirmation to feel things were following regular patterns.

The chief nodded. "You know the drill. Get your supplies to Helitac by Monday morning. Right now it looks like reservations are pretty light, so I expect it will be a quiet eight days down there." With a nod, Chief Miller dismissed Kes, who was already deep in her own world, running through her packing list, remembering what food she'd need, and making plans to depart in just four days.

Chapter 4

After that April day when Shitstorm Terese tore back into her life, everything changed. In the whirlwind of upheaval and the onslaught of Terese's sudden reappearance in her life, Mae was thrown into a state of uncertainty and fear. Returning to work, Mae kept her head down and did her best not to recoil or run every time Terese walked by her desk, which was uncomfortably often. Even before she saw her, Mae always knew when Terese was coming. The frigid storm that raged in the cavity where Terese's heart ought to be seeped out into the room before she entered, harkening the ice maven's entrance. Where Terese's presence would have once set Mae's heart skipping a beat, now it just felt like a blow to the gut every time Terese broke her concentration. And Mae wasn't the only one who felt the difference; Terese's presence in the office had caused a stir of activity and confusion for everyone, though none of Mae's coworkers knew their heads were soon to be on the chopping block.

It pained Mae to think that the stories she'd poured her heart into would soon be outsourced to people who didn't understand why the tidal chart was printed in every edition, what a soft shell lobster was, why the annual bed races were such a hit, or what a Nor'easter was. It would be the same people who didn't understand that the correct response to "Didja see that storm ov'r tha hahbah last night? It was a wicked pissah. I saw some folks getting stuck on tha bah." is "Ayuh, probably a couple of Mass-holes."[1] (That was a pretty common conversation that was inevitable before you could start interviewing any of the old-timers.) Current Tides was as much a leading character on the island as were the people Mae wrote about every week. Losing the newspaper to people from away would mean losing the common thread that held the island community together amidst the crazy tourist peaks and deepest winter lows.

Mae pushed through her fears for her future and that of those around her as much as she could and focused on what she needed to get done and done quickly. She finalized her writing assignments, wrote thank you notes to her colleagues, and left a list of ideas she had for future articles for whoever would replace her. She quietly cleaned out her desk gradually over the course of the week, so as to not arouse suspicion. On Friday, unwilling to deal with Terese's pervasive toxicity leaching into every corner of her life and finally ready to sever all ties with the woman who broke her heart time and time again, Mae marched into the office and dropped her notice and work keys on Terese's desk without glancing up or uttering a word. She could feel Terese's cruel

---

1 Translation: "Did you see the storm last night? It was horrible. I saw some people getting their cars stuck on the sand bar." "Yep, probably a couple of people from Massachusetts."

grin burning into the back of her head as she turned on her heel and walked out the doors directly to Cabot's.

Bursting in through his door out of the cold wind, Mae finally let her breath escape. She felt the gravity of what she'd just done and the fear of the unknown future weighing on her. But in front of her, Cabot stood, arms open with a bottle of wine in each hand. "Caber-yay or Que Syrah Syrah?" Cabot said with a warm and understanding smile. He continued, "I also have Chardon-gay and Hakuna Moscato." Mae had to crack a smile. Cabot was pulling out all the stops for her benefit and she could not express how grateful she felt that he opened up his home to her without question. Without another job lined up, Mae couldn't afford to keep her apartment, so until she found something, she was crashing in his spare room. "You had me at Merlot," Mae was able to squeak out. Cabot beamed at her pun and pulled her into his hug as tears streamed down her face.

As soon as the adrenaline that had been pumping through her veins all week wore off, the pressure and fear she'd been staving off crashed over her. Tears flowed freely as she finally felt safe to let them go. Cabot held her close for a minute or two and then moved them to the couch where he had two empty wine glasses and a plate of her favorite foods waiting. After the tears finally slowed, and a bottle of wine was happily polished off, Cabot broke the silence.

"You need to get out for a bit. Go somewhere. Do something. What have you always wanted to do?"

Without thinking, Mae responded "Write a book. Travel out West. Find myself in nature."

"Okay, done!" Cabot said triumphantly.

He stood up abruptly and walked to his computer. Mae shivered at his sudden disappearance and peered across the room with teary eyes following his movements while she shoved another peanut butter cup in her mouth. When Cabot was on a mission, there was no stopping or distracting him. All Mae could see was his muscular outline as he worked. It was a bit comical to see his huge figure curled over, almost bent in half, his large hands typing delicately on the tiny laptop. Mae watched as Cabot mumbled to himself, looked off into the distance, and then returned to his computer furiously typing away.

He'd been incredible in the cafe that day. As soon as Terese had introduced her new wife, Cabot stood to his full height, and without any of his usual warmth, he turned to Lara and said, "You poor thing. Get out while you can." Mae had to hold back a laugh at the look of utter shock and complete disgust on Terese's face. Terese sputtered, ready to refute and dismiss Cabot, but without missing a beat he turned to Terese and, towering over her, he gave her a look that froze her mouth and stopped her dead in her tracks. As Terese paled and looked away, Cabot grabbed Mae's hand and pulled her out of the cafe, all the way to his apartment. Mae wasn't sure her feet ever touched the ground as they dashed over the snowy sidewalks with the world whizzing by.

As soon as the apartment door closed, Cabot fired off a string of curse words previously unknown to humankind. The words were dark and sharp, punctuated and nonsensical, though the meaning was clear. Mae just stood there in amazement and gratitude, her mind and body still in shock.

She wasn't one for anger, but damn it felt good when Cabot went off.

But now, the much calmer and warmer Cabot spun around from his laptop looking proud, stirring Mae from her memories. "You're all set. You leave on July 14th. I've got you a flight, a rental car, and camping reservations. We'll need to order you a pack and hiking boots, but I probably have a few items you can borrow," he said, his excitement and energy filling the room.

"Cabot, uh… where am I going?" Mae asked, tentatively.

It all seemed a blur. As she stood outside her rental car, she took a deep breath in. Everything felt different. The air in Flagstaff smelled sweet, like fresh-baked vanilla cookies. It was warm, even though it was after seven at night. In the distance, she could see a huge mountain towering over the town. Mae was nervous and filled with anticipation. She had never left Maine before, and now here she was in Arizona getting ready for six days of backpacking in the Grand Canyon. Grand freaking Canyon! She couldn't believe it when Cabot told her.

"Cabot, the most I've ever done is hike Mount Katahdin! And that was a day trip!" She protested, shocked, filled with equal parts doubt and excitement. As the tallest mountain in Maine, Katahdin was admittedly formidable and kicked her butt, but she didn't think it was even a drop in the bucket compared to the Grand Canyon.

Cabot smiled, "Don't worry. You're staying in a campground right next to the ranger station. There will be other campers, there are no bears to worry about, and you've got time to explore. Get out there. Be a badass. Adventure. Live up to your name, Mae West! Who knows, maybe some cute ranger will sweep you off your feet!"

Cabot's face lit up as he mock swooned, collapsing on the couch next to her as he said "Ooo a woman in uniform."

Mae laughed heartily and playfully swatted him on the arm. It felt good to laugh as her imagination and wanderlust built.

"You know 'West' isn't actually my last name," Mae reminded Cabot, but all Cabot could do was laugh.

Mae spent the next few weeks preparing as best she could. It was good to have a goal to focus on, to shake off the pain caused by the abrupt shift in her life. Cabot helped her pick out a pack, a pair of hiking boots, and hiking poles. Being a proper Mainer, she had a pretty good assortment of boots: shin-high muck boots for mud season, "Beanah" duck boots since you'd definitely get a hard time if you didn't own a pair of L.L.Bean boots as a Mainer, and an old pair of hikers she'd had since high school that were being held together by duct tape and hope. None of those would be quite right for this trip though. She needed something sturdy, that came up over her ankle, had a decent tread, and could breathe in the hot Arizona sun.

Cabot surprised Mae by sewing an "I <3 Maine" patch to the side of her brand new pack. It was red, her favorite color, with an assortment of pockets, loops, straps, and secret compartments that fascinated her when it arrived. The

first time she tried it on it felt uncomfortable as it awkwardly hung on her back, empty, flat, too long for her torso, loose
across her shoulders, and uncomfortably tight around her
stomach. Cabot pulled on the various straps and buckles,
fixing the fit, shortening the shoulder straps, adding length
to the hip belt, and correctly placing the hip belt squarely on
Mae's broad hips, not tightly around her stomach as she'd
had it. Properly adjusted, the pack fit better as Mae clipped
the sternum strap closed. But still, it felt strange on her back,
empty and light. Cabot encouraged her to make it her own,
fill it with some items to get used to the weight and feel, and
told her she just needed to break it in. That weekend Mae
drove to one of the quieter trails not far from Cabot's apartment. She hoisted the pack clumsily onto her back, laced up
her boots, and took off up a short and relatively flat path.
She had filled the pack with the new and borrowed gear
she'd need on her adventure west. She worried she'd topple over backward if she tried any of the steeper sections
of trail right out of the gate. She shuffled forward, slowly,
adjusting her movements to the new weight. It was the first
time she'd been outside since she turned in her notice. Terese was never one to explore the outdoors, so the likelihood
Mae would run into her ex was pretty slim. But still, her
senses were heightened in an effort to protect herself from
any more sudden shocks. She hiked slowly, overly aware
of the sounds all around her: the wind rustling through the
barren branches, the quick movement of a squirrel dashing
up a tree she saw out of the corner of her eye, the sudden
arrival of an oncoming group of hikers whose conversation
and energy felt too loud for Mae at the moment. She was

hypersensitive and filled with the irrational fear that Terese would know she was alone without Cabot's protection. And the idea that Terese would find her and somehow come up with another way to upend Mae's entire world felt like a real and present danger.

But with each step, Mae forced herself to focus instead on the moment in front of her, not the feared future. She focused on the beauty of the landscape around her. She noticed the small buds of deep green leaves just starting to show. She heard the chattering of a porcupine as it waddled past. She saw a yellow-rumped warbler, the good old "Butter Butt," swoop down from the taller trees to get a better look at her and sing her a song as she went on her way. Though the wind still held the last remnants of the winter's chill, she felt the warmth of the possibility hanging in the air. Her timidness and fear faded away. She became more comfortable under the weight of the pack, until it no longer felt like a burden pulling her down, but instead, like just another appendage. Here, on her island, deep in her childhood playground, surrounded by granite peaks, balsam fir trees, and greening scraggly bushes, she was safe and alive. She turned her face to the early spring sun, feeling the top of her pack cushion the back of her head.

The success of the first hike only served as a catalyst for more solo adventures outdoors. The more she went out to explore and hike, the braver she became and the farther she went. She chose longer, steeper trails, up the sides of the glacially-carved mountains Mount Desert Island was famous for. Her heart pounded in her chest and her muscles were continually sore, but the ache was a good one that brought a smile to her face. With each hike, the possibility of finally adventuring out of state seemed to be less of a wild dream and more of a possibility.

Mae read every backpacking and hiking article she could get her hands on: Top Ten Things To Bring On Your First Grand Canyon Hike, Beginner Backpacking Mistakes, and How Not to Die in Grand Canyon. To be fair the last one scared her a bit and kept her awake for a night or two after reading it, especially when she saw it referenced the park's best-selling book Over the Edge: Death in Grand Canyon, which had enough material to regularly need new editions! Thankfully, Cabot was there to talk her back into the land of reality and safety. He pointed her to some more helpful (and less dramatic) reading materials. She memorized maps and got lost in her imagination at the new and strange place names such as Cheops Pyramid, Elves Chasm, and the Great Unconformity. She downloaded bird lists and consulted her brand new Western North American Birds guide. She printed out sunrise and sunset charts. The more information, the better. She needed to know it all if she was really going to leave home, fly across the country, and hike into the wilderness solo! All the while, Cabot helped her prepare. He thought of everything, what to wear, what to eat and how to prepare food, when to go, which trails to take, and he even walked her through how to pack her gear so her water, snacks, and sketch pad were handy.

After a long day of flying, running through airports to catch all three of her connecting flights, finding her rental car, and driving for an hour and a half from Flagstaff to Grand Canyon Village, Mae was beyond exhausted. She was fueled only by the anticipation and excitement of getting to see the Grand Canyon for the first time. After checking in, she stopped in her room only long enough to drop her bags and pull out her sketchpad and pencils. Drawing essentials in hand, Mae made her way out of the hotel and walked across the sidewalk to stand on the edge of the gaping hole.

The massive, gaping hole of nothing.

Mae was astounded by the sheer blackness that stretched out in front of her. She couldn't see a thing. It was a feeling she was unaccustomed to. The sun had set an hour earlier and all its ambient rays had long since disappeared. Behind her, the hotels were lit up, as were the paths, but their lights quickly faded into nothingness. There were no lights bright enough to pierce the inky, all-consuming darkness in front of her. She hadn't considered there wouldn't be spotlights shining on the canyon walls at night. There was nothing before her but vast space. She couldn't tell exactly how far down the canyon dropped off, and she imagined herself standing on a sheer cliff teetering on the edge. There was a low wall in front of her, but even with that, the canyon seemed to be sucking her in. She crossed her arms in a self-soothing gesture to hold herself back from an almost reflexive reaction to let go and fall into the abyss.

What was she doing here? How could she ever complete this hike? What was Cabot thinking? She wasn't brave like him. As much as he wanted her to be, she wasn't Mae West.

She was Mae Ridley Mack, unglamorous, timid, and at the moment, a chickenshit. She didn't have anything close to Mae West's level of gumption.

For a second, Mae thought a soft breeze was speaking the words in her brain. "It's scary, isn't it?" She jumped when she realized the words came from a voice just behind her. Turning, she could just make out someone sitting on a bench not far away.

"Sorry! I didn't mean to startle you," the voice said again. Rising, the person moved toward Mae. Mae couldn't tell much about them since they were illuminated from behind by the hotel lights. Whoever they were, they matched Mae's height and had a very thin build.

"Hi, I'm Frankie," the voice said. "I was just sitting here thinking about how monumentally huge this place is and feeling dumber than a sack of rocks for fixin' on backpacking it," Frankie said. Frankie's voice was pleasant, soft, and had a drawn-out musical quality to it. Mae couldn't tell, but she guessed Frankie was from somewhere down south going by the slight twang and drawl in their words. Granted, relative to Maine, everything was "down south," but still, Mae was relieved. Frankie seemed to know exactly how Mae was feeling.

Mae found her voice and said "Me too! I'm headed down tomorrow. How about you?"

Frankie beamed, or at least Mae imagined they did from the way the light changed and reflected off their cheeks. "I am too! I'm planning on leaving early. Have you ever hiked here before?" Frankie asked.

"I've never done anything like this, never been out West,

and definitely have never hiked like this," Mae responded, feeling the worry building inside her catch in her voice.

"Not to worry! What do you say we dive into this adventure together? I'll meet you at the South Kaibab Trailhead around 4 am," Frankie said walking away, not really giving Mae a chance to turn them down.

"4 am!? Uh, I'll see you then?" Mae said to Frankie's retreating figure, not completely sure what she had gotten herself into.

Chapter 5

Ten hours? *It had never taken ten hours before*, Kes thought as she entered the ranger station. Typically she hit the trail by 5 am (aka butt crack o' dawn) and arrived at the bottom no later than 8 am. But today wasn't a typical day.

Last night she ran through her usual rounds. She double-checked her pack, charged her radio, set out her uniform, and prepared the coffee grounds. After a quick run, she showered and laid down to get some sleep.

Sleep, that elusive mistress, did not come. She bounced her leg, flexing and relaxing the muscles in her calf quickly. She willed her brain to shut down the nervous thought circles that usually involved her mind spinning tales that were rife with emotional pain and catastrophic tragedies. She drew the inside of her lip between her teeth and gnawed slightly at the tender flesh there. She stared up at the ceiling of her bedroom, following the textured pattern long since out of fashion, though not likely to leave government quarters anytime soon.

Kes had always struggled with anxiety but found it

usually faded the moment her uniform was on. When on duty, she could focus and stay calm in the face of anything. She was well trained and handled stress and moments of uncertainty with ease. But in these quiet minutes alone, especially at night, sometimes it felt overwhelming. Kes felt even more nervous than she had before her first tour years ago. She knew what she was doing and the chief wouldn't have sent her down if he didn't think she was ready, but she couldn't calm her brain.

Closing her eyes she focused on her breathing, counting to four on the inhale and six on the exhale. With each exhale she tried to focus on something calming. Oceans didn't do it, too many sharks. Mountains had avalanches, and forests had Sasquatch. Logically, she understood that she lived in the desert, and that sharks, avalanches, and Sasquatch, or even Sasquatch riding a shark on an avalanche, could not attack her in her mind, but reasoning had no place when her anxiety was high.

Finally, Kes stilled her trembling leg and focused on a landscape she was comfortable in. She imagined herself sitting on a cliff overlooking the canyon. The warm rock conformed to the shape of her back and she sank deeper into the place. She could smell the dry dirt that hung in the air, the salt that clung to her skin, the desert sage floating on a breeze. She felt the warmth of the sun comfort her and center her. She could hear the crashing roar of the river. This place had been home forever, and its consistencies and patterns were calming. She breathed in deeply and felt a presence next to her, light pressure on her side, warm and soft. She sighed, smiled sadly, and ached for it to be real as her throat tightened and she drifted off.

After her alarm jarred her awake, she felt jittery and disoriented. Getting ready took significantly longer than usual as she fumbled through her tasks, rusty from being out of practice. Grabbing her pack she arrived at the trailhead only to realize she had forgotten her coffee and radio. After another quick trip home, she finally set off on the trail, already a solid two hours behind her usual start time.

Her body quickly fell back into stride, making her way down the steep and rugged trail. It felt good to move like this again, to find her way. The trip down had been filled with visitors asking questions and needing assistance. This wasn't uncommon but the later start time meant more people on the trail and more interactions. Simple requests such as identifying birds flying overhead and questions about her life as a ranger were common and usually only took a few minutes. Most of her interactions with visitors were quick and pleasant, but there had been two more involved medical calls that extended her hike on the way down. The first happened very near the top, at Ooh Ahh Point, aptly named as it was often the first stop hikers took on their way down where they exclaimed "ooh" and "ahh" over the views. One such hiker thought it would be cute to get a selfie while feeding a squirrel only to be shocked when the wild fluff monster bit his finger, drawing blood. Kes cleaned and bandaged the wound, and sent the young man up the trail to be checked out at the local clinic. He'd likely end up with a couple of stitches and a shot or two for his trouble. Not exactly the memory you want to take home from a day at the canyon.

As she hiked, Kes hid under her solar umbrella, an ingenious device that looked like a silver parasol. It was designed to provide a portable shade shelter and an escape from the desert heat. In the inner canyon, the dark igneous granitic and basaltic rocks soaked in the sun's warmth all day and radiated that heat right back out, making the scorching sun all the less forgiving. The one saving grace portion of the trail was called Big Shade, so named because a nearby rock formation rose so high above the south side of the trail that there was inevitably a large patch of shade underneath it throughout the day. It was often the last bit of shade Kes would find on her hike down, and she planned to take full advantage of the quick reprieve. But as she arrived, Kes found a young man on all fours vomiting profusely. Immediately she switched into rescue mode and moved swiftly to the man. From what she could tell he seemed to be alone. His small day pack was on the ground next to him. It wasn't big enough to carry any necessary overnight gear but he was too far down the trail for a reasonable day hike, even for the fittest, most experienced hikers. Kes assumed the young man had decided to chance fate and ignore all of the warning signs along the trail he had attempted to hike to the river and back in a day.

Kes tried to get the man's attention, squatting down next to him outside the splash zone and placing a hand on his shoulder. But he seemed unable to keep his eyes open and trained on Kes. He was disoriented, he couldn't answer any of her questions, including what his name was. Kes had seen this countless times before. Immediately, Kes radioed Park Dispatch and requested help and a Medivac. As soon as she heard confirmation that the helicopter was on its way, Kes got to work. Within minutes another inner canyon ranger, Matt, arrived on scene. He was just wrapping up his tour and was on his hike out when he heard Kes's call. The two worked efficiently and hurriedly, knowing that if they didn't, things could go horribly wrong very quickly.

In the desert heat, most hikers knew they needed to drink a lot of water so they wouldn't become dehydrated. What most seemed to miss is that they also had to replace all the salts they were losing as they sweat. Hyponatremia, or the lack of enough salt in their system, could take a patient from grogginess and vomiting to seizures or falling into a coma within a few hours for more drastic cases. Though anyone could be susceptible to hyponatremia, Kes had treated more fit, young men than any other age group. There was something about that super hero, indestructible complex that thrived in young men that meant they pushed the limits when they ought not to. There was no honor or reward in hiking to the river and back in a day unless you counted feeling really shitty and being unable to walk normally for a couple of days. Usually, it was a slow miserable slog on the way up trail and there was never a gospel choir waiting to sing your praises when you finally made it out. The canyon did not discriminate and sometimes took the lives of those arrogant enough to think they were beyond Mother Nature's grasp.

Kes hoped that wouldn't be the case this time. Matt and Kes needed to get the man stabilized as best they could before transporting him to a place the helicopter could land. Working alongside the hot, dusty trail was not the most medically clean environment, but they had to work with what they had. Kes inserted an IV and started the young man on a saline solution that had a higher amount of sodium than the usual bag of saline. This was the quickest way to get some more salt into the patient's system and hopefully help balance out his chemistry again until he reached a hospital. While she worked, Matt ran up the trail to where there was a medical cache chest hidden behind some rocks. Grabbing the necessary pieces, Matt rushed back down to join Kes and build the litter carry. They lifted the man into the metal gurney portion of the device and secured him tight. He was still mostly unconscious, though every so often he moaned and mumbled. Usually, a team of at least six trained people was needed to carry a litter any distance. Two passing hikers dropped their packs and were able to lend a hand, but the quarter-mile carry took a solid thirty minutes. It was an awkward balancing act, pulling, lifting, keeping the man balanced, and moving over the rocky terrain. Once the young man was finally safely in the helicopter and on his way to the hospital, Kes and Matt broke down the litter carry and parted ways.

Arriving emotionally and physically exhausted, Kes needed some quiet time to regroup and get in the right mental space for the week ahead. Medical calls like those from her hike down were common and took up the largest portion of her time when she was in the canyon. On busy summer days, medicals could keep her running at all hours of the day and night. In the quiet moments just before being thrown into the fray, she wanted to catch her breath and let the feelings crashing over her subside. But before she had even shut the door behind her, she heard Ranger Trudy Thatcher rushing through the station excited to greet her. As much as Kes adored her coworker, being around anyone else right now felt daunting and overwhelming.

Trudy wrapped Kes in a hug and held her for a beat too long for Kes's liking. As Kes unpacked, Trudy filled her in on changes around the station and visitor numbers, her words tumbling out of her mouth at a mile a minute.

"It looks like we'll have about 15-20 campers each night and the cabins and bunkhouse should be near full. We may have some thunderstorms this week, but nothing too bad. Between the two of us, I figure we'll be able to split the busiest hours."

While Trudy rambled on, Kes organized all her belongings, unpacked her food in the shared kitchen area, and made a snack. After twenty minutes of Trudy's incessant, nervous chatter, Kes was well beyond her tolerance.

"So, how are you doing? Feeling ready?" Trudy asked.

As innocuous a line of questioning as it might be, that was the tipping point. The minute the conversation turned her way, Kes felt her walls jettison up around her and she neither wanted to nor could she stop them. Kes couldn't handle the pity dripping from Trudy's words or the way Trudy tilted her head with concern, her knowing eyes burning through Kes. The anxiety building inside of Kes was unbearable. The jittering in her leg started again as she bounced her heel up and down. She didn't want to put on a brave face. She didn't want to think about it. She couldn't delve into those feelings and talk about what had happened. That would make it too real. She needed to escape, to flee the fears and pain creeping in. Kes didn't feel completely in control of her vocal chords as she squeezed her fists so tightly at her sides that her short fingernails dug into her palms. She had to keep everything together.

"I'm fine," Kes snipped, more abruptly than she intended. Immediately she felt a twinge of guilt. No matter their history, Trudy had never been anything but kind, and she didn't deserve Kes's anger. Trudy had felt the loss too. The edgy energy filling Kes's body was intolerable, causing everything to feel a little too loud, too bright, and too much. She felt the room getting smaller as she stood under Trudy's gaze. She needed to get out, to break free.

"I'm going to go for a run," Kes said, spinning away from Trudy, not willing to see the hurt look she was sure was there. Grabbing her radio, running shoes, and water, she took off out the back door, hoping she could right her mind. She needed to find some release from the tightness in her throat and the pain in her chest. But the loss felt harder and greater down here, as if the open expanse of the canyon just allowed the pain building in her chest to grow and fill the empty space between the canyon walls. Without looking back, she took off, hoping the burning in her lungs would distract her from the burning ache in her heart.

An hour later, after a punishing run, Kes's mind and body were sufficiently numb. Out of habit, she'd taken off up Clear Creek Trail. The first section of the trail rose steeply

along the inner canyon wall above Phantom Ranch in a grueling climb. No matter how many times she'd done it, the
trail still took her breath away, and the first part of her run
was more of a glorified fast walk than anything else. After
the initial rise, the trail wound along a mostly flat plateau
for nine miles. After what she figured was around five miles,
Kes turned around and slowly made her way back toward
the station. It was inconsiderate to leave Trudy alone to handle the calls, and Kes chided herself for doing so. Even if
it wasn't uncommon for only one of them to be on duty at
a time and even if no medical calls had come out over the
radio while she was gone, it didn't excuse her behavior. Kes
knew Trudy had also hiked down that day, and if anything,
Kes ought to be there to at least catch up with her friend.
She couldn't literally run away every time the topic came
up.

When she was still a half-mile from Phantom Ranch,
Kes's feet led her to a natural rock bench looking out over
the ranch, the Colorado River, and the two bridges that
crossed the river. It wasn't her intention to end up there. But
with her mind still reeling, she sat down on the bench and
let out the breath she was holding. She had been nervous
about this tour ever since the chief had called her into his office. But she didn't think it would be this hard. Everywhere
she turned, Sara was there. Kes could hear Sara's laugh in
the bubbling of Bright Angel Creek. She saw Sara running
ahead of her on Clear Creek Trail, goading her on as her
long legs outpaced Kes's. Even now, the constant presence
never really left her mind. Sara was everywhere and yet...
nowhere.

How could she be gone? Sara seemed so vibrant, energetic, and alive when she and Kes last sat on this bench, looking out over the canyon. Strong, full of laughter, and active—nothing like the frail figure Kes had last seen.

Kes's breathing was labored, even though her heart rate returned to normal. She felt the panic building in her chest and knew she needed to do something. Her stomach churned and felt icy cold. She couldn't lose it, not here. Closing her eyes, she took a deep breath and held it, focusing on her heart pounding in her ears.

She felt the pressure of a hand on her shoulder and then a warm presence next to her. She remained hard and cold, the pain still squeezing her chest, but slowly her breathing returned to normal. Still, she knew she couldn't open her eyes just yet.

"I'm not going to say the right thing, Kes. I don't know what this feels like for you. I miss her every day and I cannot imagine the pain you are feeling," Trudy's voice was like a calming balm, and as much as Kes wanted to resist and remain stoic, she could feel her body relaxing. "She's still here," Trudy said with a sad smile.

Kes nodded, willing her eyes open, and swallowed hard. "Tru, I'm sorry. I shouldn't have snapped at you." Kes apologized, her jaw set and her eyes trained on a rock between her feet, unable to meet Trudy's kind eyes. Kes's face betrayed none of the pain she was feeling.

Trudy smiled lightly. "It's okay. I know that wasn't about me. Remember, you don't have to run away just because you're scared of feeling the loss," Trudy said, squeezing her closer, Kes unbudging. Kes nodded again, her eyes unmoving, her face stony and silent, unable to trust her voice.

"Now, how about some dinner?" Trudy said with a smile. She was ever the caretaker and would not be deterred by Kes's controlled responses.

Chapter 6

The next morning, well before dawn's light was even a hint on the horizon, Mae stood at the South Kaibab Trailhead. (Granted, before she heard Frankie pronounce it she was pretty sure it was Shish Kabob Trailhead and that thought made her stomach rumble.) Her pack was securely strapped on her back, hip belt and sternum strap fastened, her hiking poles threaded onto her wrists, and an entire passel of hummingbirds rattled around in her stomach. Was it a passel? Perhaps a vibration of hummingbirds? A thrum? A glitter? A chorus?

In any case, the nervousness in her stomach was peaking as she bounced back and forth from foot to foot, chilly and nervous. She still couldn't make out the canyon other than to notice the cavernous blackness in front of her. Looking out over the edge, Mae imagined she was looking into the pitch-black night sky, the only difference being stars were missing from the bottom half of her view. A blacked-out sky full of possibility and the great unknown; if Cabot were here he'd probably quote Captain Kirk or something equally as geeky.

From where she stood, she could just make out the start of the trail before it careened haphazardly and disappeared into the inky abyss. That didn't help her nerves in the slightest as the chorus of hummingbirds doubled in numbers. What had she signed up for? Maybe she should head back to her hotel; there was still time to chicken out and put this whole ridiculous plan to bed.

"Oh good! You're here!" Frankie's soft voice piped up behind her, equally startling and comforting. Thank goodness she wasn't headed into the darkness alone. Mae felt the tension in her shoulders relax a little bit. With one final water fill-up and balance check on their packs, they set out, Frankie leading the way. The dust Frankie stirred up with every step reflected in the narrow beam of light from Mae's headlamp. Outside of the beam of light the world around her was inky black, even more so thanks to the sheer contrast between the brightness of her headlamp and the darkness of the canyon. Glancing toward where the trail dropped off, the glow of Mae's headlamp was quickly dispersed and was overcome by the sheer magnitude of the canyon. Mae returned her gaze to the section of trail between her and Frankie. The dusty trail was punctuated by large rocks, steep steps down over large wooden logs laid across the trail, and uneven terrain. Mae minded each step down, careful not to trip on the impossibly narrow trail. To be fair, the trail had to be at least 5 or 6 feet wide but it felt significantly more precarious. One edge of the trail was the ever-rising canyon wall and the other edge dropped off into nothingness. It was easier to just keep looking down than to let the rising fear of the unknown consume her thoughts.

The pair hiked in silence. That's one thing no article ever told Mae about the canyon, how immensely quiet it could be. In the early morning, away from the village, the darkness and silence engulfed the trail and Mae's consciousness. All she could hear were her hard, steady breaths, her heart pounding in her ears, the crunch of gravel under her boots, and the occasional ting of the metal tip of her hiking pole catching a stone step. Neither Mae nor Frankie was willing to break the solemnity of the silence with conversation. There was something sacred about hiking into the canyon, as if they were entering a great cathedral, an occasion that called for reverence, attention, and respect. The quiet companionship was comforting. Mae matched Frankie's pace and stride in a consistent rhythm, their hiking poles striking the ground in sync. Mae made no effort to break the moment, and instead stayed wrapped in her own thoughts.

She thought of the joy on Cabot's face when she agreed to his ridiculous plan. She thought of how proud he looked when he dropped her off at the airport, probably aching to join her but knowing it was something she had to experience on her own.

She thought of how natural it was to hike with her pack now. The weight felt bearable and comforting; something familiar in unfamiliar territory. The benefit of backpacking Grand Canyon in the summer was that she would not need a tent, nor much in the way of a sleeping kit. Though it was only in the low 50s this morning, at the bottom of the canyon, down almost 5,000 feet in elevation, the nightly temps would be comfortably in the mid-70s, and a lightweight sleeping bag and pad would be amply sufficient to keep her warm.

Mae imagined what Terese's face would look like if Cabot told her Mae was hiking the canyon. Mae felt a bit of pride at the idea of Terese being shocked and impressed. Then again, Terese wasn't one to acknowledge anyone else's accomplishments. And this trip isn't even about Terese anyway, Mae reminded herself, quickly dismissing the thought. Yes, Terese may have been the impetus for the recent upheaval in her life, but each of the decisions Mae made in the months since that day in the cafe was about realigning her life to match who she truly was and who she wanted to be. Mae quit her job because she no longer believed she had to play it safe or continue to be controlled by Terese. She agreed to go on this crazy adventure because it was something she'd always wanted to do and she was finally willing to be brave and try. With every step, Mae grew more confident, capable, and strong. For the first time since she boarded the plane in Bangor, she started to feel like she could do it. She could hike down to the bottom of the Grand Canyon, and she was on her way.

After what Mae guessed was almost an hour of silent hiking, she noticed Frankie stopped a couple of steps ahead of her. Frankie rested heavily on the ends of their hiking poles, switched off their headlamp, and turned to look back at Mae. Mae looked up at Frankie's smile and, for the first time that morning, she broke out of her inner universe and took in the view around her. Mae's jaw dropped as she saw the outline of the canyon just before the sun broke over the horizon.

"Are you serious?" Mae said, disbelieving, her voice barely above a whisper. Tears sprung to her eyes and she let out a quiet nervous laugh. She'd seen photos of the Grand Canyon before, and as magical as those were, the two-dimensional likeness was nothing compared to the real thing. In front of her, the canyon walls stepped down, getting progressively smaller and longer until they were merely elegant fingers reaching out across the flat platforms. Plateaus and cliffs overlapped as far as she could see, which was farther than she could have imagined, echoing toward the horizon until they faded off in the distance. The hues of rusted reds, burnt oranges, and soothing purples mixed together in the pre-dawn glow. The light was still soft, emphasizing the mystical and dreamlike feel of the canyon. On the backbone of a rock formation reaching toward the deepest section of the canyon, Mae had a vantage point to fully take in the depth and dimension of the world around her. The sting of tears overflowed and streamed down her cheeks. Mae took a deep breath in and let the clear, wild air fill her lungs. It felt different than the air in Maine; drier, rich in earthy scents, and it carried with it the feeling of being connected to everything at a core level.

Mae turned again to face a beaming Frankie, who pointed a hiking pole toward a sign that read "Cedar Ridge." Mae remembered the location from the trail maps she'd studied. The topographic lines and artistic representations of the hues and distinct layers of the canyon had not prepared her for the reality of physically being here. Neither of the hikers said a word as they stood alone at the point, adventurers in the wild.

After a few minutes, Mae pulled out her drawing pad and made a quick, crude sketch with shaking hands, well aware nothing could capture this feeling. Elated. No, it was more than that. Euphoric. Here she was fulfilling a lifelong dream, adventuring out west, sketch pad in hand, wandering into the wild. She was doing it! And not only that, she was rocking it. She looked back up the trail to see the winding path. The trail weaved and wound its way through the layers of rock above her. Some layers sloped gradually down and were covered with low scrub brushes while other sections were sheer cliffs, where the well-engineered trail clung to the walls to make the steepest parts passable. There were hairpin turns in tight groupings to get through the steepest sections, and a long expanse where the trail hugged the wall, slowly making its way ever downward. It was absolutely astounding to see just how far they'd come in a short time.

Turning back to the view in front of her, Mae met Frankie's eyes and brilliant smile.

"Well, where are my manners? I ought to formally introduce myself if we're fixin' to hike this crazy place together. My mama would be ashamed." Frankie reached out a warm hand, an extension of the warmth emanating from somewhere deep within. "It's good to put a face with your voice, Mae. I'm Frankie, your enby, queer fairy, hikin' pal." Frankie's drawl was adorable and charming.

"Enby?" Mae asked, taking Frankie's offered hand.

"Non-binary. Neither M nor F on my driver's license; more like BAMF. I use they/them pronouns. How about you? Should I say yes ma'am, yes sir, or yes your royal awesomeness?"

Mae let out an easy laugh that resounded in the quiet morning. There was something incredibly likable about Frankie's demeanor, inviting and direct. "I guess I've never thought about it, but I suppose out of those choices, I'd go with yes ma'am."

"Well then, yes ma'am, it is!" Frankie tipped an invisible cowboy hat, really laying the drawl on thick. "Shall we continue on our way? We've still got a ways to go."

Receiving a smile and nod from Mae, Frankie turned on a heel and moved on down the trail.

For the first time, Mae could observe her hiking partner. Frankie's wiry frame moved fluidly, barely leaving a mark with every step. Their back was ramrod straight as if their pack weighed nothing at all. Their lithe forearms and upper arms rippled with every placement of their hiking poles, and Mae imagined Frankie was likely deceptively strong. They seemed open, welcoming, and warm; something that resonated like a hug in Mae's mind.

"So, what do you think?" Frankie asked. It was still early and the pair had yet to see anyone else on the trail. Frankie was grateful for the mostly-quiet hike thus far. Always the "social butterfly," in the words of their sweet mama, Frankie had plenty of experience in finding ways to drop the "non-binary" bomb early. By leading with it, they prevented any later confusion or awkward conversations, and it usually weeded out the people who would be disrespectful. After years of dealing with "a bunch of redneck hicks who wouldn't know their asses from a hole in the ground, bless their hearts," (another Mama-ism), Frankie could read people pretty well and knew whether or not they'd be accepting.

Even in the pitch dark the night before, Frankie could tell Mae would be welcoming. She had a very calming and open presence. Though Frankie could feel the nervous excitement that thrummed in Mae's smile and words, the energy never felt draining or overwhelming. Frankie was glad for the company on the hike, feeling more at ease sharing this experience with someone else, even if much of the time they walked in silent companionship.

"I can't believe I'm actually here," Mae said, her voice stronger than it had been the night before, invigorated by the fresh morning desert air.

Frankie agreed, "It's astounding. I remember seeing it for the first time. I stood at Mather Point with my parents and just stared at it. I couldn't have been more than nine. We were on one of those epic family road trips where everyone packs into a clunky old RV like a bunch of sardines. I think we were here for only a few ticks, but I felt the pull then. I wanted to explore, to march into the depths of the canyon, and face the wildness. I came back a few years ago, but only for a day. I've never made it past Cedar Ridge before. This is all new territory for me."

"The next point is Skeleton Point?" Mae asked from behind.

"Yes'm. You know the trail well!" Frankie said, impressed.

Mae blushed at the easy praise. "I tried to research everything before coming here. I must have read every guidebook I could get my hands on. Cabot laughed every time I brought home a new book from the library about this place. He said, 'You know, there is a thing as too much research.' I just wanted to know what I was getting myself into," Mae giggled self-consciously.

"And Cabot is your honey?" Frankie asked, without a hint of judgment.

"No…" Mae laughed easily. It wasn't the first time she'd heard that question. Townspeople often tried to pair the two of them up together or called them a cute couple. Over the years, it became a running joke. "We're not each other's type…" Mae let the last word hang in the air. She'd never been comfortable being direct about her identity, certainly not as direct as Frankie had been. But she felt she could be honest.

"Ah, another rainbow pal!" Frankie said excitedly, proud their acutely-tuned gaydar had performed spectacularly once again. "So, do you have a sweetheart?"

There didn't seem to be any hint of agenda in Frankie's question, nor did Mae feel like she was being put on the spot. Frankie's natural curiosity and sincerity made it easy for Mae to be real and open with her responses.

"No girlfriend for me," Mae said, sadness lingering in her words. As much as she'd like to remove Terese completely from her mind, old habits die hard. She remembered the look of triumph in Terese's eyes when she had introduced her wife. There was an edge there, a bitterness in her words as if she hoped to cause pain. It's not that Mae wanted Terese back, not by a long shot (and not just because Cabot would lock her away before that happened). It was more the worry of being unlovable that always followed the sharp pain of any encounter with Terese.

Frankie felt Mae's energy shift and stopped to look at her. "You alright?" Frankie said, reaching over to place a hand on Mae's arm.

Mae smiled gratefully. "Yeah," Mae said, letting her voice trail off. Frankie squeezed Mae's arm and remained quiet. In their experience, when people need to talk, giving them silence was the best invitation to open up. Mae sighed and continued hiking, for the first time leading the pair. Frankie followed along behind and listened intently as Mae relayed the story of Terese the Terrible and the encounter that was the catalyst for setting out on this adventure in the first place.

The whole time Mae was speaking, Frankie listened without judgment. Occasionally, they'd nod, shake their head, or add in a thoughtful "oh no," just so Mae knew she wasn't alone. After another half a mile of hiking, Mae was finished relaying the tale. Behind her, Frankie took a quick breath and said, "Well ain't she just the curly end of a prize hog."

Mae stopped mid-step, caught off guard. From deep within her soul, a laugh bubbled up until it burst forth from her mouth ringing out clear and beautiful. She turned to look back at Frankie and was rewarded with a brilliant, mischievous smile. In that moment, Mae felt completely seen and accepted under Frankie's gaze. Outside of Cabot, no one knew the whole story of what had happened with Terese, and she'd always feared telling anyone, certain they would find fault in her being, just as Terese had. Yet here was an almost complete stranger who saw Terese for exactly who she was and wasn't afraid to call it as they saw it.

Frankie leaned on their hiking poles and said, "Some-one like that sounds like nothing but pain. You're well rid of her." Mae nodded and wiped a few stray tears from her eyes.

"Sometimes we have to experience those moments of complete and utter pain to remind us of what we want and what we don't want. You are a bright and beautiful soul. Don't let her dim your glow." Frankie smiled earnestly at Mae.

"So, you're my hiking pal and emotional guide?" Mae asked, smiling.

It was Frankie's turn to laugh. "Yes ma'am. I'm a full-ser-vice friend. Now, as your guide, I prescribe a couple of deep breaths of this delicious desert air, a smile, and a long hike."

Mae laughed and nodded.

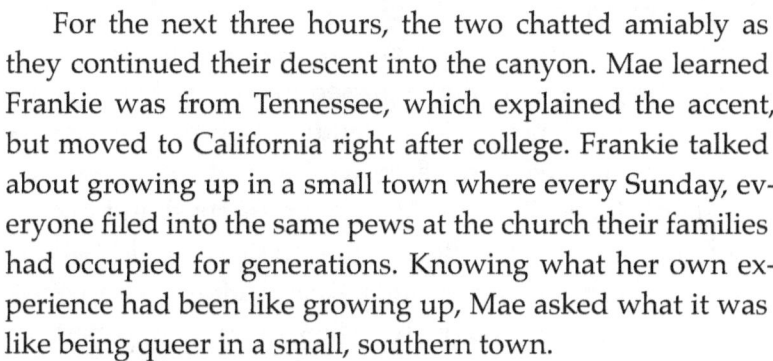

For the next three hours, the two chatted amiably as they continued their descent into the canyon. Mae learned Frankie was from Tennessee, which explained the accent, but moved to California right after college. Frankie talked about growing up in a small town where every Sunday, ev-eryone filed into the same pews at the church their families had occupied for generations. Knowing what her own ex-perience had been like growing up, Mae asked what it was like being queer in a small, southern town.

There was a sense of pride in how Frankie described

their childhood; something golden and nostalgic that made Mae wish she'd been there. Frankie told stories of their fierce mama and how she'd made Frankie's childhood safe, warm, and amazing. Growing up in the "belt buckle of the Bible Belt," as Frankie put it, Mae expected being queer would have been an issue. Frankie laughed as they relayed the story about the time Mama stood up in church one Sunday and reamed the pastor a new one when he tried to preach a sermon on the sin of homosexuality. Mae laughed easily at the image of the preacher packing up and high-tailing out of town that same day, terrified of the little spitfire that was Frankie's mama. From that point on, Frankie's mama gave the sermons each Sunday and nobody had any problem with that.

As they spoke they took turns leading and following, easily passing the conversation back and forth between them. Frankie talked about their life in San Francisco as Mae relayed stories about the quiet tourist town she'd lived in all her life. By 8 am, it was already well over 80°F and in the sun it felt even hotter. With the temperature at Phantom Ranch predicted to reach 115°F in the shade, Mae quietly thanked Frankie's back for getting her butt on the trail so early. Along the way they'd passed hikers on their way up out of the canyon, and Mae couldn't help but notice how fit they all looked and yet how slowly they trudged up the steep slopes. She looked back up the trail and gulped, knowing in just a few days' time, she too would have to make her way back up the long, steep path to the top. Shaking the worrying thought from her mind, she turned her attention forward.

Having dropped into the inner gorge at Tip Off, Mae could clearly see the mighty Colorado River, though it still seemed quite small. Mae had read somewhere that it was 300 yards across, wide enough to fit a football field in the long way, though she couldn't imagine that was even possible from this angle. With every long step downhill, the sound of rushing water grew closer, crescendoing to fill every space within the walls rising up next to her. After nearly five hours of hiking, seven miles, and a 5,000 feet drop in elevation, Mae's legs shook from exhaustion. Her thighs were not used to what equated to hours of split leg squats. The trail wound its way through the dark rocks of the inner gorge, impossibly snaking back and forth, ever descending without feeling like it was making any progress toward the bottom. Mae hoped they were close as she leaned heavily on her hiking poles with every step, desperate to shed the heavy weight of her pack and sit down in the shade. The strap of her hiking poles had rubbed a quarter-sized section of her hands raw from the constant sweat and dirt that clung to her hands. The space between her shoulders felt pinched and tight as she shouldered the pack that felt so light hours ago. She imagined the refreshing wind on her sweat-laden back, her heavy boots off, and her feet soaking in the cool stream. She longed for a cool drink and a break from the constant pounding of her feet on the rocky trail.

"Shit!" Mae exclaimed, losing her footing on a loose stone. In a split second, she felt her stomach drop and her arms lunge forward, as she struggled to find a solid foothold. With the momentum of her heavy pack on her back, she fell hard, crashing painfully onto her palms and knees.

A sharp pain in her knee caused Mae to wince. Tears stung in her eyes and swirled her vision. For a moment, the world faded away as the pain settled in. Ego bruised and covered in dirt, her confidence was shot, and fear and doubt quickly rushed in to fill the void.

Why did she think she could do this? She wasn't outdoorsy. She wasn't fit. She wasn't strong. She wasn't cut out for this. She felt the negative thoughts swirl in her mind and tears sting. A searing pain coursed through her knee as an acrid scent burned through her nose. Blinking the tears out of her eyes she noticed the damp dirt under her hands and realized she'd landed in a rancid puddle of day-old mule piss. The smell was beyond terrible, as it seared her senses. The pack leaned awkwardly, tipping forward, threatening to push her face first into the pee puddle. Frustration and self-doubt screamed deep within her, pushing out everything around her as her tears flowed freely.

Somewhere outside her pain, she felt a presence by her side. "Hey. It's okay, it's okay," Frankie said, seeing Mae's tears. "You've got this. What would an adventure be without a few bumps along the way?"

Frankie continued, their genuine and kind smile shining light through the darkness building in Mae's mind. Mae grinned slightly and allowed Frankie to help her to her feet.

"Okay, now what hurts?" Frankie asked, reaching for Mae's hands to inspect them. No visible issues. Looking down, Frankie noticed a deep cut on Mae's knee. Blanching slightly at the blood dripping down Mae's shin, Frankie had to look away before their stomach betrayed their mock bravery. "Well, we're definitely going to need to do something about that," Frankie said, pointing at Mae's knee while looking away. Mae looked down and for the first time registered the source of the stinging pain radiating through her knee. The cut didn't appear too deep though Mae knew she'd need to take care of it. What concerned her more though was the stark paleness of her new friend's face.

"Hey Frankie, are you okay?" Mae asked.

Frankie simply nodded, without turning around. "I can't do blood," Frankie said, barely getting the words out before walking ahead.

Mae felt horrible, knowing she caused Frankie discomfort. Dropping her pack quickly but carefully to avoid the still-stinking piss pond, Mae pulled out a bandana and crudely tied it around her knee. She knew Cabot told her to keep the first aid kit handy, but she had stuffed it in the bottom of her pack, certain she wouldn't need it on the well-traveled path. Unwilling to completely empty the contents of her pack, she hoped her makeshift bandage would be sufficient. It wouldn't be enough to stop the bleeding, but at least it would slow it down and, more importantly, cover it until she could properly clean the wound. She knew Cabot would give her an earful when he heard what happened. Donning her pack again, Mae winced as she hobbled over to where Frankie was standing. "Hey, it's okay now. No more blood." Mae said, placing a hand on Frankie's shoulder.

Frankie took a deep breath before responding, "Sorry 'bout that." Their voice was small and soft.

"No worries! Just another bump in the adventure," Mae said smiling easily.

Frankie returned Mae's smile. "Are you okay to keep hiking?" Frankie asked, genuinely concerned. Mae was grateful for Frankie's honesty and care. Though her knee stung and she couldn't walk without pain, she felt a strange confidence building inside her. Yes, she'd tripped, but it wasn't the first time. And she was okay. The gash wasn't too deep and it would heal. She was better than okay. She was on an adventure and she'd made it this far. She wasn't broken.

"I'm okay. I can do this."

"Yes, you can," Frankie said, their voice returning. "And you know what happens when we get there, right?" Frankie asked, a grin growing. Mae looked puzzled. "We're going to soak in the creek and drink ice-cold, sugary sweet lemonades," Frankie said triumphantly. Mae's mouth watered as she imagined how delicious that would be.

"We're almost to the tunnel, so it's not much farther now," Frankie said, pointing to a dark cavernous hole in the side of the canyon wall just up ahead. The trail disappeared into the pitch-black darkness, echoing the sound of the river that reverberated off the walls around them.

"If it's alright by you, I'd like to go through the tunnel by myself," Frankie said. "It's just something I want to experience alone," Frankie stated. Mae nodded, thankful for a moment to compose herself before continuing. "See you on the other side!" Frankie said with a wink.

Mae watched Frankie's pack disappear into the inky darkness of the tunnel. With a blink, Mae was alone. She took a deep breath and closed her eyes. The river noise dominated all her senses. The wind smelled like a mix of salt, dirt, and mule piss, not a scent she expected to get out of her nose anytime soon.

"I'm on an adventure and I can do this," Mae whispered to herself and took a few tentative steps into the tunnel. A few feet in, she found herself blinded by the darkness and stopped to give her eyes a few seconds to adjust. With barely enough light to make out the sides of the tunnel, Mae held her poles out in front of her like two swords to stop herself from walking into the walls. Slowly and steadily she hobbled forward, moving toward a blinding light at the far end. The outline of a round opening grew larger and clearer with each step forward. The fear and pain she felt faded into the darkness as she moved into the light. With one final step, she exited the tunnel and stood at the end of the Black Bridge.

An engineering marvel, the Black Bridge spanned out over the raging, muddy brown Colorado River. At the far end, Mae could make out Frankie's form holding up both their hiking poles and waving excitedly. Stepping out over the bridge, Mae was astounded. The wooden planks under her feet were well worn by hikers and mules alike. She touched both sides of the narrow bridge at the same time and slowly moved forward. She felt the suspension bridge move slightly with every step. It was barely wide enough to let two people pass, and Mae felt grateful she didn't run into any mule trains while crossing, as there would be no place for her to go but backward toward the tunnel. The water rushing below was disorienting and cleansing. It drowned out her internal doubt and removed any last fears she had with its rapid current. The tempo of the river coursed within her, bubbling through every part of her soul in excitement. She was here! She had actually done it! With every step, the smile on her face grew until it beamed from deep within her as bright as the hot Arizona sun.

"Welcome to the bottom of the Grand Canyon," Frankie said with a bright smile across their face as Mae stepped off of the end of the bridge. The pair hugged as best they could with their awkward packs and hiking poles. Giddy, a bit slap-happy, and energized by the accomplishment, the two moved quickly, giggling most of the way to the campground. Finding their sites, they quickly shucked their packs and made their way down to the banks of Bright Angel Creek.

They were both roasting and sweaty, and nothing sounded nicer than a long soak in the cool water. Within seconds the pair were lying in the creek, fully clothed, and delighting in the incredible landscape around them.

"How's your knee?" Frankie asked and instinctively looked away. Mae lifted the edge of the bandana to check and flinched slightly. The cut was deeper than she had realized and hadn't stopped bleeding fully.

"I should clean it and get a better bandage from my first aid kit, I think," Mae said, as she tried to disguise the fear in her voice.

"It may not be a bad idea to have someone look at it," Frankie offered. Mae shook her head, feeling bad for having already inconvenienced one person with her clumsiness.

"No, no, I'm okay," Mae insisted. She figured she'd bandage it properly once she'd cooled down and rested a bit. Frankie looked doubtful.

"Well, at least let me go get you a lemonade from the

ranch." With a smile, Mae agreed and with that Frankie was off.

Chapter 7

With every breath, Mae's lungs filled with warm desert air, and with every release, she felt more at home. Lying in the chilly creek water, Mae's knee was comfortably numb. There was nowhere she needed to be but here. She had done it. She'd made it to Phantom Ranch. The juxtaposition of the warm desert air against the cold creek water was invigorating and refreshing. Her body was wonderfully sore and well-used. She was exhausted and closed her eyes, allowing her body a moment to rest.

In the heat, Mae let her mind wander and she drifted somewhere in the limbo between awake and asleep. Real noises from hikers walking past, birds rustling in the leaves above, and the soothing plink of water cascading over boulders mixed with her mind's wanderings, and she found herself deeply caught up in her daydreams. She was exploring a narrow canyon. The twists and turns of the impossibly tall rust-red walls mirrored the bends and curves of the cool, clear water running over her bare feet. She felt the sun warm her, gently kissing her eyelids, her face upturned. The wind whispered through her hair and over her ears, caressing her skin. She felt completely free, unburdened, and untamed.

A smile pulled at the corners of her heart, brightening and lightening her body until she felt like she was lifted from the river suspended a few feet off the ground. A warm wind current lifted her higher as she spread her arms out to steady herself. She felt the joy rise in her chest, the air tossing her around gently, lifting her even higher. The updraft of air swept her up and spun her delightfully, releasing any ties that held her fastened to the surface.

With a deep inhale, she opened her eyes and looked out over the vast expanse, floating high above the river bed she'd stood in. From this vantage, she took in every corner of the carved landscape with heightened senses. She soared over the land, diving down into the canyons, weaving in and out of the various mesas and plateaus, playing and floating on the currents. This feeling of pure exhilaration was intoxicating; she never wanted to land again, drawn to the farthest horizon, desperate to see what lay beyond.

Somewhere far away a faint voice beckoned to her. It resonated deep within her body, awakening parts of herself she'd forgotten were there. It was music in harmony with the song in her heart and she felt drawn to it. She circled back, searching for the voice's owner.

"Mae?"

She heard it again, this time louder. The voice was tender and familiar and it caused her heartbeat to quicken. Slowly, it became louder and clearer until she felt a warm hand pressing on her arm.

As Mae blinked her eyes open, it took her a moment to

come back down to earth. She looked down to see a tanned, wonderfully warm hand resting on her arm. Following the hand up to the owner's face, she felt her breath catch. Glacial blue eyes, a peppering of freckles across the bridge of her nose, that charming grin and melodic voice.

She felt the cool creek flowing over her legs, the rocks digging into her back, the wind in the trees, and the sun on her face. This felt more real than a daydream. She looked toward the bank and saw Frankie standing nearby, smiling. She was definitely at Phantom Ranch, so she hadn't lost her grip on reality too much.

Mae turned back to those piercing eyes and felt her heart jump. A small "wow" slipped through her lips, caught off-guard by the incredibly beautiful woman kneeling before her. "Kes?" she whispered, wondering how she could be awake, as it was only in her dreams where she saw those impish, twinkling eyes.

A wide grin broke across Kes's face and she gently squeezed Mae's arm. "You remember me?"

Mae felt the warmth of Kes's hand flood her body as she nodded slightly. A glint caught her eyes, the sun reflecting off the gold nameplate on the park ranger uniform Kes wore. "Oh fuck," Mae said nearly inaudibly.

Startled and wide-eyed she looked up at Kes's surprised look. She hadn't meant to say that out loud and felt blood rush to her face as her heart pounded in her chest. She didn't think Kes could be any hotter, but the uniform definitely put the icing on the cake.

Kes laughed wholeheartedly at the quiet, unexpected expletive and embarrassed look on Mae's face.

"You work here?" Mae asked, in an attempt to regain her composure. She wasn't sure if she was actually drooling or if that was just in her mind.

"No, I'm just a sucker for a polyester uniform," Kes said, her face sincere until a slow grin spread from ear to ear. She was stunning and Mae couldn't help but giggle, feeling excited and completely overjoyed by Kes's sudden arrival and brilliant smile. Mae could stay here all day, just looking into Kes's eyes.

"Your girlfriend says you banged up your knee. Can I help?" Kes asked. Her voice was still very kind, but there was an authority there Mae hadn't heard before. It only added to her sexiness factor, Mae decided. To be honest, Mae had completely forgotten she had any appendages at all, as she had gone altogether soft. Her brain hadn't yet processed Kes's words.

Frankie piped up from the shore, bringing Mae back to reality. "First of all, darlin', not a girl. And secondly, don't you worry, her dance card is wide open."

"Well, that's good," Kes said, returning her focus to Mae.

Mae blushed again and shot Frankie a glare, causing Frankie to laugh and retort without taking their eyes off of Mae, "Yes, ma'am. As sweet and free as tea on my grandmama's porch."

"Frankie!" Mae chastised, which only made Frankie laugh harder until they were in tears. "I'm just gonna leave you to it," Frankie said walking away, their laughter echoing after them.

Kes smiled slightly to herself and donned a pair of medical gloves before gently lifting Mae's knee, thankful for something to focus on. She cradled the back of Mae's calf in the palm of her hand as she gently removed the bandana. Methodically and tenderly Kes moved her fingers around the wound, checking the edges of the cut. It was free of debris, having soaked in the river, but it looked painful.

Mae couldn't take her eyes off of Kes's face the entire time. She watched the care and kindness in Kes's eyes and her every touch. She completely forgot about the pain in her knee. All she could feel were Kes's hands, her gentle fingertips, and the warmth radiating from her palms all the way up Mae's legs. Mae was grateful Kes was not taking her pulse as her heart pounded in her chest. She was sure her feelings were written all over her face already.

"How does it feel?" Kes asked, meeting Mae's eyes for the first time since Frankie walked away.

Kes's eyes were inviting, deep, and full of emotion. Mae could hardly find her words but managed a weak, "I'm okay." Kes was mesmerizing, and being this close to her again only heightened all of the feelings Mae had harbored for years.

"Does it hurt when I do this?" Kes asked, bending and extending Mae's knee slightly while keeping her eyes locked on Mae's.

"Just a little," Mae squeaked out, distracted by the electricity thrumming through her system.

"Okay. I'll clean the wound and bandage it for you. The bandages will need to be changed a few times and you'll need to keep them clean and dry so it doesn't get infected. I don't think you'll need stitches, but I want to keep my eye on you." *That's not all you want to do*, Kes thought, her mind immediately taking her back to the feelings that hadn't faded since the first time she'd laid eyes on the beautiful woman before her. *Keep it together, Wylde,* Kes thought, *you're on duty dammit.*

Clearing her throat and dismissing the naughty thoughts strumming through her mind, she continued. "You'll likely be sore and hiking will be painful for now. You'll want to rest and ice it as best you can to keep swelling down. How long are you down here for?" Kes asked with concern on her face.

Mae furrowed her brow and her anxiety started to build in her chest. "I'm here tonight and tomorrow. But then I'm supposed to hike up to Cottonwood for a couple of nights before coming back here," Mae recited her itinerary quickly. What if she couldn't hike? What if she'd done more damage than she had realized? What if she didn't get to see Ribbon Falls? What if… Before her mind could fill in the next concern, she felt Kes's hand squeezing her own and looked up.

"I bet we'll have you up and dancing in no time. I promise you're in good hands," Kes said with a wink and a genuine smile.

Mae felt her blush return and smiled shyly at Kes. Her eyes stayed locked on Kes's and she felt like the world faded away around them. She couldn't feel the pain in her knee or hear the hikers walking by. She didn't notice the mule deer who wandered into camp. She forgot she was sitting waist-deep in a cold creek. All she could see was the grin on Kes's face, the twinkle in her eyes, and the warmth in her look. Although she'd hate to inconvenience anyone and it would break her heart if she was not able to hike, she wouldn't mind staying at Phantom if it meant she could be near Kes.

Kes's radio burst to life on her hip, breaking the moment between them. Kes dropped her hand from Mae's arm and rose suddenly to her feet. "Get some rest today and I'll be back to check on you later," Kes said with a smile before walking away.

Chapter 8

Kes bound in through the back door of the ranger station, a smile still pulling at the corners of her mouth hours after seeing Mae. There was a feeling building deep within her core fueling an energy that buzzed through her muscles and made her feel like every cell in her body was vibrating. Mae had that effect on her and had since the first moment they met. Something about Mae felt like home to Kes, and it had taken no more than a minute in her presence to pull Kes right back to those feelings.

It had been a busy day since the moment Kes left Mae's side, her radio crackling to life at regular intervals, sending her running around in the heat. Kes assisted with unloading the mule train, weaving in between large piles of grassy green dung, and relieving the dirty, dusty, ornery animals from their canvas packs. She filled up a wheelbarrow with marked packages of food and medical supplies and pushed the uneven load a mile up the trail to the station, before returning for three more loads of necessities.

She was sweaty and worn out, her muscles reeling from

the long hike and stupid punishing run from the day before. Unable to fully focus on any of her tasks, everything took a little bit longer than usual. Her thoughts kept returning to the pair of mossy green eyes, adorable dimple, and grin that made her lose track of time. It had been over two years since she last laid eyes on the woman she found in the creek this morning, but still, the memory of the first time Mae made her heart skip a beat was fresh in her mind.

Mae had glowed back then too. Backlit by the last fingertips of sunshine, she was stunning. Her wild hair was extra curly in the salt spray and caught the light, giving her a heavenly aura. Mae's eyes shimmered and brimmed with sappy tears and she stood in the happy moment. She was magnetic and bright. Kes was immediately drawn in, excited, and brought to life, a feeling that had not faded with the years.

"Hey, K, the maintenance crew needs help hauling some gear up. Are you free to lend a hand?" Trudy said, jarring Kes back to the present.

Kes was startled, pulled from her dreamy thoughts. "Huh?" Kes asked, ever so eloquently.

"Maintenance needs help," Trudy said again, more slowly this time, unsure if her words were making any impact on Kes. Her friend seemed eons away, lost in some pleasant thought, Trudy guessed from the smile that still lingered on Kes's face. Whatever Kes was thinking about, it was good to see some of her lightness and joy returning.

"What's going on?" Trudy said smiling. "Why do you have that goofy grin on your face?"

"It's nothing," Kes said defensively, her characteristic

professional exterior returning. She shut down the wonderfully lovely thoughts she had about Mae, not willing to share them with anyone for fear she'd have her hopes dashed again.

"Kestrel Mead Wylde, don't you lie to me," Trudy teased. It had been far too long since Kes had shown even a hint of a genuine smile or any true measure of joy. Trudy wanted to fan those flames, keep the fire within burning, hopeful it wouldn't go out again. She knew she had to tread lightly though, for fear Kes would clam up again or run.

"Really, it's nothing," Kes said, though the look on Trudy's face made it clear she wasn't buying it. As much as she wanted to close off this part of her heart, Trudy wasn't likely to stop asking.

With a sigh, Kes relented. "Remember the report of the hiker with the banged-up knee from earlier? Turned out to be a woman I met at Sara's wedding a couple of years ago," Kes confessed, unable to stop a slight grin from crossing her face. She couldn't help it.

Kes remembered the shock she felt when Frankie led her to Mae. She'd been so caught off guard seeing Mae here, in her canyon, her safe place, her home, that she couldn't stop herself from reaching out to touch Mae's arm if only to confirm she was real. Kes's heart pounded the minute Mae opened her eyes, and a thrill coursed through every cell in her body. Over the years, she was certain her mind had improved Mae's features, making her more beautiful as a memory than she could possibly be in real life, but quite the opposite was true. She was even more lovely than Kes had remembered. Mae's eyes hadn't faded even a smidge and neither had their effect on Kes.

She may have been more thorough than medically necessary in her examination of Mae's wound. She needed time to regain her composure, to bring herself back to the present, and not let her mind run off wildly into her dreams again.

As reserved as she was with most people, there was something about Mae that lit her up from deep within. She had no fear of being open and completely transparent with Mae. In fact, in the short time they had spent together years earlier, she was more herself with Mae than she had been with just about anyone else in her life. She'd asked about Mae's itinerary, not because she was worried about the gash on her knee changing her plans, well, at least not completely. She hoped she'd get to spend some time with Mae and that their moments together wouldn't be cut short this time.

The excitement and joy she felt bubbling up inside her surprised her. For so long it felt like those pieces of herself were gone, like they had shriveled up and died with Sara.

"Wait, do you mean Mae? Mae is here?" Trudy asked, interrupting Kes's thoughts again.

Kes paled and ice filled her gut as she felt her armor snapping back to attention again. All pleasant thoughts of Mae were flushed from her mind. How could she have forgotten?

Chapter 9

"Okay, so what's the deal with Ranger Dreamy?" Frankie asked, breaking the silence between the pair.

Mae blushed and nearly spit out some of her dinner (tuna and crackers, which was pretty tasty, if she did say so herself). She couldn't help but grin widely, so much so that she was sure anyone in the campground could probably see the way she felt about Kes.

"I knew it! There is something there. Spill it, honey."

Mae thought back to that first moment she saw Kes.

Mae smiled broadly at her childhood friend, Marie. From the moment they met on the first day of preschool, the two girls were inseparable. Just after parent drop-off, Marie stood by the door wailing her eyes out, her sad face pressed on the glass. Mae walked over and put her arms around Marie's middle in an awkward little kid hug. When Marie turned around Mae picked up the teddy bear she'd brought from home and handed it to Marie. Marie smiled slightly as she pulled the teddy bear to her chest, squeezing it tight. Without a word, Mae walked over to the corner of the room and started coloring. Marie followed her, teddy bear still firmly held in her little arms. Quietly, Marie sat down next to Mae, who passed her a piece of paper and pushed a few crayons her way. From that point on, wherever Mae went, Marie was sure to follow.

Back then, Mae was a wild whimsical child, always shoeless, wandering the woods and hills of the island, a fearless adventurer, her curls flying off in every direction as she dashed down the trail. She was found high in the branches of trees more often than she was found on solid ground. She'd climb as high as she could and lie with her stomach across a branch, her legs dangling down on either side. For hours she'd watch a downy woodpecker hard at work pounding its sharp beak into the side of a tree. Or she'd have a staring contest with a barred owl as it slowly blinked at the flightless creature far above the ground. From deep within a hidden pocket, Mae would pull out a small sketch pad and scribble away at one with the world.

Marie was the more sensible, grounded, risk-averse of the pair. While Mae wandered high above in the canopy, Marie would sit patiently at the base of a tree, her nose deep in a book, lost in the words and worlds within. As different as they were, they could not have been closer. They spent every moment together growing up, so much so that most of the townsfolk assumed they were twins. There was no memory Mae had of her childhood that did not include

Marie.

Then, in their first year of high school, they were suddenly and painfully ripped apart. The fishing industry on the island had been slowly dying, forcing fishermen to venture farther from shore every year to haul in enough just to get by. Both Mae's and Marie's dads were struggling to stay afloat with the price of fuel skyrocketing and the abundance of massive commercial fishing enterprises pushing the smaller boats out of business. Unwilling to spend another winter unsure whether they would have enough money to keep food on the table, Marie's dad sold his boat and all his gear and took a job with an oil rigging company off the coast of California.

When the girls heard the news, they held each other tight and bawled for hours on end. They promised to stay connected, and for a few months, Mae received postcards and letters from Marie's adventures out west. She'd kept all of Marie's letters, and spent hours daydreaming about all of the places she'd love to adventure with her best friend.

But over time, the letters and phone calls came less and less frequently. Mae was heartbroken, feeling like half of her was missing from the equation. Everywhere she went, she wished Marie was there with her.

One evening years later, Mae found herself home alone again, her confidence and self-worth destroyed by a particularly painful lecture from Terese. In between tears, Mae heard the ping of a new notification on her phone. Checking it, Mae felt a warmth fill her heart as she saw it was a friend request from her oldest and dearest friend. That night, Marie and Mae spent hours catching up over chat. They picked up again as if no time had passed. Marie was engaged to be married and was coming back to Maine for the wedding. To Marie, it seemed only natural that her childhood best friend stand up with her at the wedding, and Mae graciously accepted.

The small wedding party gathered on Sand Beach. Well, everyone but one very late officiant. Mae was slightly nervous showing up and only knowing Marie. But when she arrived, Marie's fiancee, Sara, gleefully embraced her, heartfelt and open. Sara introduced her to everyone as Marie's childhood partner in crime, a sentiment that warmed Mae's heart and endeared Sara to her forever. For the better part of an hour, the party explored the beach and talked about the happy couple. Mae teared up as she watched how genuinely adorable Marie and Sara were. Marie glowed every time she looked at Sara. Sara was so tender as she tucked a stray hair behind Marie's ear. And Marie was equally as kind and open. It was beautiful to see.

Sara let everyone know the officiant would be arriving shortly, calling them all back from their respective wanderings across the beach. Mae pictured her childhood minister, frumpy, always out of breath, white-haired, a little too handsy, and paler than a ghost.

So when a dark-haired blur ran past her, Mae was surprised. Kes flashed a brilliant but apologetic smile at Sara, who stood in mock scolding. Mae thought her heart might pound out of her chest. Kes was absolutely stunning. The depths of love in Kes's blue eyes as she recited her lines reminded Mae of the color of the waves. They glittered and sparkled, dancing playfully while communicating the sheer expanse of her affection for her friends. Mae saw the kindness and adoration on Sara's face when she looked at her best friend and felt it acutely. Sara adored Kes and the feeling was obviously mutual. Kes beamed a brilliant smile to rival the glow of the setting sun from the moment the ceremony began, and when that smile turned her way, Mae felt the brightness fill every fiber of her being.

As Kes recited her part of the wedding, Mae was touched by her words. She spoke truthfully and openly about the love Sara and Marie shared, never holding back her admiration and affection. She laughed from the deepest parts of her abdomen, genuinely and infectiously. It was the most joyful sound Mae had ever experienced, and she couldn't help but feel tears sting her eyes with joy upon hearing it. Throughout the rehearsal, Mae's eyes stayed trained on Kes. Her movements were easy and graceful, like a peregrine in flight; agile and strong.

After the rehearsal, most of the wedding party remained on the beach, enjoying the beautiful colors after sunset. Sara's young nephews ran up to Kes and launched themselves into her open arms. She easily caught one child per arm and spun them around. When she set them down again, they giggled wildly and took off running, with Kes not far behind. Mae watched the trio run with abandon, sand flying with every step. Whenever Kes caught the boys, she lifted them high and swung them out over the waves, threatening to let go and toss them into the cold water. They laughed with the uninhibited glee reserved for children and begged for mercy.

At one point Kes caught Mae watching and winked. Mae felt an electric pulse course through her stomach when Kes's eyes caught her own. Mae felt her old self stirring inside her. Being around Marie again had that effect, and she was sure the twinkling, devilish eyes of Kes only inspired that desire more. She wanted to run after Kes and the kids. She wanted to follow them into the wild waves, letting the salt spray, cold water, and gritty sand wash her clean. She wanted to throw her head back and laugh like the gulls nearby, fully embracing the moment, the life that surrounded her. But she held herself back, the voice inside her head still cutting her down before she could break free.

When the boys were thoroughly exhausted, which Mae didn't think was possible, Kes scooped them up, one under each arm, and returned them to their waiting parents. Within a few steps, Kes was by Mae's side. "So, you're the infamous Mae, Marie's childhood accomplice? As I hear it, the two of you wreaked havoc in town."

Mae smiled brightly. "I'm sure Marie exaggerated the tales. I promise you I'm innocent," Mae protested.

"I doubt that's true, or at least I very much hope you're at least a little bit naughty," Kes said with an impish glint in her eyes.

"So, you're crushing on her pretty hard? Your long-lost dreamboat?" interrupted Frankie, stirring Mae from her memories. "And now she's here, rescuing you in that sexy uniform? Well, that just dills my pickle! Got yourself the sweet beginnings of a romance novel, I reckon," Frankie said teasingly.

Mae cracked up laughing, partially because she hoped Frankie was right, and partially because she was a little embarrassed. Deep within, a budding hope was beginning to take shape, and she was excited but also worried. She didn't want to be hurt again. But there was something to the glint in Kes's eyes when she said Mae would be up and dancing again soon that made Mae believe she had reason to hope.

But, in the span of a single breath, another voice entered Mae's mind. Sneering, ridiculing, abusing. It was the familiar voice that piped up whenever Mae started to feel joy. The words often changed, but this time the words were ones carved in her brain from that same wedding weekend. "Don't be an idiot, Mae. I bet she was only talking to you out of pity," the voice scoffed.

Chapter 10

Kes sat on the sand at Boat Beach, completely covered in sweat and out of breath. As was her habit, she came down to the beach after sunset to work out and get some quiet time. Tonight it seemed even more crucial.

After the awkward moment with Trudy that afternoon, Kes had done everything she could to avoid going to the ranger station. Thankfully, the day had been full of projects and work to do, so it was relatively easy. Still, she didn't like the conflict and tension.

Digging her toes into the sand, she looked out over the Colorado River and remembered that night on Sand Beach. For years she had heard stories of Marie's childhood friend and admired the spunk and fearless soul from Marie's tales. She heard about the time Mae made up a song filled with the most ridiculous phrases to distract Marie when she froze on a cliff face during one of their adventures. Kes heard about the little devilish sprite who swam across the frigid harbor stark naked on a dare. She heard about the time Mae went missing for a night at age 10. She wandered into town the next day, bleary-eyed and covered in mud. When her parents asked where she'd been, she explained she needed to return a baby loon she found stuck in the mud to its nest and she waited hidden nearby all night to make sure the parents came back. Kes had laughed to the point of tears at the description of a little mud-streaked, red-cheeked, wild-eyed ruffian, who walked into town barefoot with tears in her eyes having saved a baby loon.

On Sand Beach, Kes knew in a heartbeat the gorgeous, curvy, teary-eyed woman standing behind Marie was the infamous Mae. Kes saw the glimmer of an impish scamp in Mae's twinkling eyes and sexy smile, but she was so much more than the girl from Marie's tales. Kes felt drawn to Mae as if something deep in her core was magnetically pulling them together. She wanted to know Mae, to make her laugh, to be bathed in the light of her heart. She remembered feeling utterly jittery with nervous excitement walking up to Mae and how quickly she was put at ease by Mae's lilting laugh and warm heart.

That evening, the wedding party had dinner together at a local restaurant, and Kes made a point of sitting next to Mae. As soon as she could, Kes tried to engage Mae in conversation, longing to know her, what made her smile, what she hoped for, what made her heart warm. Sara watched the whole scene with a knowing look. Sara could always read Kes like a book and easily cut through any bravado or strong front Kes put up. She hadn't seen Kes's heart on her sleeve often; usually it was tucked well below the many protective layers she'd built up over time. But it was good to see the way Kes's face lit up every time Mae turned her way.

With everyone around, Kes couldn't very well hoard all of Mae's attention, as much as she would have liked to. Instead, she resigned herself to little tidbits of conversations and being able to sit back and watch Mae when others stole her attention away.

Kes loved the way Mae's lips curled up in one corner when she was trying to contain a smile. She loved the way Mae bit her bottom lip when she was thinking and the genuine way she showed her care in everything she did. She loved seeing the colors of Mae's eyes change and the way they often looked moist with tears upon hearing a particularly sappy story about Sara and Marie. Kes wanted to wrap her arms around Mae in those moments.

Kes asked Mae a barrage of questions, loving the sound of Mae's sweet voice and the fire in Mae's eyes. She loved the excitement and passion Mae had when Kes asked her about her sketches. She couldn't remember everything they talked about, only that she didn't want the night to end. Kes had long been enamored with the Mae from Marie's tales, but the Mae of real life was even more swoon-worthy.

After hours of talking and laughing, Kes still longed for more time. As Sara and Marie stood to leave, Kes rose to give them a hug goodnight. Sara gave her an extra squeeze and whispered "Now, don't keep my bridesmaid out all night. We need you both to be alert and ready tomorrow." Kes blushed, unsure she was ready to share what she was longing for in her heart.

In her pocket, Mae's phone vibrated against her leg. She felt her stomach drop as if it were suddenly filled with a

brick of lead as she looked at the time and noticed 37 text no-
tifications, all from Terese. She braced herself as she opened
the messages, each one more demanding, asking where she
was, when she'd be home, who she was with, and so on.
Dread, guilt, and shame flooded Mae's senses, deflating the
joy she'd felt just moments before.

Mae stood abruptly, her face pale and concerned. She
knew she had to leave as quickly as she could but didn't
want to be impolite or rude. She hugged Sara and Marie
goodnight, thanking them for inviting her. She felt the
warmth in Marie's embrace, but even that could not touch
the guilt she felt deep in her core. Just minutes before, she
had felt so alive, intrigued, and excited, but the text messages altered every feeling she'd felt and moment she'd experienced that night.

Kes stood by the door, watching the change in Mae's
demeanor. It was subtle, but after studying Mae all evening,
Kes could feel the shift. Mae smiled sweetly at Kes, but the
smile didn't quite reach her eyes. Kes opened her arms to
give Mae a hug goodnight. As Mae's arms wrapped around
her body, Kes melted completely into their warm and welcoming embrace. Kes took a deep breath in and was completely lost and equally at home. Mae smelled like vanilla,
balsam fir, and fresh ocean air. Kes struggled to clear her
mind as Mae let go. With one last heart-stopping grin, Mae
was gone.

The next day was a whirlwind. Kes barely saw Mae before the wedding, but when she did, Kes felt like she couldn't breathe for a second. Mae was wearing a smart, well-fitted button-down, green bowtie highlighting her eyes, and a pair of khakis with the bottoms rolled up. She looked sexy as hell, and Kes felt at a loss for words. She longed to take Mae's hand in her own and walk along the waves, just getting to know her more. Kes hadn't realized she was staring until she felt Sara hip-check her. "What?" Kes said, failing to look innocent.

"Talk to her," Sara prodded. "Come on, Ranger. Lay that Wylde charm on her."

"Hush your mouth!" Kes said, in a whisper, hoping Mae couldn't overhear their conversation. "Let's just get you married."

"Fine, but you'll talk to her after you get me hitched. She deserves someone who looks at her the way you do, and it's my wedding day, so you can't say no," Sara said, in mock bossiness, making Kes smile in spite of herself.

During the wedding, Kes willed herself not to look at Mae, knowing if she did she would completely stumble over her words or forget to have the brides exchange rings, or something equally taboo. But the minute her officiating duties were completed, she allowed herself to look over, and in that moment she fell in love with Mae all the more for the beautiful tears of joy streaming down Mae's face.

The reception was held on the second floor of a local pub. Kes hoped she could find a seat next to Mae, again, but those hopes were dashed the moment she realized their assigned seats were at separate tables. She tried to catch

Mae's eye, but every time she looked in her general direction, Mae was looking in her lap. It was as if the bright light that had glowed throughout Mae's entire being a mere hour before had been completely extinguished. She was sullen, she looked pale, and her eyes were vacant. Kes wasn't sure what was wrong and longed to go to her side. Seeing her opportunity when Mae rose to use the restroom, Kes quickly excused herself and followed suit.

Opening the bathroom door she found Mae in tears, completely crumpled in on herself. Instinctively, Kes wrapped her arms around the sobbing figure and pulled Mae's head to her chest. Mae molded to Kes's body perfectly and wrapped her arms tight around Kes's middle. Kes pressed her lips against Mae's forehead, unsure of the source of the tears but completely certain of her role right then. She wanted nothing more than to take away any and all of the pain Mae felt at that moment. Silently she stroked Mae's back, feeling Mae calm slightly with each passing breath. The world melted away until time had no meaning to Kes. She didn't want to let go. She placed another kiss on the top of Mae's forehead, causing Mae to look up into Kes's eyes. She could have happily gotten lost in those mossy green pools. More than anything she longed to see them glow again.

That's when all hell broke loose.

The bathroom door slammed open, causing Kes to jump. Instinctively, she put herself between Mae and the door and looked straight into two piercing black holes. The expression on the woman's face in the doorway was terrifying and evil.

"What are you doing?" The voice hissed in the doorway, barely audible but frightening. The tone in the bitter voice filled Kes's veins with ice as she felt all of the blood drain from her extremities. Something about this woman sent Kes's protective instincts into overdrive. She'd dealt with more than her fair share of homophobes in the past, but this woman didn't strike Kes as one of them. Who was this and who did she think she was talking to any human being like that?

"Is this why you got home so late last night?" The voice continued, blaming and writhing with every word. Kes felt her stomach drop. Home?

Mae's voice was barely above a whisper and she stepped out from behind Kes. "Terese, I'm sorry. It's not like—"

"I bet she played the 'poor me' card," Terese said addressing Kes, interrupting Mae, dismissing and diminishing her all in the same breath. "It's her way of getting attention," Terese continued. Turning to Mae, Terese said, "Why is it every time I turn my back you're off flirting with someone new? I can't even let you go to the bathroom without worrying you'll run off. As if anyone would be interested in you, my pudgy little one."

Kes felt her dinner lurch in her stomach. The abusive ridicule and cruel sentimentality made Kes absolutely sick. She was astounded by the vile lies spewing from this woman's mouth. Even without knowledge of their past, there was no way Kes could ever believe Mae was anything but sweet, faithful, and giving, likely to her detriment. As real and as genuine as Mae was, Terese was the exact opposite: narcissistic, abusive, and brutal. Kes's heart went out to

Mae and she longed to take her away from all of this. But in the shock, she found she was frozen in place, terrified and enraged.

And then almost as quickly as the rage started, it dissipated. Kes was left feeling even more uneasy with the new version of Terese standing in front of her. "You always do this, don't you. We're having a really good time and you find a way to ruin it and make me get really mad at you," Terese said with a huff. She acted so hurt and even pouted slightly. Her whole face changed, but Kes could still see the sharp bitterness that never softened in her eyes.

"I guess I'm just not good enough for you. I'll go home by myself, then." Terese turned on her heel, not even waiting for a response from Mae. Like a puppy cowering with her tail between her legs, Mae walked out the door chasing down the retreating icy figure.

Kes was dumbstruck and for a solid five minutes, she didn't move. What just happened? Where was the ass-kicking young punk she'd heard so much about? How could anyone ever put out that inner spark and why on earth would they want to?

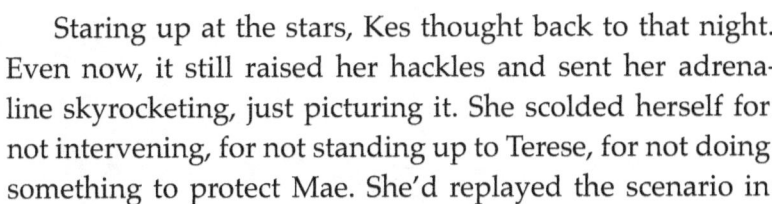

Staring up at the stars, Kes thought back to that night. Even now, it still raised her hackles and sent her adrenaline skyrocketing, just picturing it. She scolded herself for not intervening, for not standing up to Terese, for not doing something to protect Mae. She'd replayed the scenario in her mind a thousand times, without feeling better.

She remembered every moment of that night clearly, every word spoken, every time she saw Mae shrink a little more as Terese's words cut her down, and the emptiness she'd felt when Mae left. She remembered everything. Every single moment... except for one.

The one thing she forgot, the memory that had made her avoid the ranger station all day, was that it was Trudy's sleeping face she woke up to the next morning.

Chapter 11

With a deep breath, Mae relaxed deeper into the warmth that surrounded her. She was loved. She was cared for. She was safe. Those feelings coursed through her whole body as she felt two arms pull her closer. Instinctually she nuzzled her face deeper into the soft skin, taking in a familiar, intoxicating scent. She could feel her heart soar as a hand stroked her back and two lips pressed against her forehead. There was something so incredibly endearing and loving in these small touches.

Mae knew this embrace well, though for two years she only ever experienced it in her dreams. When they first started, she felt guilty for dreaming about someone other than Terese and worried Terese would know. At the same time, she longed for the dreams, because it was in those moments where she felt truly at home, truly loved. In the minutes before Terese stormed through the door, Mae felt completely safe with Kes and completely accepted. Kes didn't ask why she was crying nor did she admonish her for her tears. She simply accepted, without expectation or conditions, and pulled Mae into an embrace that calmed and soothed the pain in her heart.

It was a feeling Mae had unconsciously chased for years. She'd ached for it, without understanding what it was she was missing. There were brief, fleeting moments when she felt like she found a taste of that feeling when she was with Terese. But then it would vanish again, leaving behind an even bigger hole and ache. For years she tried adapting herself and clung to the little love nuggets when they came. She tried to figure out who she was in the moments Terese was affectionate, or at least some sad facsimile of the affection Mae longed for. She wanted to be that person all the time because if she was, then just maybe Terese would be happy and loving and Mae would be enough.

But stepping into Kes's arms, everything clicked. She didn't have to pretend or try to be someone worthy. She was home, and she was accepted for exactly who she was. In those moments, she was seen and loved. Simple, yet not simply found.

The feeling always lingered for a while after she woke, and she'd find herself trying to cling to the last few moments of sleep, willing the dream to go on.

This morning was no different. The first birds twittered above her, beckoning her from her sleep. Instinctively, Mae squeezed her eyes shut, aching to dive back into her dreams. Unable to stop her mind from stirring awake, she sighed and reached for her phone on her nightstand. It wasn't until her hand touched dirt that she opened her eyes and realized she wasn't home.

Mae sat up with a smile and enjoyed the view. It was

almost dawn, as far as she could tell. The sky was a pale pink and the light made the inner canyon seem even more romantic than she imagined it would be. Mae heard a beautiful songbird singing nearby, the same one who had stirred her from her slumber. The song was brilliant and resonated clearly in the morning air. Excitement bubbled in Mae's chest even though her entire body felt beaten up. The hike had worked out muscles she didn't know she had, and she felt as if her age had doubled overnight. Stretching skyward, Mae creaked and untangled herself. Tentatively, she stretched out her knee. It was sore. She felt the bandage pull uncomfortably at the healing wound, but overall, she was pleased it didn't feel worse.

Mae slipped into her dust-covered hiking boots and moved silently out of the campground, sketch pad in hand. On the hike down, she'd noticed a beach not far from the Black Bridge and she set off along the trail hoping to find it. It seemed like the perfect place to enjoy sunrise and maybe spot a glimpse of the trilling songbird that started her morning.

As she walked, Mae took in the smells of the inner canyon. They were distinct and very different from the new scents she experienced on the hike down, and not just because it lacked the pungent "Eau d' Mule Piss," though that was a relief. Instead, this place smelled crisp, like new life. There was the fresh smell of the creek splashing over boulders on its way downhill. Creosote, cactus, pomegranate, and fig trees added to the natural perfume. It was glorious and Mae smiled broadly as she enjoyed each deep breath.

After a few missed turns, Mae finally made her way to

the beach, only to find she wasn't the first one there. Ahead of her, she could just make out the outline of someone standing at the water's edge. The figure stood relatively still, looking down. The deafening roar of the river hid her arrival from her fellow hiker. Mae noticed a slight movement but didn't register what was happening until she saw the figure shed a button-down shirt, exposing well-toned shoulders and a white sports bra. They turned slightly, and Mae caught the distinct outline of a face she recognized. Mae coughed slightly, choking at the sight of Kes's nearly bare torso.

When the first things she saw were the twinkling stars above, Kes realized she'd spent the whole night on the beach. She hadn't meant to, but after a long day in the sun and feeling responsible for whatever Trudy might be feeling, she was utterly exhausted. She'd only closed her eyes for a moment but was quickly lulled to sleep by the roaring river and her warm sandy bed.

With a full night's rest under her belt, Kes felt a little stronger. She promised herself she'd talk to Trudy. They would be working together all week, and running away and avoiding the problem wasn't going to help.

As she sat up, she felt the gritty sand cling to every inch of exposed skin. She was completely covered. As bone-chilling cold as the river was, she was willing to brave the temperature to rid herself of the coarse grains. She removed her shoes, socks, belt, and radio, and emptied her pockets. Deciding it would be best to look semi-presentable, she removed her uniform shirt, but kept on her shorts. In the early hour, she felt safe no one else would be awake to catch her in her state of unprofessional undress.

Kes was startled slightly when she saw someone standing at the top of the beach but when she saw Mae's adorable face glowing in the pre-dawn light, she felt joy soar through her, making her heart race. Kes wanted nothing more than to walk up and pull Mae into her arms. She wanted to run her hands through that curly mop, kiss her face tenderly, and tell her how beautiful and incredible she was. Something about the morning felt like she was still in a dream, without restrictions or caution.

Damn, I really do need to cool off, Kes thought to herself with a giggle.

She pointed to a pile of belongings next to her feet. "Can you watch these for a sec?" she shouted, unsure her voice would carry. All Mae could manage to do was nod.

Kes grinned and walked waist-deep into the chilly river. Water closer to the shore was calmer, but even there she needed to be careful not to be swept downstream by the mighty Colorado. Kes studied the surface of the water and chose a spot not far from shore that was deep enough she could submerge herself, but still placid enough to mitigate any risk of being pulled away. As she dipped below the surface of the water, she felt her muscles constrict suddenly, forcing her to the surface to catch her breath. Though it was already well into the eighties in the early morning hours, the fifty-degree water always took her breath away, regardless of the air temperature. It was like being dunked into an ice bath; a good shock to the system. The heat coursing through her core didn't fade completely though, but she was able to temper it a little. Kes rose again and raked her hands through her hair, forcing the individual grains of sand to extricate themselves from her scalp. She dunked under again and this time her body didn't panic. Rising, she arched her back and stretched in the water, pulling her tightened muscles loose again. It was half a perfect start to her day; the other half being still on the shore.

Mostly clean and unable to keep herself away any longer, Kes returned to the beach to collect her belongings and join Mae. The draw Kes felt to be near Mae hadn't lessened with time; if anything, it was only stronger and Kes felt it grow with every step she took. Mae's focus was elsewhere, which Kes was grateful for. It gave her a moment to study Mae's face unnoticed. Mae's eyes were alight with excitement as she stared off into the brush that lined the edges of the beach, searching for something unseen. Her hair was wildly curly and askew. It was endearing. As Kes knelt before her, Mae turned toward her with a smile.

"How's your knee?" Kes asked softly, her voice a warbling whisper carried on the wind. She was lost in those green eyes, how they reflected the hues of the sage and desert brush all around. She could feel the warmth radiating from Mae's body, and felt the full impact of having her this close again. It was exhilarating. Mae's face was still sleepy and a soft warmth clung to her features, making her look even more angelic and inviting to Kes.

"A little sore, but okay I think," Mae shyly responded.

Having Kes this close so soon after the dream she had this morning was dangerous. She longed to reach out and touch Kes if only to confirm she was real and really here.

"May I take a look?" Kes asked, her eyes laced with concern. Kes gently placed her hand on Mae's leg. Mae gasped slightly at her touch. Kes's fingers were still chilled from the cold water, but that wasn't what took her breath away. Deep within, the feelings she'd woken up with reverberated again, filling her senses. She felt her heart pounding in her chest as Kes's long fingers rested lightly against her skin. All Mae could do was nod.

Kes pulled the bandage back slightly, careful not to cause Mae any undue pain. Looking for any signs of infection, Kes was pleased to see the wound was still mostly clean, save for a few grains of sand, and healing well. Kes shot Mae a smile. "It's looking good," Kes reassured Mae, keeping one hand on Mae's leg, just above her knee, unwilling to break contact. She didn't want to let go, afraid if she did, Mae would disappear. She wasn't ready to lose her again.

"I can change the bandage later today," Kes said, her voice still quiet in the early morning. She looked up and caught Mae looking at her. For a moment, neither of them said a word nor broke eye contact. Kes stayed kneeling in front of Mae, her hand still on Mae's leg. She studied Mae's face, the hint of a smile at the corner of Mae's sweet lips, the way one of her curls fell perfectly between her eyes. Kes noticed the way the river reflected in Mae's eyes, swirling and teeming with all of the feelings Kes held below the surface. Kes noticed the rise and fall of Mae's chest and found herself matching Mae's breathing pattern.

"Am I okay to hike tomorrow?" Mae said, breaking Kes's train of thought. "I was hoping to find Ribbon Falls on my way up to Cottonwood campground. I've heard it's stunning and absolutely magical." Mae's face lit up as she talked about it, and her eyes never left Kes's. The passion and intensity of her excitement were contagious, and Kes felt her heart rise with every word.

"It is amazing. There's a little trail off of the main trail that will take you out to the falls. It can be tricky to find and it's really rocky and uneven, so be careful. Make sure you take your time and bring enough water for the whole day," Kes said automatically from the script in her brain. She'd given the same speech about the falls thousands of times before to just about every hiker headed up the North Kaibab Trail. She didn't mean to flip into "ranger mode," but did so completely out of habit, without even realizing it. It was her duty to keep everyone safe and make sure hikers understood what conditions they would face so they could be adequately prepared.

Mae's face fell ever so slightly as she pulled the corner of her lip in between her teeth. Anxiety and doubt lurked in the dark corners of her mind. Her fears taunted her quietly. Maybe this wasn't something she could find on her own.

Seeing the light dim almost imperceptibly in Mae's eyes, Kes kicked herself for defaulting to work speech. She quickly moved to sit next to Mae, placing a hand on her forearm, leaning into her slightly as she did.

Mae looked up into the warm glow of Kes's gaze and felt her self-doubt fade. There it was; the feeling she longed for over the years. She felt empowered, strong, capable, and even beautiful. She felt herself relax under Kes's touch and allowed the light back in.

Kes smiled, "Ribbon Falls is incredible and you can absolutely go there. You made it all the way here. That's pretty badass. It's a long way to Cottonwood and Ribbon Falls, but you've got this."

Kes's words were genuine and spoke intimately to Mae's heart. Deep inside, Mae felt her strength returning. She wanted to believe Kes was right. Wasn't that why she was here? She'd already traveled across the country on her own, hiked this far, and even survived nearly face planting into mule piss. This time, she wouldn't let fear stand in her way, wouldn't let the voice of self-doubt color her reality.

Mae beamed and her eyes twinkled with excitement and gratitude. Kes's heart jumped. There was something so authentic about how Mae expressed her feelings. Without a doubt, she was truly herself in all moments, whether that was showing doubt or being unabashedly joyful. Kes loved watching Mae's eyes and the way they showed her delight. Kes didn't want to see Mae go but she would never get in the way of Mae's happiness.

"I'm not sure if I'll be able to, depending on how busy we are tomorrow, but if you'd like the company, I'd be happy to hike with you up to Ribbon Falls," Kes offered. She would do anything to extend the time she got to spend with Mae. She knew it was something she'd need to work out with Trudy, but whatever she had to do, she wanted to make that happen. The smile that spread across Mae's face was enough to melt Kes completely.

"Absolutely!" Mae said excitedly, her voice rising higher with each syllable. Mae felt warmed inside and out by the glow of Kes's brilliant smile. Kes's thumb lazily drew circles on Mae's arm, from where her hand still rested. The sensation sent an electric current coursing throughout Mae's body, heightening all of her senses. She felt the warmth where the length of Kes's side pressed against her. Everywhere Kes touched her, Mae felt as if her cells were overly excited and thrumming with energy. With Kes around, Mae couldn't hear the voice of self-doubt ringing through her ears. She couldn't hear the worry that she'd been trained to feel over the years. She couldn't hear the pain.

But she *did* hear something. Mae quickly turned her head in search of the source, causing Kes's hand to drop from her arm. There that sound was again. Somewhere nearby a songbird sang one of the most beautiful songs she'd ever heard. It was a descending trill, punctuated by a pattern of slowing tones at the end. It was the same call that had led her to the beach that morning.

Kes watched in utter fascination as Mae craned her head one way and then the other, eyes peering through the thick brush. Mae was incredibly cute, her hair bobbing with every sharp twist of her head, a smile seizing her lips, and her deep dimple popping out.

The canyon wren's call was one of Kes's favorites. She remembered when her grandmother first held her hand and in hushed tones pointed out the wren sitting atop a prickly pear cactus, its head tilted back, sharp beak wide open, singing its song to the skies. Kes could still feel the warmth of her grandmother's large, dark hands and see the way the wind played at the white wisps of hair peeking out from under her grandmother's oversized sun hat. Every memory of her brought to mind the scent of sage and cinnamon that always clung to grandma's clothes.

"Canyon wren," Kes whispered.

Mae turned wide-eyed to Kes, excited. "I heard it this morning when I woke up," Mae said. "I followed the noise down here, but I haven't seen it yet. I want to add it to my notebook." Mae glanced down at the sketchpad in her lap.

Kes noticed the small pad of paper for the first time. Mae opened it to her first page. Kes reached for the journal, but before she touched it, she looked at Mae and silently asked permission. Mae nodded meekly. Kes picked up the notebook and silently tabbed through each page, looking at sketches of birds, wildlife, and stunning scenic landscapes. The drawings were incredible, as detailed as scientific drawings but with an emotional depth that sucked Kes into the very moments they represented. She saw one of Sand Beach and could hear the crashing of the very real-looking waves. Deep within, all the feelings she felt on the beach the first night she met the incredible woman sitting next to her came rushing back in. She was astounded how deeply Mae's drawings affected her and captured a moment, a feeling, a memory. Turning a few more pages, she stopped on an unfinished drawing of a regal-looking falcon.

"American kestrel," Kes whispered.

"Yes!" Mae beamed. "I saw him back home this spring. I'd never seen one before."

"Absolutely stunning. My grandmother loved kestrels. She loved how they soared on the wind currents in the canyon. We used to watch them for hours, gliding on the updrafts, ridiculously fast. I think she wanted that sense of freedom too," Kes said, a mixture of pride and sadness in her voice. "She loved them so much, she named me after them."

For a moment, Kes simply stared at the drawing, unable to look away. From time to time, the loss of her grandmother hit her particularly hard. Seeing this nearly lifelike drawing of her namesake, it was almost as if her grandmother were there, reaching out through the universe to touch her heart. It caught her off guard, as grief sometimes did. With a deep breath, Kes looked up into Mae's warm eyes. She felt safe and unafraid of showing her true feelings.

"You two were close?" Mae asked, longing to learn more about the incredible woman next to her.

"Very. She raised me. My mom died giving birth, so Grandma took me in. I couldn't have asked for a better friend or parent."

"What brought you to the canyon?" Mae asked, hoping she wasn't prying too much.

"I've been here my whole life," Kes said with a smile, used to the shocked look that answer often elicited. "Grandma was a park ranger, one of the first female rangers ever. So I grew up, went to school, and got my first job, right up there," Kes said, looking toward the canyon's rim.

"Grandma was strong, independent, tough as nails, and hilarious," Kes continued, lost in her thoughts. "My grandfather didn't like that she wanted to tromp around the park, especially not in boots and pants, so she up and left him. She didn't follow convention, nor was she willing to compromise herself. She was wild, free, and untamed, much like the canyon itself." Kes's face lit up with obvious admiration.

"When I was little, Grandma used to take me with her whenever she went into the canyon to monitor migrating birds. I would run all over the park with my backpack and my little notebook, find a small perch to sit on, and listen for birds, while Grandma caught up."

Kes stared off for a moment, with a smile across her face. There was something peaceful yet impish about the grin that gently lingered on Kes's lips as if she were caught up in a particularly funny memory.

Mae was fully engrossed listening to Kes's story. She could imagine a young Kes, running around the canyon, studious and silly. She could see the depth of love and respect Kes held for her grandmother. Mae instinctively placed a hand on Kes's arm and smiled. Kes looked back at Mae and felt her throat burn with tears aching for release. She didn't want to cry in front of Mae or in front of anyone for that matter. But there was something so welcoming and warm about Mae's heart that made Kes feel she wouldn't be judged if a few slipped out. Swallowing hard, she willed them back down. To recenter herself, Kes looked down at the notepad again.

"You've really captured the spirit; energized and focused, yet incredibly calm," Kes said.

"I haven't finished it yet," Mae said, slightly crestfallen. Mae looked up at Kes apologetically, remembering the bitter April day when she had seen her falcon friend. Kes smiled, "I think it's beautiful just as it is."

Kes turned a few more pages. The last drawing in the

notepad caught her eye and stole her breath. She could make out a woman rising from the water. She was topless, arms outstretched as she raked her fingers through her hair. The water goddess's back was arched, exposing her taut stomach and well-defined hip bones. Kes looked at the figure's face and noticed her own familiar half-grin lining the drawing's lips.

Before she could study it any further, Mae deftly retracted the sketch pad and quickly closed the cover. The blush that flooded Mae's face filled Kes's heart with compassion. Mae was stunning, genuinely herself in all of her emotions, and it drew Kes in again.

After Sara and Marie's wedding, Kes had wanted to reach out to Mae, to connect, to get to know her on a deeper level, to check in, and to save her from whatever was going on with Terese. But even Marie couldn't reach Mae after that day; she was just gone. No presence online and she didn't answer any of Marie's messages. Marie, Sara, and Kes were all concerned, but from the other side of the country, there was little they could do. Kes was certain she'd never see Mae again, and yet here she was.

"You're beautiful," Kes whispered, in a voice barely audible. She was caught off guard by her own words, unsurprised she felt that way, but surprised she'd spoken her feelings out loud. Mae turned, amazed and unsure she heard Kes correctly. Kes looked uncharacteristically shy. She hadn't meant to let those words slip out from between her lips.

Kes cleared her throat and begged her voice not to betray her feelings again. "Have you seen a condor yet?" Kes asked. She fought her inner defenses threatening to rise. It had been too long since she was fully herself with anyone, but Mae had a way of getting past her armor. And for the first time in a really long time, Kes actually wanted to let someone in.

Mae beamed. The joy that filled Mae's face echoed deep in Kes's heart, erasing her embarrassment for having let her feelings show. Mae didn't say a word, just shook her head no, excitedly.

Kes stood up and dusted herself off. It was about time to start work for the morning. "I'm sure Trudy is wondering where I am and I suppose I ought to get to work, but I was planning on searching for condors in a few hours, if you would like to join me?" Kes asked hurriedly, nervous energy coursing through her system. Condor monitoring was one of her favorite responsibilities while she was stationed at Phantom Ranch, and she felt pretty certain Trudy wouldn't mind if she completed that task this morning. The smile that spread across Mae's face put another crack in Kes's armor. "It's a date," Kes said with a grin as she turned to leave.

Chapter 12

Mae trudged out of breath up the steep trail. With every step, she leaned heavily on her hiking poles, grateful for their assistance. Her muscles ached and twinged, tightly wound after the long descent the day before. Although it was still pretty early in the day, the temperature was already well over ninety degrees Fahrenheit. When she and Kes started hiking, Mae worried about keeping up with the lithe figure in front of her. Kes's well-defined calves and taut behind moved gracefully and surely, climbing the trail with ease. With every granite step, Mae was treated to the sight of Kes's well-defined muscles tightening and releasing, a fluid motion that was mesmerizing. As soon as she realized she was staring, Mae dropped her gaze, embarrassed. From the darkest places within her, she heard Terese's icy cruel laugh mocking her hope.

Tears stung the corners of her eyes as she tried to push the voice out of her mind. Right pole, left foot, left pole, right foot. Deep breath. Right pole, left foot, left pole, right foot. Deep breath. *Not this time*, Mae thought to herself.

The internalized version of Terese living in Mae's mind rent-free represented the worst of all of her self-doubt. The evil, sneering voice seemed to pop in to cut down any moment of happiness and every second when Mae allowed the hope deep within her to build again. Focusing on the ground in front of her, Mae tried to clear her mind of the toxic stench that lingered anytime Terese popped in uninvited. Terese lived in Mae's fears and fed off of them in a negative feedback loop that tended to snowball if Mae didn't cut the chatter immediately.

Taking another few deep breaths, Mae focused on the world around her, bringing her mind back to the present. She noticed the way the air smelled, the feeling of joy that had been steadily building over the last 24 hours, and the rhythm of her heart drumming in her ears.

Suddenly, Mae realized Kes was no longer hiking. Looking up, Mae was caught off guard by Kes's brilliant smile and the way Kes's eyes were locked on her own. She felt Kes's grin cut right through the last of her doubt and touch her heart. She felt the joy Kes sparked inside her alight again. And most of all, she felt seen.

"It's a date." When Kes had first said those words, Mae was certain she imagined them. So much so, that when she arrived at the ranger station, she was sure Kes would be too busy to hike, or worse, that Kes had invited her out of pity or a sense of duty and regretted it.

For years, Terese convinced her that anyone who spent time with her did so out of a sense of obligation or because they saw her as a charity case. But she never felt that with Kes. Kes seemed genuinely overjoyed to be in Mae's presence, and the radiating beauty that stood before her now had even gone so far as to call this a date!

"It's a tough hike up," Kes said, still out of breath. She paused for a moment, mid-sentence, to take a long pull of water from the bite valve of her water pack. "But totally worth it," Kes said, finishing her thought. "It kicks my butt every time."

Mae felt relieved knowing she wasn't the only one struggling with the elevation gain and terrain. Silently, Kes looked up the trail with a questioning look on her face, and with a nod from Mae, the pair continued the slog uphill. After another twenty minutes in silence, Kes led Mae off-trail to a small outlook. Removing her pack, Mae felt sweat on her back immediately evaporate as a warm wind blew by. It was an odd but not unwelcome sensation. Mae teared up looking out over the view. From here, she could make out the entirety of Phantom Ranch, the beach she found Kes on, the Black and Silver bridges, and the muddy Colorado River. Directly below she saw the camper cabins and canteen, the ranger station, and Bright Angel Creek, the small creek she was lounging in when Ranger Kes found her.

"It's pretty incredible, right?" Kes asked. Mae could only nod.

"You can even see the Yavapai Geology Museum from here," Kes said, looking across the river toward the South Rim of the canyon. "It's not far from where you started your hike, I'm guessing."

"You can?" Mae questioned, squinting toward the rim of the canyon, searching for any sign of a building. Kes smiled to herself at the studious look of scrutiny on Mae's face and moved to stand behind Mae to help point it out. Kes pointed her arm over Mae's shoulder toward the rim, squatting slightly to line her eyes up with Mae's. Without thinking, she placed her free hand on Mae's hip to steady herself.

With her body so close, Mae felt heady, as if an overload of energy was coursing through her entire system. Mae could barely focus. She felt Kes's breath caress her cheek and felt the heat emanating from Kes's hand on her hip, sending signals that overwhelmed her senses. She knew if she moved ever so slightly she would be pressed against Kes's body, and the mere inch between them was electrifying. She was immediately drawn into memories of their hug, but now the feelings were more alive and more vivid than she remembered. She took a deep breath to clear her mind, but that only filled her senses with the scent of Kes's salt-stained skin.

"If you look closely, there's a small building right there on the very edge of the canyon," Kes whispered, her lips not far from Mae's ear. Her words were warm, and they ran over Mae's cheek like a caress. She felt Kes's presence with every inch of her body and blinked hard to rid herself of the desire she felt. With a deep breath, Mae looked again, struggling to clear her mind. "Wait, that little speck? That's a building?" Mae gasped when she finally saw what Kes was pointing at.

Kes laughed heartily and squeezed Mae's hip slightly. Mae felt Kes's rumbling laughter vibrate throughout her rib cage and she wanted nothing more than to lean back into Kes's arms. She looked back at Kes. "Crazy, right?" Kes said, her gorgeous smile beaming, eyes filled with light. "I know it's tiny, but believe me, it's really there."

"I hiked all the way from there?" Mae said quietly to herself, searching the canyon wall for any sign of the South Kaibab Trail. From this angle, it was all but hidden in the natural breaks and scree slopes of the many layers of the canyon as they made their way down to the river. She was utterly shocked. Logically, she knew it was a long way. But it was one thing to see it on a map and know the distance and completely another to actually feel it. She was astounded by the sheer magnitude of her accomplishment as she felt the vast space around her. Mae realized just how far she had come, literally and figuratively. She could never have imagined she would be brave enough to embark on an adventure like this. It was incredible.

"Yeah, you did," Kes said, moving out from behind Mae to stand by her side. Quietly she watched Mae's facial expressions cycle through a range of emotions: surprise, shock, confusion, and finally joy. Kes enjoyed a few private seconds studying Mae. She loved the way Mae's eyes flickered and reflected her emotions. She loved how authentic and genuine Mae was with everything she felt; how it was written on her face without judgment or fear.

Kes acutely remembered the woman she found in the bathroom; fragile, drained, and lost. She remembered seeing the depth of pain Mae must have felt in that moment and the way she ached and wanted to reach out to protect Mae. It completely broke her heart watching Mae follow Terese out that door. She felt frozen in place, in shock and unable to comprehend what had just happened. Kes felt like she failed in some respects, knowing she just let Mae leave when there was no way she would be safe with Terese.

But the woman standing next to her had somehow survived without Kes. And more than survived. She was flourishing more and more with every passing moment. She seemed fully her own person, no longer hidden, belittled, or controlled. There were moments that Kes could see the lingering scars and influence of Terese, but even those seemed outweighed by the joy that shone so brightly from deep within Mae. It was as if she were coming into her own again.

Kes wanted to pull Mae into her arms and not let go. She wanted to tell Mae just how much she admired her. She wanted to apologize for not following her out of the bathroom and standing up to Terese. She wanted to tell her how she felt holding her close back then, even if it scared her. She wanted to open her heart and let Mae in, fully, without questions or conditions.

That feeling was terrifying. Kes had really only ever let in two people in her entire life, a sad fact she tried not to dwell on. Those were the only two people who never expected anything from Kes in return. But they were both gone now; losses that absolutely shocked and devastated her almost beyond repair. She wasn't sure she was willing to open herself up to that risk again.

A smile played at the corner of Mae's mouth and broadened ever so slowly until it spread across her entire face. She turned and was surprised to find Kes's eyes already waiting. In every single moment, Kes looked at her with such kindness and compassion. Mae didn't feel like the floor would suddenly drop out or that Kes would flip on a dime and snap at her. It was a new feeling, and she approached it with cautious optimism. She wasn't sure if she should trust herself and believe that this incredible woman wanted to spend time with her. But here they were, and the smile shining at her gave Mae every indication Kes wanted to be here.

"So, condor time?" Kes asked. Mae nodded excitedly.

As long as they weren't too swamped with medical calls, once a day one of the rangers would climb up to this vantage point to scan the skies for condor activity. They kept active logs of anything they found, noting the location and number of each bird. Each week the condor report was relayed up to the biologists at the South Rim to be compiled with observations from volunteers and staff scanning elsewhere in the canyon. It was an important study and a job Kes took very seriously.

Kes moved to her pack, extracted a weird metal contraption, a long cable, and a small receiver box. The metal contraption looked like an old radio antenna. Kes connected the cable to the antenna and receiver. Carefully, she turned the dial while slowly sweeping the antenna through the air. Kes moved the antenna from left to right, holding it parallel to the ground. Then she rotated her hand so the tines of the antenna pointed toward the sky and ground. Methodically and fluidly, Kes swept the antenna back and forth. When the wind picked up, she held the receiver closer to her ear.

Suddenly, Mae heard steady beeping coming from the receiver pressed against Kes's face. Kes turned and beamed a brilliant smile at Mae. "That's 280. She's a proud momma. She and 187 just bred successfully near the Battleship Formation." Kes pointed off into the distance at a large rock plateau.

Kes continued excitedly. "Condors usually mate for life. Condor 280 is mated to 187, and they have been a successful pair for many years. It's always exciting when they have a chick. Trudy and Sara used to bake a cake every time they had another baby, and we'd have a little party down at the ranger station." Kes smiled wistfully.

"Do you usually see condors?" Mae asked.

"They are still pretty rare. Back in the early eighties, there were only twenty-two California condors left in the entire world. The remaining condors were captured, and a captive breeding program was begun. Condors usually only lay one egg at a time, which makes increasing the population pretty difficult. But things are getting better. There are just over 400 condors now. In the mid-nineties, six condors were released to the wild not too far from here." Kes loved the story of the condors and told it many times over the years. She hoped she did it justice, remembering all of the times she heard her grandmother give the same spiel.

"Condor populations declined to near extinction due to human interference. It was our fault they were almost completely gone. My grandmother had a particularly soft spot for condors. I think she identified with coming back from the brink of destruction and finding a way to soar again. She and I would travel to the rehabilitation site every other week hoping to catch a glimpse of them." Kes continued her story without pause. Talking to Mae was easy, and she wanted to share her amazing grandmother with Mae, so maybe Mae could see her the way Kes did.

"That little spitfire somehow managed to talk her way into assisting with the initial condor release. I think seeing them up close solidified her connection. She longed to soar on the thermals rising over the canyon with them, and given the chance, I think she would have." Kes's smile was tinged with sadness. She'd never opened up like this to a relative stranger, but with Mae, she felt safe.

"Even into her nineties she still volunteered to monitor the condors. By then she was barely five feet tall and weighed about 100 pounds soaking wet. But she'd stand up on the rim with her spotting scope and antenna, searching for her condors and talking to anyone who walked by. She used to do the best imitation of the condor mating dance," Kes said, laughing.

"I wanna see that," Mae said, a little hint of deviousness twinkling in her eyes.

Kes's breath caught in her chest. There she was, the impish Mae she'd heard so much about. She wanted to see more of that spark, and if that meant completely embarrassing herself by imitating a condor mating dance, so be it.

"Okay, but this only works on condors," Kes said.

Feeling a little foolish, Kes extended her arms to either side of her. She tucked her head down between her shoulders and looked sheepishly down at her feet. She danced back and forth from foot to foot, keeping her arms stretched out at her sides.

Mae laughed openly from somewhere deep within. Her face lit up, and a fire glowed in her eyes. In that moment, Kes believed she could soar like a condor, riding on the columns of air rising out of the canyon.

"I think you could get that to work on whomever you wanted." Mae laughed.

"Promise?" Kes said hopefully, never taking her eyes off of Mae's.

It was Mae's turn to blush. Did she just openly flirt with Kes? Did Kes flirt back?

Kes held her gaze for a few moments before dropping her arms and continuing.

"My grandmother would happily perform that dance whenever she could, for whomever she could. Whenever I was sad, Grandma would condor dance up to me, making me laugh until I couldn't breathe. She always believed joy and love were paramount in life. She was such a hoot." Kes shook her head remembering her grandmother's antics.

The two stood in silence for a few moments. "Your grandmother sounds incredible, Kes. I can see her in you," Mae said.

Kes smiled gratefully. Talking about her, Kes felt her grandmother's spirit stir inside her. *Let it in, Kestrel.* Kes felt a little pressure in her chest hearing her grandmother's words echo in her mind. *Let it in.*

Kes studied Mae for a moment. Mae was absolutely beautiful. She was free, expressed her feelings openly, and never held back when it came to joy.

As Kes observed Mae, she saw a large black blur out of the corner of her eye. She smiled, knowing what was coming, and continued to watch Mae's face.

Mae's jaw dropped as the massive bird flew overhead. A hot wind gust followed behind and Mae's breath stopped. She turned quickly to follow its majestic flight as the bird soared and rose higher and higher over the plateau. She could just make out the large white underarm patches and the wing bands that read 194.

If she didn't know better, Mae would have sworn the condor was a small Cessna plane, turning lazy circles. She knew condors were large birds, but nothing had prepared her for the nine-and-a-half-foot wingspan that flew so close she could see every feather lining its long, graceful wings. Not a conventionally beautiful bird, but majestic nonetheless, Mae was in awe of their sheer power and freedom.

After a long moment of shocked silence, Mae broke into a laugh that bubbled up from the deepest parts of her heart. As she laughed, her eyes filled with joyful tears. She closed her eyes tight and turned her face skyward. The pleasure she held in her chest was too much, and it overflowed, pouring freely down her face. She laughed so hard she couldn't catch her breath.

"What! Kes! What!" Mae said, completely flabbergasted. She couldn't form a coherent thought.

"Amazing, right?" Kes said, with a knowing smile. Seeing the unabashed joy on Mae's face, Kes fell a little harder for her. Kes could see Mae's heart shining. It was incredible to be bathed in Mae's light. Mae felt everything, every moment, with all of her being. Usually when emotions were too strong, whether too happy, too sad, too angry, or in general, too much, Kes ran. Deep emotions like that scared her because to feel meant being vulnerable and letting someone else see you fully.

But she didn't want to run. She didn't want to hide her feelings. She wanted to feel it all, regardless of what feeling she might also open herself up to. Kes admired Mae and basked in Mae's joy. She didn't want to break the moment. Everything inside of her was drawn to Mae. Kes longed to wrap her arms around Mae's waist and pull her close.

"That's 194. She likes to buzz visitors, catching them unawares. She's a sass," Kes said, with a grin.

"I like to think my grandmother lives on in 194. She was born just after my grandmother passed, and she certainly has her spirit. Grandma would have loved soaring over the canyon, swooping down to check on me, scaring the crap out of visitors, and delighting young children," Kes said quietly, her words tapering off at the end. Something, or more like someone, inspired Kes to be more vulnerable and to share the feelings she'd kept hidden for so long.

Grabbing her pack, Kes turned to Mae. "I want to show you something," she said, reaching for Mae's hand.

Chapter 13

Mae stared down at her hand. When Kes reached out, Mae didn't hesitate to take the offered hand even though she was trembling. Now Kes's long fingers were intertwined with hers, leading her down a side trail. Mae's heart was pounding, but slipping her fingers in between Kes's had felt like finding a missing piece. She fit there and she didn't want to let go.

Looking up, Mae noticed they were at another viewpoint, though this one seemed a bit wilder, less visited. The view was just as astounding, but the privacy made it feel more intimate. Kes moved to a flat rock and shed her pack, motioning for Mae to join her. Mae followed suit. The rock was small, and Mae had no choice but to sit very close to Kes, her thigh pressed against Kes's. Mae couldn't see or hear anyone or anything nearby, and she easily imagined they were the only two people deep in the wilderness. She smiled to herself.

"Sara brought me up here after my grandmother died," Kes said quietly, gently opening the armor she'd held up for far too long. She looked out over the view and remembered the moment. Other than her grandmother, Sara had been the only person she felt safe being vulnerable around. Sara knew her—her faults, her fears, her tendency to run… she knew it all and still loved Kes.

After her grandmother passed, Sara gave Kes her space. For a full week, Kes was wound tight and was uncharacteristically short and agitated with everyone around her. Sara knew as long as Kes was in the ranger station or wearing her duty belt, she wouldn't let her armor down and let her tears fall. One night, Sara invited Kes out for an evening run, and after a grueling ten-mile slog, she led Kes here. The two sat in silence for a half hour, just watching the clouds pass by. Finally, Kes let go. She bawled, tears flowing freely for the first time, having been tucked away in all of the corners of her mind. Her throat burned and her head pounded as she cried openly. Sara simply sat with her, her arm wrapped around Kes's shoulders holding her tight.

"I miss her," Kes said quietly. She hadn't intended on saying that out loud. She wasn't exactly sure why she brought Mae here. She'd never shared it with anyone but Sara.

"Your grandmother or Sara?" Mae asked.

"Both of them," Kes said, with a sad smile. In the months since Sara passed, Kes refused to acknowledge the loss. She couldn't eat, focus, or make it through a day without feeling like she would collapse. She couldn't fathom the reality that Sara was gone. Every day she felt the absence and every day she pushed it away or tried to fill the void with yet another carved candlestick or spoon. Even now, it was tempting to distract herself and redirect her thoughts of Sara.

Mae reached for Kes's hand and wrapped her fingers around Kes's palm. Mae's hand was warm, and her grasp was firm and comforting, and it beckoned Kes back from the darkness. Sometimes in moments of deep grief, the best thing you can give someone is simply time and a safe place to grieve. Kes smiled and lazily rubbed her thumb over Mae's hand. Taking a deep breath, Kes leaned toward Mae and pressed the side of her body against Mae's.

It was such a subtle movement, Mae wasn't sure it was intentional at first. It was equally comforting and thrilling. When Kes squeezed her hand and turned to shoot her a smile, Mae believed she hadn't imagined it and reciprocated. Mae wasn't sure what was going on in Kes's mind but sensed pain and wanted to reassure Kes she was there.

"For a long time, this is where I would come to reconnect with Grandma. I'd feel her in the condors soaring overhead, the warm canyon air on their wings. Just when I felt I was at peace with her passing, we lost Sara. I didn't think I would have to go through the pain of loss again, and not with someone so young and fit. I've not been back to Phantom since Sara passed. I didn't think I'd ever come back here." Kes paused for a moment, taking a deep, ragged breath in. She felt the weight of all the pain she carried around; the guilt, the shame, the responsibility for Sara's passing. She could no longer ask for Sara's forgiveness. The depth of her pain called to her like a dark temptress, and she feared being drawn into the hole again. Pain stung the backs of her eyes, so she closed them and focused on her breath. She focused on the warmth of Mae's hand in her own. She grounded herself in the feeling of Mae's side pressing against hers.

She felt Sara inside her, and she let the warm love flow throughout her.

For so long she had felt completely shrouded and dulled from feeling, unwilling to let herself feel any joy. In the last month, she'd finally started to feel the initial beams of light returning, but with it came more pain. It felt like a constant struggle, like she couldn't hold on to the good. She didn't know if she should allow herself to feel the good after everything that happened. She wasn't sure she deserved to feel happy. But here, next to Mae, finding the light was easy. With Mae, she remembered her own goodness and could feel the love Sara had shown her without cutting her feelings off.

Overhead, a few clouds dotted the skies, breaking up the deep blue that stretched as far as Mae could see. The sun cut deep shadows across the plateaus, mesas, and towers that cascaded along the canyon's spine. The bench they sat on was tucked in behind a vertical slab of basalt. The dark rock was warm and for now, the pair was in shade, but by Mae's prediction, that wouldn't last long. Sitting here holding Kes's hand felt like the most normal thing in the world, and Mae didn't want to break the moment. She ached to rest her head on Kes's shoulder and snuggle into the warmth of Kes's neck.

Kes turned to Mae and grinned slightly. Mae thought Kes's smile, in all of its forms, was the most beautiful thing she'd ever seen. The shy smile, the warm and playful smile, the troublemaking smile, the sexy smile—Mae loved them all. But now, being mere inches away from Kes's lips, it was nearly impossible for her to resist the desire to lean in and taste them for herself. She felt her heart pounding in her chest. She imagined taking Kes's lower lip between hers and running her tongue over its fullness. She was sure Kes could read her thoughts and she blushed and averted her eyes.

"We should probably start heading back down," Kes whispered, sounding disappointed. As they rose, Mae dropped Kes's hand to reach for her pack. Kes felt the loss immediately, the coldness left behind. She ached to reach back out and pull Mae in close.

The pair made their way to the main trail and started a slow hike back down to the bottom. Mae followed Kes, lost in her thoughts. She still felt Kes's touch burned into her hand and wanted desperately to have another reason to reach over and restore the physical connection.

"Grandma was my favorite person in the world. She was tough but loving and giving. She loved me just as I was," Kes said, breaking the silence.

"She knew you were gay?" Mae asked.

Kes stopped for a moment on the path and grinned slightly remembering the moment. "I was a pretty precocious kid and I knew I was gay very early on. When I was about eight, Grandma came home from work and I blurted it out as soon as she walked in the door. I had prepared a speech, but I was too anxious to wait."

Mae giggled as they hiked on. The image of a little wild-haired, freckle-faced Kes shouting "I'm gay" at her grandmother was adorable and endearing.

Kes loved the sound of Mae's giggle and joined in.

"Grandma pulled me close and kissed my head. She said,

'You are exactly perfect, just as you are my Kestrel, and I love you with every part of me.' I couldn't believe it. I think I bawled for a while. I was bullied at school for being too much of a tomboy and for not acting like a little girl. I was afraid and had prepared for a fight, like she wouldn't love or accept me."

Kes smiled remembering the interaction. Her grand-mother then said words she repeated often throughout Kes's life. *Let love in, Kestrel. Love yourself, love wholly and deeply. And when you find love, let it in. Life is too short to deny love the opportunity to blossom in you.* Kes didn't share these words with Mae, too afraid to say them out loud.

Mae smiled and nodded. That was exactly the reaction she'd wanted when she had come out to her parents. When they couldn't love her like that, when they outright rejected her, she was left searching, feeling like the hole inside her would never be filled.

For years, she lived off of the small love kernels she received from Terese. Despite the way Terese treated her, Mae stayed, convinced no one else would love her and that maybe she wasn't worthy of love. It was a script deeply in-grained in her mind, though she wasn't sure how it started. But time away from Terese made her see the abuse for what it was, a lashing out due to self-hatred and a severe lack of self-love. Mae was certain the only person Terese ever really cared about was herself.

Cabot and his sweet mama loved Mae, truly and deeply, but even that relationship was tainted by Terese, who found a way to poison everything. Mae wondered when the last time was she'd truly felt loved. She felt entirely grateful to

Cabot and his mother for taking her in, but still that pit in her heart remained.

"What did your family say when you came out?" Kes stopped to face Mae.

Mae's face fell. Kes's heart hurt seeing the pain on Mae's face, and she ached to pull her close. "I'm sorry. I shouldn't have pried." Kes quickly apologized.

"No, no. It's okay, Kes." Mae sighed and reassured Kes with a weak smile. With a deep breath, Mae passed Kes to continue hiking in the lead. She didn't want to see pain in Kes's eyes when she told her story.

"They didn't take it well. My mom asked me how she'd ever be able to face her friends, asked why I was doing this to her, and mostly just cried. My dad wouldn't look at me but told me I had a half hour to get out of the house. I haven't spoken to them since." Although the memory stung, it was as if it had happened to someone else. She'd shed too many tears over the years about her parents, and she just couldn't mourn the loss anymore.

Kes's heart broke, and she was absolutely dumbfounded. How could anyone reject Mae? Mae was an incredible, loving, genuine person with a gigantic heart. Kes couldn't imagine any parent turning her away.

"As far back as I can remember, I worked alongside my dad on his lobster boat every summer. It was tough and smelly work. If I never had to smell salted herring lobster bait again, it would be too soon." Mae chuckled slightly. "But he treated me like an employee, not a daughter," Mae said with a sad smile.

"Mom was always distant. As a kid, I was too wild and

always too dirty. As a teen, I was too curvy, too sensitive, too boyish, and I never measured up. I spent all of my childhood feeling like I was too much of something and still never enough. The littlest things seemed to set my mom off, and I would run away to the forest to get away. It's a wound that's taken a long time to heal," Mae admitted.

Mae stopped for a moment to catch her breath. She wasn't sure she wanted to turn to see Kes's face, afraid she'd reveal the childhood pain she felt that still lingered somewhere deep within. She felt emotionally and physically drained; the sun's intense rays bearing down on her. She hadn't realized how hot she felt. The wind felt as though someone was holding a hair dryer right in Mae's face. It was completely taxing the little energy reserves she had left, and she longed for the coolness of the creek. Mae could hear the refreshing burbling of the water nearby as they approached the ranch.

"I should get back to work," Kes said, hoping her voice didn't betray her feelings. Deep within, she felt that same protective streak shine through, the one that had wanted to save Mae from Terese. She could see Mae didn't need saving now, but she still wanted to take her in her arms and remove the pain. Something within her was on high alert, afraid of not being able to protect Mae, afraid of letting her in and being hurt again. But first and foremost, she was on duty and needed to return to the responsibilities that waited for her. Focusing on work was an excuse to escape those feelings for a little bit, albeit a valid excuse.

Still, the desire to see Mae again pulled on her mind and she couldn't stop herself from reaching for Mae's hand again. "Would you meet me at Boat Beach after sunset?"

The brilliant smile on Mae's face was the only answer she needed.

Chapter 14

The scent of cinnamon and sugar filled her senses as Kes entered the ranger station. The cooler was working overtime, trying to keep the station's interior at a reasonable eighty-five degrees. Trudy, on the other hand, was standing in front of the open oven door, red-faced and sweaty. As she withdrew a bread pan, the delicious aroma increased tenfold. Kes's stomach rumbled, and hunger hit suddenly. In the rush of the morning, she'd forgotten to eat. She hoped to all that was holy that Trudy had made her famous cinnamon rolls.

Trudy turned and saw Kes's hunger-stricken face. She knew if she didn't let Kes get at the baked goods, she might have a drooling hangry monster on her hands. Trudy laughed, "Yes, you can have some. Go grab a cup of coffee, let me grab the frosting, and I'll serve you one." Kes sat down and grinned at Trudy like a goofy child. Trudy laughed and shook her head again. Carefully, Trudy pulled the largest, gooiest bun from the batch and smothered it in frosting. She had spent the last hour covered in flour, dirtying every dish in the cabinet.

The rangers were scheduled to work a ten-hour split shift; half of their hours in the morning and half of their hours in the afternoon and evening, with a break during the worst heat of the day. But it was rare they were ever able to follow that schedule. Between medical calls that had them hiking to all corners of the inner canyon, rafting trips needing information, mule trains needing unloading, trail work, condor monitoring, visitor questions, and other various tasks and issues that arose during the day, they worked from well before dawn until late into the night, without stopping. So, in a lull between calls, Trudy jumped on the opportunity to make some comfort food. It was the best way Trudy knew to communicate her love, and right now Kes needed to feel loved.

As protective and guarded as Kes was sometimes, Trudy knew her friend well and was justifiably concerned. After Sara's death, Kes hid herself away, didn't answer Trudy's texts, and didn't let anyone in. Undeterred, twice a week Trudy dropped off food on Kes's doorstep. She needed to know Kes was eating and taking care of herself. Kes never said a word about the quiet arrival of casseroles, lasagnas, and baked goods that kept her from fading away to nothing. It had been a long three months, but Trudy was excited to see light coming back to Kes's eyes. So when Kes came into the ranger station, smiling like a schoolgirl with a crush, Trudy was overjoyed. It warmed her heart to see some life back in Kes's step, some real emotion shining through, the hardened exterior partially removed. It had been too long since Trudy had seen Kes's smile reach her eyes or heard her laugh. She wanted to see joy in Kes again, and she knew Sara would want that too.

Seeing Kes completely shut down and literally run away when Trudy realized Mae was the injured hiker felt like a slap in the face to Trudy. She couldn't understand what had changed inside Kes nor what she'd done to elicit such a response.

Trudy thought back to the morning she woke in Kes's hotel room only to find Kes long gone. She never pushed the topic with Kes, respecting that something had scared her off. She wanted to be a safe place for Kes, a friend, a confidant. She had been patient and understanding when Kes needed space. She never took it personally when Kes shut her out. But this had to stop. Kes needed to face whatever it was that scared her, or she'd miss out on her second chance with Mae.

Trudy set the aromatic cinnamon roll in front of Kes as a peace offering and took a seat next to her friend. She prepared herself. She couldn't let Kes brush it off again.

"Kes, we need to talk about what happened at the wedding," Trudy said, steadily meeting Kes's eyes. Immediately she felt Kes shrink and glance at the door as if she were debating whether or not she could make a run for it.

"Don't run away from this again, Kes," Trudy said, firmly yet kindly. "Sooner or later, we need to talk about it, and right now seems like as good a time as any."

For a solid two minutes, Trudy sat still, afraid if she moved Kes might dash off. She hoped Kes hadn't completely shut down and locked her out. Trudy knew she was pushing her luck by being so direct with Kes, but it was necessary. Finally, Kes took a deep breath in and cleared her voice.

"I woke up in the hotel room, and all these feelings came crashing in around me. Having Mae ripped away from me, feeling foolish about getting wrapped up in her so quickly, feeling ashamed over letting you see me like that. Also, I couldn't remember what happened between us, what I had done in my pain. I felt guilty that maybe I led you on or hurt you. I couldn't handle all of that right then," Kes said slowly, processing her feelings out loud. Her voice was small, uncertain, fragile.

Trudy sat dumbfounded, unsure what she expected Kes to say, but certain it wasn't that. "That's what you've been worried about? Is that why you ran away from me yesterday?" Trudy was annoyed, though she couldn't quite explain why.

"I ran away because all of those emotions came flooding back in. I didn't want to feel like I had hurt or disappointed you, and I didn't want to let anyone see the excitement I felt about seeing Mae again, for fear I'd lose her again," Kes admitted.

"Okay, well, first of all, nothing happened that night. You got drunk and Sara was worried about you, so I promised to get you home safe. I stayed to make sure you were okay, but nothing happened between us." The hurt in Trudy's heart built. She didn't know why she was feeling defensive and angry, but she needed Kes to know what she felt.

"I wasn't hurt or disappointed. Sure, there was a time when I hoped maybe you and I might get together, but I gave that up years ago. You and I would never have worked

out. And I saw you with Mae. No one could deny the connection you two had and, from the looks of it, still have. I've
never seen you light up the way you do around her." Trudy
felt the anger in her heart dissipate. She'd said what she'd
always held back. She needed Kes to trust and respect her
enough to know she wasn't easily hurt and wasn't pining
over something that never was.

Trudy took a deep breath. Kes was one of the most giving people she'd ever met, but when would Kes get it into
her head that she wasn't responsible for everybody else's
happiness or safety? She could see the pain in Kes's eyes,
the way she felt responsible for things far beyond her control. She reached across the table and put a hand on Kes's
arm.

"My beautiful, wonderful friend. I love you dearly, but
let me take care of myself. You're not responsible for me or
my feelings."

Kes simply kept her eyes trained on the table in front of
her. She didn't seem cold or shut down, it was just as though
she was processing. Trudy knew Kes heard her words, even
if she wasn't responding.

"You have an amazing heart," Trudy continued, tears in
her eyes. "You can't be responsible for everyone else. You've
got to let that go and let people in. And you really need to
stop running away when you feel something, good or bad."

Quietly, slowly, Kes looked up at Trudy, the pain evident in her eyes. Kes simply nodded, unwilling to voice
her feelings. She felt her walls rising, although more slowly
than before. She didn't want to isolate herself again, but it
was hard not to retreat into that safe space she was used to.

All Kes could manage to squeak out was "I know I don't let people in…" before her voice cut out again.

Those simple words completely melted Trudy's heart. "Let her in Kes, and this time, don't let her go. You can't let your fear of loss hold you back. She's here now. Make the most of it."

Kes pondered Trudy's words. She thought of Mae and felt a light build steadily inside her. Trudy was right; Mae was here, and Kes didn't want to see her go again. Kes felt deeply for Mae, but opening herself up again meant she made herself vulnerable to pain and loss. Loss, like the one she felt the minute the blistering ice-storm had slammed open the bathroom door and whipped Mae out of her arms. Or how lost she felt when Marie had called to let her know Sara passed away.

Trudy read Kes's face and saw the worry and darkness lapping at her thoughts. She squeezed Kes's arm again, pulling Kes from her fears.

"Kes, vulnerability isn't weakness. Being vulnerable means you will feel loss and heartbreak, sure, but without vulnerability, you'll never feel joy and love. You can't have one without the other. And living your life without feeling isn't living. You've got to love."

Trudy paused and let her words sink in. She imagined Kes was dealing with demons she wasn't willing to voice yet. Trudy wanted to respect Kes's need to process. She suspected it would just take a little more time, a little more love, and probably another couple of doses of honest conversation to get Kes to release the pain she held. Nearby, Trudy and Kes's radios crackled to life and, in stereo, broadcasted a report of an injured hiker a mile up the trail.

Trudy stood and placed her hand on Kes's shoulder to keep her from rising. "Eat your cinnamon roll and take a break. You can get the next call out." Trudy squeezed Kes's shoulder and grabbed her go-bag. *Guide her,* Trudy thought, and she sent a silent prayer to Sara as she walked out the door.

Kes's eyes burned as she stared out into the middle distance. *You've got to love.* She played those words over and over again, feeling drawn back to memory. Sara had said very similar words to her a few months before she passed, and just hearing those words brought her right back to that moment.

The two of them were lying in Sara's hospital bed, giggling over something long forgotten. Kes hadn't seen Sara in a week and was shocked to find her friend so quickly deteriorated. Sara's beautiful face was gaunt. The cancer and chemicals had ravaged Sara's body until she was a mere skeletal clone of her former self. Her eyes were deeply sunken in her skull. But she still smiled and laughed just as she always had. Kes brought out her worst jokes and did everything to get Sara to laugh.

Suddenly, Sara's face flinched and contorted in sheer pain. Kes went pale, and her stomach dropped to the floor. She fumbled and desperately pressed the nurse's call button. Nurses rushed in, checked the machine attached to

Sara, and pushed a syringeful of pain killer into Sara's port. Kes stood back, feeling frozen in place as she watched the pain etched into Sara's sweet face. Her stomach churned as her heart pounded in her chest. She was terrified she'd hurt Sara and she could do nothing to help ease her pain.

As the drugs kicked in, Sara's face calmed, her breathing slowed, and she collapsed back against her pillow. Within seconds, she drifted off into a deep, drugged, exhausted sleep. Kes stood next to Sara's bed unsure what to do.

For a few moments, she just looked at Sara's peaceful face, haunted by the image of the pain Sara had been in. Kes needed to be useful. She tidied Sara's room, reorganizing the many "get well" cards hanging on the walls, and watered the flowers by her bedside table. She worried Sara would be cold, so she found a blanket and covered the sleeping form. She slipped into the hallway to refill the bucket with ice chips. She moved silently, desperate not to disturb Sara's sleep.

After a half hour, Sara opened her eyes, still groggy from the drugs. She placed her hand on Kes's cheek and lovingly stroked away a tear. "Kes, it's okay. It's okay to cry, to grieve. But love first and love wholeheartedly."

Chapter 15

Filled with excitement, Mae arrived at Boat Beach early. A few hikers were hanging out on the beach savoring the last bits of light reflecting off the canyon walls. There was no sign of Kes yet. Mae found a good place to sit down and wait. She enjoyed hearing the laughter and comradery of the group, but as much as she enjoyed their company, she hoped they would leave before Kes arrived.

As the night set in, the other group packed up and headed back to camp. Mae had the beach to herself. She was nervous and kept looking toward the path, hoping to see Kes every time she heard the brush rustling or footsteps fall on the sandy gravel trail. Lying back, exhausted from the long day, Mae looked up at the ever-darkening sky. Heavy clouds clung around the rim of the canyon, but directly overhead the sky was clear. A few planets appeared and Mae pressed back into the sand, trying to take in as much of the sky as she could at once. Every so often she noticed a new star spark into existence. She watched the sky change from purple to slate blue, and finally settling into an inky pool.

As darkness set in around her, Mae's fears and doubts slowly crept in. It started quietly, so much so that she didn't notice at first. But the voice grew stronger the longer she sat there. *Of course she didn't come. Why would she?* Clearly, distinctly, she heard Terese's voice echoing in her mind.

Mae bit her lower lip and felt the tears well in her eyes. The skies blurred, obscured by the pain building and running freely down her face. Her chest hurt and she felt all of her pain flooding her system. She'd worked so hard to mute Terese's bile and to instead give her own feelings a more dominant voice. She repeated practiced words to drown out the bitter sting. "You are worthy. You are loved. You are enough."

In the darkness, the bitter voice inside her won out. It sneered, *Yeah right. You are nothing.* From deep within, Mae replayed her time with Kes over the past day, reviewing every feeling, every word, hopeful she didn't do anything to scare Kes away. The doubt inside her changed and shifted. It didn't sound like Terese anymore. A little stronger, she mouthed the words while she said them to herself, "I am loved."

Love? Who would love you? What is wrong with you? The words were new but not completely unfamiliar. Mae felt the acid in her stomach rise up into her throat, threateningly close to the surface. She hadn't heard that voice in years, but in a second it took her back. The voice continued, but instead of spinning new lies, it replayed from Mae's memory. *What is wrong with you?*

Mae was transported to the moment she stood in her parents' kitchen, barefoot and covered in mud.

"Do you know how many people were looking for you, Mae? And for what? So you could live out some fantasy of saving a bird? You really are an idiot."

She remembered proudly walking into the kitchen excited to tell her parents all about the beautiful loon family and the way the little one called to his parents. But what she'd found was only hatred and pain.

Mae remembered every line on her mother's face, the way her voice rose at the end of every statement, the bitter hatred that had poured from her eyes. She felt reduced to nothing, belittled to the point she could no longer remember the joy that had filled her when she was crouched in the thick bushes waiting for the loon's parents to return to the nest. Mae was right back to being that scared little ten-year-old again.

Tears streamed steadily down the sides of Mae's face now, falling toward her hairline. Whether it was Terese's or her mother's voice that berated her, it was hard to block them out and break free of the pain, especially when her self-doubt played in her mind. Those same scripts and ways of processing information were well-worn and too easy to fall into.

"Mae? Mae, are you out here?"

Mae sat bolt upright. That voice was kind and searching.

"I'm here." She managed to croak out, her voice shaking as she looked toward the path.

Mae could just make out Frankie's figure as they walked the path to the beach. "Oh thank goodness! I hadn't seen you all day and I was getting worried." Frankie plopped down next to Mae.

Up close, Frankie could make out Mae's features and saw the pain that poured out of her eyes. Without thinking, Frankie wrapped their arms around Mae's shoulders and pulled her close. "Who do I need to beat up?" Frankie asked.

Mae laughed through her tears. She couldn't imagine Frankie's tiny, wiry frame taking on either Terese or her mother, but it was a hilarious thing to picture.

"Okay, you didn't have to laugh that hard," Frankie said, feigning offense.

Mae smiled weakly and leaned into her friend.

"So, what's going on? You know I've got a flask of whiskey if that would help?" Frankie asked.

Mae took a deep breath. "I was supposed to meet Kes here after sunset. She didn't show." She let out a heavy sigh.

"You're disappointed? Worried?" Frankie said. They sensed the depth of pain in Mae's heart, but it wasn't clear why Mae was hurt.

"Yeah. She said she'd come but she didn't." Mae was surprised at herself. She'd never expressed disappointment outright before. That's not how she was raised. Women were supposed to yield to others' desires, to give without end, to put others before themselves. She'd never simply stated what disappointed or hurt her before.

Mae continued. "When she didn't show, my mind took over. I got worried and started hearing all this doubt fill my mind."

"Who was blathering on?" Frankie asked.

"At first it was words I heard from my ex pretty regularly. All of those jabs were familiar."

Frankie nodded, urging Mae to continue.

"But the voice shifted and it took on words I had forgotten about," Mae admitted. "I heard my mom berate me. I felt worthless."

Mae's tears subsided, and the ache inside dulled considerably. Mae named the doubt inside her and in doing so reduced its utter control of her thoughts.

"Are they telling the truth?" Frankie asked, knowing the answer.

Mae stopped for a moment, surprised. She'd never considered that before. Were the voices inside her head filling her head with lies?

She thought back to Terese's words and favorite taunts. Every single one of them focused on an aspect Mae treasured about herself. Terese called Mae stupid and ugly, but Mae knew herself to be very intelligent and knew she was beautiful, even if she never met the ideal body type Terese expected. Her mom told her she was too sensitive, a crybaby, and needed to grow up. But Mae knew that the depth of her compassion allowed her to connect with people and care for them. Her mom told her she was unlovable, but she'd met people like Cabot and Marie who loved her for exactly who she was.

"It wasn't about me," Mae said, in a whisper.

"Exactly," Frankie said with a smile, letting Mae sit with that realization, giving it a moment to sink in.

Frankie remembered the moment they had come to the same realization and how freeing it was. They could tell Mae was just on the cusp of understanding, so Frankie pushed a little further. "It never was about you and it never will be. People's reactions to you are completely steeped in their own shit. Whatever your mom or your ex said in real life or in your mind tonight, it has nothing to do with you. It was a manifestation of their own fears, expectations, or self-doubt."

Mae stared blankly at the river while her mind raced. She thought of all the bitterness spewed her way over the years. She believed wholeheartedly that somehow she had caused it and had to fix what was broken. Mae had been raised to believe she was responsible for others' reactions and feelings. If only she could love Terese enough for the both of them, maybe Terese could love herself. The same held true for her mom. If Mae could only be her mom's idea of the perfect daughter, then maybe she might love Mae. For years, Mae had clung to the brief moments of affection when her mom was in a good mood. Those moments got her through the rough days.

"My ex, Terese, used to run away. She'd just suddenly be gone. She'd usually come back after a few days without any explanation for where she'd been. I never knew why. But I'd blame myself and do everything I could to make her feel safe as soon as she returned. I'd go out of my way to be good and not scare her off again. But I never knew what I did wrong," Mae said.

"No need to get tore up about her, you ain't done nothin' wrong. By the sounds of it, Terese is a right fool and fighting demons deep within. As my momma says 'God love her, 'cause ain't no one else gonna.' But by being your loving and open self she got exactly what she needed to fill her complete inability to love herself; undying affection and attention. I reckon it both fed her and scared her shitless because she didn't want to need you or anyone. She used abuse to keep herself above you and make you feel like you were dependent on her when really it was the opposite," Frankie said.

It took Mae a moment to really cipher through what Frankie said, once she figured out the Southern slang and adorable drawl, but every word rang true to her experience. "It wasn't me." Mae sighed deeply, feeling relieved. A small smile spread across her face. It made sense. The fear she'd seen in Terese and the hateful words her mother said were manifestations of their own doubts and self-hatred. For the first time in years, she felt lighter and not so afraid of the dark. The abusive voices were silent, not because she was suppressing them, but because they'd lost their power over her thoughts.

Mae listened to the river rushing and felt with each lapping wave a bit more of her pain wash away. The tears that had blurred her vision cleared. She looked upward again and was astounded by the number of stars in the sky. Absent of all light pollution and with nothing to obscure her view, Mae looked up into the depths of the heavens. With new eyes, she saw the wonder of the universe. She glowed too, from somewhere deep inside. She felt it radiate out through her eyes and her heart.

"Still, Kes didn't come," Mae said, in a whisper.

Frankie smiled, knowing it was difficult to rewrite the narrative that has spent years in your mind, especially when you've only ever heard it told one way. "Just cause it's pissing rain, don't mean dandelions comin'," Frankie said.

Mae turned to Frankie, with a confused look creasing

her brow.

Frankie continued, switching out of their Tennessee colloquialisms. "Don't add meaning to an action. She didn't show up. That's an action. But that action doesn't have any inherent meaning until you assign some. She didn't come. Your training is telling you that means she's not interested or you assume you did something wrong. Right?"

Mae nodded silently.

"But it's just an action. There are a lot of possible reasons that could have prevented her from coming that have nothing to do with you. Maybe she got a sudden bout of food poisoning. Maybe she had to wrangle a wild mule on the loose. Maybe she has narcolepsy and fell asleep at her desk. Maybe she's writing you a love sonnet but got caught up trying to find the right word that rhymes with Mae and lost track of time: bae, gay, oy vey, old bay, andale, cafe au lait."

Mae laughed. Frankie had a way of lightheartedly taking the pressure off.

"Your turn. What are three possibilities for why Kes didn't show up that have nothing to do with you?" Frankie asked.

"Maybe.... Maybe she had to capture a rabid bat but got bitten and turned into a vampire. Maybe she had to help a momma bighorn sheep give birth. Maybe she got carried off by a condor," Mae rattled off, feeling the lightness return to her chest.

"See? It could be anything and it likely doesn't have anything to do with you. I saw the way she looked at you yesterday, Mae," Frankie said.

Mae's heart skipped a beat. How had Kes looked at her?

"Something had to keep her from coming here tonight, but whatever it was, it wasn't you," Frankie said gently and gave Mae another side-hug squeeze.

Chapter 16

She drifted somewhere between awake and asleep, lost in her thoughts. She felt a warm pressure around her middle, almost as if she were wearing a lead vest that was dragging her down. Voices and figures mixed in her mind lost somewhere in a strange dream. Unfamiliar but not unwelcome. She was in a crowd with people pressing in around her on all sides. She searched for someone she knew but couldn't remember who. She felt stuck in place, unable to fully focus. Deep within, she felt the compulsion to move, prompted by ever-growing anxiety and urgency. She pushed, hoping for an opening in the restrictive crowds around her. They needed her. She had to go. She had to find them. She had to help. Where were they?

For a moment, she went airborne only to come crashing down hard again. Jolted awake, the wind knocked out of her, Kes's eyes flew open in a flurry and she tried desperately to make sense of the scene around her. A frigid wave crested over the side of the raft and caught her right in the chest. She was awake now, definitely awake. Cold, wet, and awake. Readjusting, she looked around wildly trying to re-member how she came to be wrapped in a life vest, crash-ing through a rapid, on a strange raft in the middle of the Colorado River.

Suddenly, it all came flooding back.

Shortly after Trudy left, another medical call-out crack-led over the radio. There was an older man with a head wound just upriver at Clear Creek Beach. The rafters had secured him as best they could, but he needed more medi-cal attention. All afternoon, high winds and lingering storm clouds grounded the park's helicopter up on the rim. It was too risky to fly in, and none of the other rangers were within range. Clear Creek Beach was almost ten miles away on a rough, unshaded trail. Kes grabbed her ready go-bag, add-ed a few extra foodstuffs, refilled her water bladder, and began hiking.

Clouds dotted the sky in heavy clusters around the North and South rims of the canyon, but they did little to provide any relief from the heat. It took her all afternoon and into the evening to safely make it to Clear Creek Beach. When she arrived, she was utterly exhausted, but seeing the gaunt, pained, bloodied face looking up at her, Kes's adren-aline kicked into action. Luke was an older man from Texas on a rafting trip through the Grand Canyon. His group was exploring Clear Creek to cool off during the heat of the day when Luke lost his footing and went down hard, hitting his head in the process.

The oarsmen were able to get the bleeding to stop, but they were worried, understandably so. Luke struggled to keep his eyes open and complained about pain in his chest and difficulty breathing. Kes checked the deep, nasty gash across the right side of his forehead and eyebrow ridge. It wasn't actively bleeding, but he'd need to get it checked out. Kes continued to examine him and placed her hands on either side of his ribcage to check his breathing. Immediately, Luke winced and drew a sharp breath in between his teeth. Kes hadn't even asked him to take a deep breath in yet. She lifted his shirt and held her breath, willing her face not to show any sign of worry. His right side was deeply bruised from his armpit almost down to his hip bone. He couldn't seem to get a full breath and flinched with every inhale. She touched him as tenderly and as gently as she could. Kes was sorry to cause him any more pain, but she needed to assess the structure of his rib cage.

"Well, that must have been quite a fall, Luke. It feels like you've got a few broken ribs and I would guess a concussion. I'll do my best to make you comfortable, but I'm going to need you to stay awake. I'll get you on the next helicopter out as soon as I can." Luke smiled weakly, and Kes beamed at him. She projected strength and compassion and assured him he would be okay. He needed her to be calm, in control, and ever steady.

But behind the uniform, her heart pounded, and her mind filled with dread as her stomach dropped. She was pretty sure he hadn't punctured a lung, but the amount of bruising and his confusion worried Kes. He could be suffering from internal bleeding, and if he was, there wasn't anything she could do about it here in the field.

She called over one of the rafting guides and asked them to watch Luke while she stepped away to report to Dispatch. She calmly and emotionlessly filled them in on the situation and her assessment. But the light was fading quickly and the winds hadn't died down on the rim, keeping help at bay. Fear rose in her throat, and she felt her mind whirl. "We'll send down a helicopter at first light. For now, do your best to keep him stabilized and awake."

Kes acknowledged the order and clipped her radio to her belt. When she returned to Luke's side she found a camp chair, a hot cup of coffee, and a delicious dinner waiting for her. She looked into the guide's eyes, surprised. "We'll support you as best we can. The other guides and I will rotate in on two-hour shifts to keep you company and make coffee. Eat up and then you can take over again."

Kes was incredibly grateful as her stomach rumbled and a pang of hunger shot through her core. She gladly picked up the bowl of food and devoured it within a minute, barely tasting it as it passed over her tongue and straight down into her stomach. It was going to be a long night, and she'd need to be on top of her game. Being alone in the dark as the only life support for Luke was terrifying, but knowing someone would be looking out for her was a great comfort.

Every half hour, Kes took Luke's pulse and asked him a couple of questions to test whether he was cognizant and could remember where he was. She had him tell her stories about his life and then told him all about her wildest experiences in the canyon. Anything to keep him awake.

He told her about his wife, LuAnn, and how he fell in love with her the first moment he saw her. "LuAnn and me met during senior year in high school. She was the prettiest darned girl I'd ever seen. She smiled and I was a goner." Luke's Texas drawl was endearing. Kes loved the way his eyes crinkled as he described his wife.

"She had the bluest eyes, like the Texas midday sky when the sun is high and the winds are rolling. She was smart as a whip. When she laughed I felt like everything was alright in the world. I used to memorize jokes just to see her smile." Luke teared up. "When we were still in high school, I asked her to marry me. She said no. She said she wanted to go to college and get a real job. I said that sounded fine by me. I don't think she expected that."

Kes could see Luke obviously adored his wife to this day.

"I waited, worked any job I could to help support her dream, and on the day she graduated from medical school, she finally agreed to marry me. We've been together almost 50 years now." Luke beamed, obviously proud of his wife.

Kes loved seeing the joy on his face. She longed for that kind of beautiful bliss and enduring adoration in her own life. Luke talked about his wife as if he were still just as in love with her as he had been the moment he first laid eyes on her. His genuine and deep affection for his wife was endearing, and it reminded Kes of the budding feelings that were brought to life every time she thought about Mae. They hadn't spent much time together, but it wouldn't have mattered if it had been five minutes or several years. Kes was drawn to Mae. Something within her resonated and came to life with the hope, the possibility, and the desire for a deep and real love they could someday share.

Kes kept Luke talking, clinging to his every word, and not just because she knew the happy memories helped keep his mind off the pain. She'd given him a pain killer, but it was a mild dose, only enough to take the edge off. It couldn't be too strong or he might drift off.

"How about you? Do you have yourself a sweetheart?" Luke asked. Kes smiled broadly, her mind immediately turning to Mae. She wasn't Kes's sweetheart, but Kes hoped maybe she would be.

"I'm working on it," Kes responded, honestly. A slight smile pulled at the corners of her mouth. Suddenly her stomach dropped; she'd missed their date. As soon as the radio called her into action, her mind had been focused only on getting to Luke's side and getting him stabilized. She'd completely forgotten she was supposed to meet Mae after sunset. She imagined Mae sitting on the beach all alone waiting for her, and her heart broke a little. She knew there was nothing she could have done differently, there hadn't been time to get a message to Mae, but still, she felt disappointed in herself for unintentionally standing Mae up. Kes's face visibly fell and Luke, being the perceptive bugger that he was, quickly picked up on it.

"What did you forget?" Luke asked, a smile on his face. He knew that look of guilt and worry well.

"I was supposed to meet... my date tonight," Kes admitted, stuttering slightly over her words. She was never sure if she should use the correct pronouns in front of visitors. It crossed the line into her personal life that she wasn't comfortable with revealing to strangers. Over the years, she'd faced enough discrimination from visitors as a young, female ranger. There was nothing she could do that would stop people from being assholes and dismissing or demeaning her for the obvious ways in which she was different, but that didn't mean she had to let them have any more ammunition than necessary.

"What's her name?" Luke asked, with a little grin.

Kes's jaw dropped. "Darlin', I may be from Texas, but I'm not small-minded. My son is gay, and I remember the hesitations he used to take whenever he talked about a 'friend'."

"Mae. Her name is Mae." Kes smiled shyly.

Luke reached for Kes's hand and squeezed it. "She'll understand that you had to rescue this old geezer." His gaze was steady and his deep brown eyes were comforting.

Kes returned his gentle smile and reached for her coffee. In her mind, she saw the twinkle in Mae's eyes, felt the warmth of their fingers intertwined, and longed to be close to her again. But right now, she didn't need to get lost in her daydreams. Kes took a deep breath to clear her mind and enjoy the delicious scent of the fresh-brewed coffee. She knew one of the rafting guides was awake nearby. She never noticed them refilling her coffee and yet there was always more. For that, she was incredibly grateful.

Kes pointed out the stars and told Luke stories about growing up in the canyon, hiking at night with just the light of the full moon to guide her way. He laughed at her antics, but seeing him wince, she tried to find less funny stories to tell.

Sometime just after 4 am, Luke's speech became slurred and he slowly stopped talking, mid-story. Kes reached for his hand, and her stomach dropped at the cold clamminess. "Luke?" She called but received no response. Dread filled her mind, and for a second she faltered, frozen in place. "Please, please hang on," she begged.

Shaking her head, she jumped up from her seat and quickly kneeled beside him. Though delayed momentarily, her instincts and training finally took over. She felt for a pulse and pressed her ear to his chest. He was still breathing, and his pulse was there, albeit weak. Kes waved over the guide. "We're going to need blankets and some strong bodies. We need to get him out of here now."

Without waiting for a response, Kes returned her focus to her patient. "Luke, I need you to wake up," Kes said loudly, rubbing his hand. Luke didn't stir. Kes needed him to stay conscious. The worry that had frozen her in place earlier started to stir in the edges of her mind. She couldn't do this. She couldn't lose him too. Firmly, she grabbed his hand, pinching hard the fleshy area between his thumb and first finger. If she did it right, it should be incredibly painful, and enough to stir Luke. She heard him moan and was grateful. He was still there.

Kes unsheathed her radio and depressed the button, "Dispatch, Ranger Wylde." The radio crackled, and Kes craned her ear, praying for a quick response. After a few torturous moments of sheer silence, a voice answered back, "Go ahead, Wylde."

Without wasting a moment, Kes reported, "Patient's pulse is low and thready. He's nonresponsive to verbal stimuli though I got a little response to pain. He's fading fast and we need to get him to a hospital. When can we get a medevac?"

"Standby one." Kes held her breath. It was still too early for a park helicopter to make the trip, and she couldn't tell what the weather conditions were like up top. She wasn't sure he'd make it to sunrise without some immediate, intensive intervention. A helicopter could get Luke from the bottom of the canyon to the fully equipped hospital in Flagstaff in about 20 minutes, as long as it could fly.

"Life Flight is taking off and will be at the landing zone in ten. Can you get the patient to the beach?" Kes let out her breath. Help was coming.

"Affirm, Dispatch. We will be ready and standing by."

Kes needed to find a way to carry Luke safely to the beach without twisting him or jolting his broken ribs. Usually, for a litter carry, they used a backboard on a special cart with a wheel on the bottom of it, but out here, that wasn't going to be an option. She was going to have to fashion something together and do it quickly.

Kes leaped to her feet to search for something suitable, but when she turned around, she was surprised to see all of the guides and a few sleepy-eyed visitors standing there. "We thought you might need this," one of the guides said and pointed to a weird contraption on the ground. The group had tethered a couple of oars together, creating a platform. They'd covered the makeshift backboard with life jackets, to cushion Luke.

The team moved quickly and efficiently transferred Luke onto the litter. In tandem, they carried Luke slowly down to the beach, shuffling forward at a snail's pace under the awkward load. As they trudged along, they heard the helicopter's motor cutting through the night's stillness. To Kes, it sounded like the most beautiful concerto she'd ever heard, knowing that it brought with it people who might be able to save Luke. The helicopter touched down just as the team arrived on the beach. EMTs jumped out and, within moments, they had Luke secured to a gurney and loaded into the helicopter. As the helicopter took off, Kes felt all of her energy drain, the adrenaline long burned out.

The rest of the morning was a blur. She remembered someone handing her food and coffee. She remembered packing up her things and getting ready to hike back. She remembered sitting on the inflated, tubular sides of a raft as someone tightened her life jacket. She remembered the bustle of activity around her as gear was gathered and packed into place on board.

Sitting up in the raft, she recognized the bridge looming up ahead. She guessed the crew decided she was in no shape to hike back and, considering they would be floating right past Phantom Ranch, they gave her a ride. In her exhaustion, she must have drifted off.

She ran her hands over her face, thankful for the water's chill. She looked over at the oarsman who smiled brightly as he expertly guided the boat under the Black Bridge and onto Boat Beach. She shakily made her way up to the front of the boat and jumped off onto the sand, falling to her knees. She couldn't remember the last time she felt this exhausted or weak. She'd pulled long shifts before, but having gone two nights without any solid sleep, in a real bed, she was dragging. Achingly she rose to her feet. The guide handed over her pack and radio. She could barely manage a smile or a thanks as she removed her life jacket and tossed it back in the boat.

With a tanned and calloused hand, the guide reached out for Kes's shaking palm. "Thank you for saving my dad." His words hit Kes, but it took her a minute to register their full meaning. "I called the hospital on the satellite phone just before we took off. He's stable and talking again. He asked for you. I felt so helpless seeing him like that, and I couldn't fathom what I would do without him. If it weren't for you... truly, thank you."

She watched the boats pull away, utterly dumbfounded and exhausted. She saved Luke. He was going to be alright. She was relieved and grateful that he'd survived, of course, but in her core, she felt something break. It started small, but soon the overwhelming feelings she'd held back for too long came crashing in all around her. Her throat burned, and tears stung the backs of her eyes. She couldn't stop them from flowing this time. She turned to start the hike back up to the station, longing to hide away somewhere dark and quiet. But looking up, she saw someone standing there. Kes couldn't keep up the facade anymore. Unable to carry on, she went completely limp and fell into the open arms awaiting her. Tears streamed down her face, blurring her vision. She cried for all of the guilt she was carrying, all the pain that ate away at her, all the helplessness that paralyzed her.

"I'm so sorry, Sara."

Chapter 17

The incessant pounding brought Trudy to the ranger station door. She assumed it was a visitor looking for information or a bandage. Opening the door, Trudy's heart jumped into her throat. Mae stood on the other side barely managing to hold up a limp, exhausted, crying Kes. Without question or hesitation, Trudy hurried to Kes's other side, helping lift the weight of Kes's weak form. The three of them awkwardly moved into the station and back around to the residential area. Mae and Trudy gently sat Kes on the edge of her bed.

Mae deposited Kes's backpack onto the floor. Trudy looked on with concern, frozen in place, as Mae knelt to remove Kes's dusty shoes. Tears streamed down Kes's face without end. Trudy couldn't remember ever seeing Kes cry before. Not even after a medical call ended tragically. Not when her grandma passed away and she lost her only tie to family. Not at Sara's funeral. Seeing the tears now cut Trudy to her core. Her heart ached to comfort her friend. Kes's blue eyes glazed over, and she stared out into the middle space, lost somewhere. Kes's shoulders hunched forward, and she seemed to crumple smaller and smaller with each passing breath. What happened?

Trudy struggled with her own tears, as she watched Mae caring for Kes. Mae was gentle, loving, and intentional with every movement. She looked at Kes sweetly, without a hint of pity or judgment. One by one, Mae unbuttoned the dusty uniform shirt and slipped it off over Kes's strong shoulders. Gingerly, she lifted Kes's arms to slip the garment fully off. She folded the shirt neatly and set it aside, an act that made Trudy smile. Mae showed respect and care in everything she did. Mae removed Kes's socks, taking a moment to massage Kes's calves and the soles of her feet. Mae moved to unbuckle Kes's pants, not wanting her to lie down covered in dust. Kes at least assisted with this part, though her mind was still obviously light-years away. Trudy was sure she'd never seen Kes accept help, and certainly no one had cared for her like this before. Kes curled into a tight ball on her side. Mae wiped Kes's tears away from her face, catching a few before they rolled down onto the sheets. Slowly, she pulled the comforter back and guided Kes underneath. She tucked the comforter in around Kes's body.

Trudy was overcome by the depth of love she saw between the pair. It was obvious that Mae adored Kes. *Let her in*, Trudy thought to herself.

Mae stood to slip out, but as soon as she did, Kes started to whimper and tear up again. Immediately, Mae returned to her position next to Kes. Kes wrapped an arm around Mae's middle, burying her face in deep. Mae gently stroked Kes's temple and hair. "It's okay, I'm here," Trudy heard

Mae whisper. Kes seemed to settle, and Trudy let out a breath she holding. Whatever happened, Kes was safe with Mae.

"We need sweet treats," Trudy mumbled to herself, slipping out of the room. When in doubt, Trudy knew a delectable pie, fluffy cake, or warm crisp always helped make things a little better. She could pour all the love she felt and the care she wanted to give into a pastry or a pie. She'd been baking for so long, she didn't really follow recipes anymore. She'd grab the ingredients she'd shipped down on the backs of mules at the start of each tour, and in a puff of flour, something tasty would appear. Right now baking something delicious was the only thing she could do for Kes, and she needed to do something, or the worry inside her would build to breaking.

Twenty minutes later, covered in flour and surrounded by various mixing bowls filled with deliciousness in various states of doneness, Trudy was startled to hear a noise behind her. Mae had snuck into the kitchen, closing the door behind her.

"She's drifted off," Mae said quietly, feeling awkward. She was unsure what to do, feeling like she was intruding. Normally, visitors weren't invited into the residential section of the ranger station. "I should go. I'm supposed to hike to Cottonwood tonight." Mae looked nervously at the clock. It was already well after noon, and hiking over seven miles uphill, in the 115-degree heat without shade, no less, seemed a Herculean task at the moment.

"Sit down. I just made some coffee, and I've got an apple crumble coming out in a minute or so," Trudy said.

Mae sat down heavily on a stool next to the counter. She hadn't realized how tired she was. She remembered Kes collapsing in her arms. The two had stayed wrapped up together kneeling in the sand. Finally, when the tears had slowed slightly, Mae decided she needed to get Kes to the ranger station. She remembered hoisting Kes up and half-carrying, half-dragging her along the way. It seemed to take forever, but she'd been so focused on Kes's pain that she wasn't sure how long it had actually taken. It broke her heart to see the agony Kes was in and especially because she didn't know why it was happening or how she could help. Sitting down, every muscle in her body ached deeply from the physical and emotional toll. She felt her shoulders sag forward, and she leaned against the counter, drained.

"What happened?" Trudy asked.

"I was hoping you could help me figure that out," Mae admitted, her eyebrows furrowed in concern.

"I went down to the beach this morning. When I arrived, Kes was being handed her pack from a guy on a large raft. I couldn't hear the conversation, but the person on the boat shook her hand and said something that must have affected her deeply. When she turned around she looked surprised, relieved, and deeply pained. She saw me and I got to her just before she collapsed to her knees." Mae's eyes filled with tears. Kes looked so small then, so deflated. Mae could feel Kes's pain radiating off of her.

With a deep breath, Mae continued. "Her entire body went limp, like her strength was completely drained. I didn't know what was wrong, but I wrapped my arms around her. Through her sobs, I heard her say, 'I'm so sorry,

Sara.'" Mae recited the course of actions as best she could remember. She could see the worry and guilt creasing Kes's face when she apologized to Sara. Kes seemed to be in utter anguish, but Mae didn't know why.

Trudy's face fell. Throughout Mae's retelling, she became increasingly concerned, and hearing what Kes muttered, she felt her heart drop into her stomach.

For months, Trudy worried about how Kes was coping. Kes had always been pretty private about her feelings, but after Sara's death, she took it to a new level. Throughout the memorial and graveside ceremony, Kes had stood in the back, removed from everyone else gathered, as if she was merely a spectator viewing the collective grief from a distance, untouched and untouchable. Even Marie couldn't reach her through her stony exterior and dazed look. Kes had retreated too far inside herself. After the funeral, Kes blocked everyone out, as far as Trudy could tell.

Trudy knew Kes well enough to know she tended to keep her emotions to herself and figured she was coping with the loss of her best friend in her own way. She seemed to be getting back some of her spunk and joy, especially over the last few days, though it often felt like she was still keeping everyone at arm's length. But now Trudy knew the truth. She pursed her lips together to stop herself from tearing up. She couldn't imagine trying to deal with a loss this deep all by herself. Trudy let out a deep sigh and turned to look at Mae. Mae's face was lined with worry, tears still clinging to the corners of her eyes.

"Let me get you a slice of the crumble, and then I'll tell you everything I know," Trudy said.

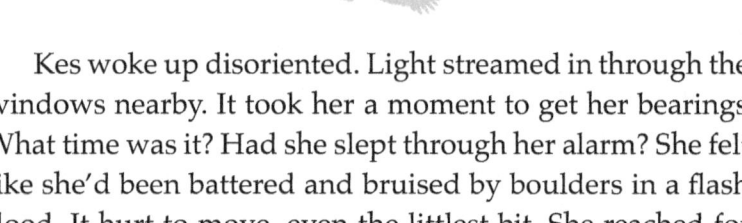

Kes woke up disoriented. Light streamed in through the windows nearby. It took her a moment to get her bearings. What time was it? Had she slept through her alarm? She felt like she'd been battered and bruised by boulders in a flash flood. It hurt to move, even the littlest bit. She reached for her clock, turning it toward her. It read 5:17. It couldn't be 5:17 in the morning because the sun wouldn't be that strong yet, so evening? How long had she been out for?!

Kes sat up and immediately placed a hand on her pounding head. She felt emotionally hungover, her body drained and exhausted. Next to her clock, she found a tall glass of water and a couple of aspirin. She gratefully gulped both down, finishing the entire glass. She slowly rose to her feet and pulled on a tank top and a loose pair of shorts. She followed the sound of joyful voices coming from the kitchen.

"Good evening, sleepyhead," Trudy said, walking over to wrap Kes in a warm hug.

Kes took a deep breath in, settling into Trudy's embrace. Trudy smelled like vanilla, cinnamon, apples, butterscotch, and flour. On second thought, no… it wasn't just Trudy; the whole room smelled like fresh-baked goodness. Kes took a deep breath in and realized how famished she felt. As Trudy pulled away, Kes saw Mae smiling shyly over in the corner.

Bits and pieces started to come back. Mae found her. Mae carried her. Mae took care of her. Kes was overwhelmed with gratitude, and she felt tears sting her eyes. She didn't think she had any left, having wrung herself completely dry earlier. A single tear slipped down her cheek, and for once she made no attempt to repress it. Without a second thought, Mae immediately crossed the kitchen to stand in front of Kes. She reached up and wiped away the tear, looking deep into Kes's beautiful eyes.

Kes's heart was bursting just looking at Mae. She was absolutely stunning, and her kindness and loving nature touched Kes to her core. "I'm okay. I'm just thankful, Mae," Kes said, reassuring her.

For a moment, they stood shyly, unsure how to proceed. Kes broke the silence and pulled Mae into a firm hug. Mae responded in kind, wrapping her arms around Kes and letting herself give without restraint. Kes breathed deeply and melted into Mae's arms. It felt like home; fully secure and fully wanted. Kes felt like every stress she carried around melted away. She felt lighter and more centered than she had in months.

"How about we get some food in you before you fade away?" Trudy said, breaking the trance.

Kes smiled gratefully at her friend.

"We've got tacos... your favorite," Trudy said with a wink and was immediately rewarded with a blush on both Mae's and Kes's faces. It was too easy.

"And for dessert, Mae made something called whoopie pies. I'm not sure exactly what they are, but they look amazing." Trudy shot Mae a huge smile.

"Keep her, will you?" Trudy said. Neither Kes nor Mae was sure which one of them she was talking to, but naturally, they turned to each other with a shy smile. Heart full of joy, Trudy walked out of the room laughing.

Chapter 18

At dinner, Kes laughed easily at the antics between Trudy and Mae. It warmed her heart to see the joy all around her. She didn't feel dead to it anymore. She let it enter her heart and fill every fiber of her being. The burden of guilt she'd carried for a few long months had lessened considerably.

Kes watched Mae laughing to the point of tears at some embarrassing story Trudy was telling about Kes. Mae's laughter flowed easily from her beautiful smile and reverberated around the room. Kes noticed Mae seemed lighter, brighter; there was no more doubt lingering around the edges of her smile. Mae turned to Kes and flashed a wink that made Kes's heart melt. Kes loved watching Mae, and having her here felt natural and wonderful. Somewhere in the middle of the conversation, Kes felt Sara's presence there with them as if she wasn't gone at all.

After dinner, Kes asked Mae if she wanted to join her for a walk. Kes was eager and impatient to move, having slept for most of the day. She still felt sore and wiped out, but she figured a walk around the ranch would feel good. Kes stayed in her "civilian" clothes, off-duty and happy for the break. Trudy was more than capable of running the station solo as she had done all day while Kes slept, and she shooed the pair out the back door.

The pain in Kes's chest rose, but this time she didn't push it away. It was time to talk about Sara, about what happened. "She had just turned 37 when she was diagnosed with an aggressive form of breast cancer. Four months later, she was gone."

Mae remained silent and waited for Kes to go on. She squeezed Kes's hand as they walked, letting her know she wasn't alone.

"When Sara passed, I felt my world collapse around me. I didn't understand why she had to go." Mae's heart went out to Kes. She couldn't imagine losing Cabot, and even thinking about it caused tears to well behind her eyes.

"After she died, I closed myself off to everyone. I tried to ignore my pain and bury my guilt. I couldn't face my coworkers or our community. I didn't want anyone to see me hurting." Kes took a deep breath and looked out over the creek. She found a good rock to sit on and led Mae to it. The two settled in and watched the canyon colors change as the sun set.

"I had a lot of leave saved up, so I took it. The chief understood; everyone in the division had felt the loss too," Kes continued. It felt good to talk about this, and looking over at Mae, she had no fear left. Mae smiled gently at her and ran her thumb over the back of Kes's hand.

"I dreamt about her today." Kes looked out over the

creek, remembering the dream as if she were right back in it. "She felt so real. She was right next to me; I could feel her there. She looked beautiful, joyful, and healthy." After holding back her feelings for so long, it felt good to open up and finally share them with someone. The burden of her emotions felt lighter as she released them.

"I felt guilty, like I'd abandoned her and let her down," Kes admitted. For so long she'd blamed herself for not being there, for making Sara go through that horrible, terrifying moment alone. "She looked at me and truly saw me. I felt her deep in my heart as if she'd stepped in there and knew exactly what I was struggling with inside. She knew what I was feeling and why. I couldn't hide it anymore." Kes smiled sadly, taking a breath to remember the next words Sara spoke to her.

I don't think you're upset you weren't there the moment I died, Kes. Neither of us thought I'd be gone so soon. You're not upset you weren't there, you're upset you couldn't save me, Sara said. Deep down Kes knew it was true.

Kes turned to Mae, "When the oarsman thanked me for saving his dad's life, everything came crashing in around me. I was grateful he had survived the ordeal, but it brought up all the guilt again. Why couldn't I have saved Sara? Why couldn't I save her, Mae? She was my best friend, my family. She needed me." The pain and guilt strangled her words and stabbed at her heart.

Mae turned to face Kes. She needed her to hear these words, to feel their full meaning. "You can't save everyone, Kes. You are incredible, talented, and there's a lot you can do, but cancer sucks." Hot tears poured down Kes's face.

"You can't change what happened, Kes," Mae continued, "but you get to decide where you go from here. You can spend your whole life beating yourself up about something you had no control over, or you can live. You get to live, and the best way to honor Sara's memory is to love her and live."

For a while, Mae and Kes sat in comfortable silence. Mae studied Kes. Her face changed, tension and pain were replaced by contented peace. With a deep breath, Kes broke the silence first. "I wasn't meant to save Sara; I was meant to love her and to learn from her." It seemed like a simple realization, but it was one that brought Kes peace and understanding.

Mae wrapped her arm around Kes's waist and snuggled her head into the warm space near Kes's neck. Kes leaned into Mae and sighed. She felt happy, loved, and at home. For the first time in months, she felt at peace with herself. She thought of Sara and no longer felt like her memories were tinged with bitterness and anguish. As Kes stared into the darkening sky, she thought back to who she'd been before she had hiked down for her tour... what was it, four days ago? Her mind was still feeling a little groggy from her midday snooze.

"Wait, weren't you supposed to hike to Cottonwood tonight?" Kes asked, looking at Mae.

Mae laughed and smiled at Kes's worried face. "I packed up my things while you slept. Trudy set me up in the spare room at the station. She thought I'd want to be there when you woke up."

Kes smiled, once again thankful for Trudy's thoughtfulness.

Mae smiled, "I'll hike up to the campground in the morning. I can't wait to see Ribbon Falls. I know you have to work, so you may be busy, but if not, would you still like to—"

"Yes!" Kes interrupted before Mae could finish her question. "I would love to."

"Fantastic, it's a date," Mae said, a flirty grin on her face.

Damn, that grin did things to Kes. She longed to lean across and kiss that delicious grin right off Mae's face. *Get yourself together, Wylde*, Kes internally chastised herself.

Chapter 19

Last night felt like a dream, Mae thought, groggily getting to her feet. At one point while they were talking,
Mae had ached to lean over and kiss Kes. She could have
sworn Kes felt the same way, but she wasn't sure if it was
the right time. As little experience as Mae had, she figured
going in for a first kiss while Kes reminisced and processed
the death of her best friend was likely not the right time.

It was just about three in the morning, and Mae could
already smell coffee brewing in the other room. She threw
on clean clothes and grabbed her pack. It had been days
since she had showered or run a comb through her unruly
curls, but she didn't care. She was living her adventure; her
dream had become reality.

Quietly, Mae snuck into the kitchen. Kes stood with her
back to Mae, busily working over the stove. Mae watched
as Kes danced a little bit to some unheard music. She wiggled her butt, slid around in her socks on the linoleum
floor, and shimmied her shoulders. She was adorable, and
Mae couldn't help but let a little laugh escape. Kes whirled

around shocked. Her mouth hung open until a slow "I'm caught" smile developed. She giggled a little and then hushed Mae, pointing at the clock.

The two worked seamlessly to prepare the rest of breakfast, quickly eat, and hit the trail. It would likely be well over 120 degrees in the sun today, and there wasn't much shade to be found anywhere along their way. It was a long, slow climb up the North Kaibab Trail from Phantom Ranch to Ribbon Falls, and Kes predicted if they left soon they could make it to the falls while most hikers were still asleep.

Mae was excited to explore a new section of the canyon and quickly felt her legs fall into a now-familiar rhythm. She felt stronger and was surprised when she realized she'd set out on this adventure just a few days earlier. She felt like she'd been at Phantom for weeks, if not longer. Mae noticed Kes stopped up ahead of her on the trail. Within a few steps, Mae caught up.

Kes pointed off-trail at a side canyon, breaking the silence for the first time all morning. "Phantom Canyon. It's a beautiful place to explore. Gorgeous little waterfalls, carved rock, and absolutely peaceful. You've got to check it out sometime."

Mae peered up the side canyon but, in the darkness, she couldn't make out much. "Maybe I can check it out on my way back down." Mae smiled. She could see the excitement and passion in Kes's eyes. If the side canyon made Kes that excited, Mae was certain it was a place she needed to see.

With a smile, Kes turned and kept on hiking. The trail widened in a few places, and the pair were able to walk side-by-side. Kes turned to Mae, "I'm curious, what brought you here?"

"Cabot," Mae said with a laugh. Kes looked confused but Mae continued.

"About a year and a half ago, my girlfriend left me." Saying those words, Mae realized how little power they had anymore. She no longer felt ashamed or like she had failed.

"A few months ago, she showed up in town again with her new wife. Add to that, she took over ownership of the small company I worked for... well, I needed to get out." As much as Mae hadn't wanted this trip to have anything to do with her ex, she knew if it hadn't been for Terese's sudden reappearance in her life, she may have still been stuck accepting a life half-lived.

"For too long I was willing to confine my adventures within the bounds of my dreams. I was comfortable simply existing. I made decisions based on what was expected of me or what others needed, never on what I wanted." Mae breathed in deeply. It was hard to admit that she had been living her life for others. She didn't feel like the person she had been on Cabot's couch crying into her wine.

"Cabot is my best friend and, in a lot of ways, a good kick in the butt. He booked and planned this trip as a way for me to realign my reality with my dreams. And he encouraged me when I was quite sure I couldn't do it," Mae said, with an honest smile.

"I will need to thank Cabot," Kes said, smiling to herself. She was thankful for the opportunity to be near Mae again and genuinely felt gratitude toward whatever force in the universe had brought them together again. She wouldn't let this chance slip through her fingers this time.

So will I, thought Mae. Cabot didn't allow her to linger in her negative emotions or to stay stuck in a place where she was ever under the influence of Terese. She would be forever grateful to him for his intervention in helping her break the cycle. He had been right. She had needed this adventure.

"Was your ex the woman from Sara's wedding?" Kes asked. Kes felt bile build in her stomach, her hackles rose, her defenses on full alert as she remembered.

"Yeah, Terese," Mae said, with a somber nod.

"I despised her then, and I can't say my feelings have changed much," Kes admitted.

"You did? Why?" Mae asked.

"Even in our short interaction it was clear to me she was toxic. Anyone who dims your incredible, beautiful heart is downright evil in my book. That's exactly what she did. She was like a poison that killed every amount of joy around her. I couldn't stand how she treated you that day in the bathroom, and I guessed that it wasn't the first nor the last time she acted that way." Kes felt protective of Mae, even now when the threat had long passed. "You are amazing, Mae. I love the way your heart shines through in everything you do. You are genuinely yourself, kind in all you do, wild at heart, and a giving soul. From what I could see, she only wanted to control you and erase all those wonderful attributes," Kes admitted.

Mae stopped and looked at Kes wide-eyed. Kes saw her for exactly who she was, where she was, and still thought she was incredible and beautiful? And openly told her without any kind of prompting or the expectation of receiving something in return? Mae's heart pounded in her chest. Kes spoke honestly from her heart, and Mae knew she meant exactly what she said. No hidden agenda or icy lash waited to strike. She was sincere.

"Thank you," Mae said in a quiet voice, unable to fully express what she was feeling.

After a few stunned minutes, Mae turned to keep walking and opened up more. "I spent a lot of time over the last year wondering why I stayed with Terese for as long as I did. I didn't have a good reason and mostly felt ashamed of myself until this trip."

Kes nodded. She knew the healing power of the canyon; it helped put everything in perspective. Out here you couldn't help but feel acutely humbled, dwarfed by the towering canyon walls, wide-open skies, and the entire universe on display every night. It was a place Kes always sought out to work through her troubles. She wasn't surprised the canyon did the same for Mae.

"After my parents kicked me out, Cabot and his mom, Rose, all but adopted me. I spent every holiday and school break in their spare room. Rose was sweet. She treated me like a daughter, was proud of me when I graduated, and I always felt welcome there. But still, I felt like something was missing."

"When I met Terese, I was excited. She was charming and good to me in the beginning. She opened my door for me, always paid for dinner, bought me presents, and was sweet to me. I thought that was what a good relationship looked like."

Mae paused for a moment to take a sip of her water. She

wasn't sure how long they'd been hiking or how far they'd gone, but she didn't care. She wasn't scared to tell Kes about her past. She wanted to be honest with Kes about it, and more than that, she wanted to be honest with herself.

"I thought maybe I'd finally found my place. For so many years, I felt lost and worried I was a bad person, or unlovable in some way. But here was someone who wanted to be with me."

"Slowly, things changed. It started small, with a few criticisms or jokes at my expense from time to time. Behind closed doors, Terese was still very affectionate. But those short negative moments happened with more frequency until I got to the point where I was living from each mere second of affection to the next. Love crumbs."

Mae sighed deeply. She remembered saving screenshots of particular texts to reread whenever she needed a reminder that deep down Terese loved her.

"I thought that even in the darkest moments, Terese still loved me. I thought, if I just tried a little harder and loved her more, she would be happy. I was used to walking on eggshells and feeling emotionally responsible for someone else. I thought that was love. It's how it had been growing up with my mom."

It had been a hard realization to come to, but Mae knew that both Terese and her mom were so absorbed in the depths of self-hate that they couldn't see their actions for what they really were. Their narcissism was a front to cope with their own demons.

Mae reflected for a moment on her regrets and all she had lost while being in Terese's clutches. "I only heard about

Sara's illness and death a month ago," Mae said, her voice aching with sadness. "I couldn't bring myself to reach out to Marie until recently." Though she didn't really know Sara well, she felt guilty about not having been a better friend to Marie during what had to be an incredibly difficult time.

After the wedding, Terese had been worse than ever before. Her victim/bully split personality reared its ugly head, and her diatribes oscillated between repeatedly accusing Mae of being unfaithful and dismissing the notion that anyone would ever give Mae the time of day. She held Mae responsible for making her look like the bad guy in front of "that bitch in the bathroom." Terese blamed Marie and Sara for trying to drive a wedge between Mae and herself. Terese saw bad behavior and hostile intent in anyone Mae associated with, projecting her worst qualities, manipulative lies, and toxic motives onto everyone else.

Mae tried everything to repair the rift between them, but all of her attempts were rebuked by Terese. When Mae asked what she could do to make things right, Terese made only one demand.

"Terese made me cut off all contact with Marie, Sara, and anyone involved in the wedding," Mae said quietly. "At the time, I thought I was doing the right thing, paying for the feelings I had no right to have, for the mistakes I made. I was trying to save the incredibly unhealthy and abusive relationship I was in, at the expense of the people who truly cared about me." Looking back, it turned Mae's stomach to see how she had allowed herself to be controlled and manipulated by Terese and how she had willingly given up the people who cared about her in an effort to keep Terese happy.

"It took me a long time to work up the courage to reach back out to Marie. I wasn't sure how to apologize and explain my disappearance. I felt ashamed for letting someone cut me off from the people that meant the most to me. Unfortunately, by then, Sara had passed. It was yet another moment in a series of realizations that opened my eyes to all I could lose and had already lost by not being true to myself."

As she spoke, Mae processed everything she was feeling, voicing for the first time the true measure of all that she had experienced and learned. She no longer felt she had to mold herself to fit whatever form best suited those around her by hiding away parts of herself and betraying her own desires and needs. Dislodging the ingrained pattern of self-doubt and pain was a slow process, but being away from the world that was filled with regrets, memories, and old habits freed Mae to retrain her brain into a new way of being and viewing life around and within her.

Kes listened to Mae intently. She didn't detect any bitterness or cruelty in Mae's voice, and she was touched by the depth of genuine compassion in Mae's being. It broke Kes's heart to imagine the pain Mae must have endured at the hands of the people who were supposed to love her the most. Stopping for a moment, she faced Mae and pulled her into a hug, unable to find the right words to express everything she was feeling. Mae smiled and settled into the natural embrace, her hand slipping into the small space between Kes's back and her pack. They held each other in comfortable silence.

Pulling back, Mae looked at Kes. "I don't regret loving my mom or loving Terese. It was a lesson I needed to learn, and it brought me to where I am today." Mae beamed a smile at Kes that caused Kes's heart to fill with hope.

"I want to be loved back, by someone who loves themselves too." Mae sighed, turning back to the trail. Until this moment, she hadn't given that thought a voice, but having said it, she felt free. She wanted to be loved, wholeheartedly, unabashedly, and steadfastly, without doubt or conditions. That had always felt like asking too much, but not anymore.

As they hiked, Mae felt lighter. She saw Terese's face in her mind, but she no longer heard her bitter words. With a smile, Mae released Terese. She let go of any pain or confusion she had carried around with her. She let go of feeling responsible for Terese's happiness. It wasn't her burden to carry, nor should it ever have been her sole purpose. She forgave herself for staying so long in a relationship that had only drained her. Next, she saw her mother's face. She sent her mother love and let her go, too. She didn't need to carry either of them around anymore.

Kes smiled to herself, allowing her heart to be open to the hope that was building within. Mae wanted to be loved. She didn't need to be loved but she wanted to be. Loving Mae... that sounded pretty incredible to Kes.

"We're here," Kes said, turning to smile at Mae.

Mae looked up and gasped. She had been so lost in her thoughts and focused on placing her feet on the uneven ground that she hadn't realized how far they'd come. Behind Kes, a long, elegant waterfall crashed deliciously over the edge of the canyon and landed on a three-story-tall mound of rock that was covered with moss and other greenery. The water was rich in calcium deposits. Over thousands of years, the water had flowed over the canyon wall, and those tiny dissolved pieces of calcium had collected together at the base, forming a travertine hill. The whole place looked like a scene out of a magical fairyland. Flora clung to every available surface, a stark contrast to the rust-red rock walls.

Mae tossed off her pack, immediately feeling the chill where her sweat-drenched shirt hugged her skin. Carefully, Mae moved through the shallow pool toward the massive green mound. The cool mist rolling off the edges of the waterfall kissed Mae's skin and felt heavenly and refreshing. Mae stood, arms outstretched, face upturned, feeling the water pour over her. It soaked into every fiber of her clothing, drenching her completely. She laughed as it trickled down over her collarbones, between her breasts, over her stomach, and down her dusty legs. It felt incredible and exhilarating.

Kes stood back and watched Mae, tears pooling in her eyes. The sight of Mae took her breath away. Joy shone out of every inch of her exuberant face, and Kes loved seeing her excitement. Ribbon Falls was one of Kes's favorite places, but coming with Mae was like seeing it with new eyes. She loved the hanging gardens clinging to the canyon walls and the hues of rust, white, and purple that tumbled down the cone-shaped mound at the waterfall's base. She felt more connected with the world here. Mae laughed and turned to face Kes.

Mae's signature curls, now heavy-laden with water, hung over her face. Her green eyes matched the moss around her and called to Kes. Mae's soaked clothes clung to her, highlighting her sensuous curves. Mae reached out her hand, hoping Kes would join her. Slipping off her shoes and uniform shirt, Kes slowly trod through the water, safely making her way to Mae.

Mae wrapped her fingers in Kes's and pulled her under the water. For a minute they stood facing each other before Mae pulled Kes into a warm hug. "Thank you for bringing me here," she whispered.

Mae's lips vibrating so close to her ear sent shockwaves through Kes's body. Kes wrapped her hands around Mae's sides, holding her close. Kes could feel the water trickle down between them, warmed by their bodies. Her heart was pounding, and she was sure Mae could feel it. Kes pulled back, just far enough to see Mae's dreamy eyes. She reached up and stroked Mae's sweet face. She desperately wanted to lean in and kiss those incredible lips.

Suddenly, Kes heard a noise somewhat akin to the low growl of a wild animal. She stepped back, alert and shocked. She looked around, searching for the source. Mae couldn't help but laugh at the look on Kes's face. "Sorry, that was my stomach," Mae sputtered out between giggles.

Kes broke into a laugh that filled her entire body. All of the joy she had felt with Mae poured out of her, like the cascade of water above them. Mae loved the sound of Kes's laugh. It was pure, musical, and magical.

"Second breakfast it is," Kes said with a grin. They found a comfy place on the nearby ground to sit and dry their soaked garments. From the far reaches of her pack, Kes pulled out a semi-frozen caramel chocolate bar. Breaking it in half, she handed a portion to Mae. It was Kes's all-time favorite treat on hot canyon hikes. The cool chocolate and slightly melted caramel did wonders for the soul.

Mae took a bite and groaned. She swore food just tasted better in the canyon. She was sure it had something to do with the number of calories she was burning every day, but it didn't matter. She quickly devoured her half.

Kes savored the chill and sweetness. With a smile, she turned to Mae. A small strand of caramel clung to Kes's lower lip. Mae nearly leaned over to lick it off but caught herself at the last moment. She'd never initiated affection before, and as much as she wanted to kiss Kes, she was a little worried that maybe Kes didn't feel the same way.

"You've got a little..." Mae said shyly, pointing to her own lip. Kes smiled and slowly slid her tongue over her lips, removing the leftover sweet. Mae's heart pounded. She leaned in closer until she was a breath away from Kes. She couldn't stand it anymore. The pull inside her was over-whelming. Mae crossed the remaining distance and, with the softest lips, lightly kissed Kes, her heart pounding.

Their kiss started slowly, a few tentative pecks, pulling back every few kisses to make sure this was okay. Mae slid her hand up to Kes's cheek and pulled her in closer, deepen-ing their kiss. Mae's tongue slid over Kes's lower lip, send-ing electric pulses straight to Kes's core. Kes moaned into Mae's mouth, melting Mae's heart. The world faded away as Kes slid her hand through the short hair at the base of Mae's skull, pulling her even closer. Their tongues danced together, and Mae couldn't help but smile against Kes's mouth.

After a few quiet minutes, the pair pulled apart, out of breath.

"I've wanted to do that since I sat next to you at the rehearsal dinner," Kes admitted shyly.

"I'm glad I wasn't alone in that desire," Mae said, with an adorable grin.

In the quiet, they snuggled up together, not willing to feel any distance, now that they'd finally embraced. Mae rested her head on Kes's shoulder and sighed deeply. Together they watched the changing light reveal different crevices and formations on the canyon walls. Kes snuggled in closer to Mae and kissed Mae's cheek. Mae turned and grinned, looking deeply into Kes's eyes. She wanted to stay right here in this moment. She wanted this feeling in every moment.

Kes placed a soft kiss on Mae's forehead. "I don't want to go, but I need to start heading back. I don't want to leave Trudy hanging," Kes said with an adorable half-grin. She hated to leave Mae's side. She'd rather spend all day exploring with her, both the canyon and each other. She wanted to make up for lost time.

Mae nodded, knowingly. "Duty calls." She grinned at Kes. Everything in that moment felt right. "I'll see you tomorrow?"

"Looking forward to it," Kes replied with a wink. She leaned down and kissed Mae, feeling the excitement inside her rise up with each passing millisecond. "Okay, I'm going, I'm going…" she said with a laugh.

Chapter 20

Even though the sun had long since passed, it was still relatively warm. So much so, that Mae laid atop her sleeping bag, sweating. She looked to the skies and enjoyed the unmarred view. She was really here, lying out under the stars, in the very depths of the Grand Canyon. When Cabot told her she wouldn't need a tent, Mae had doubted him.

"What about mosquitos?" she protested.

"There aren't any in the desert."

"What about rain?"

"It's a desert."

"What about the cold?"

"Desert."

"What abo—"-

"Sand once again, desert your persistent questioning, the answer is desert." Cabot cut her off with a ridiculous goofy grin as if he were saying "did you get it?" and wait-ed for her to laugh. She rolled her eyes and laughed at his groan-worthy puns.

She'd been making excuses, putting up roadblocks,

avoiding the possibility that she might actually succeed. First it was the tent and then, when Cabot made it clear that wasn't a problem, she moved on to one thing after the next. At one point, it was, "How will I eat while camping?" Obviously, people ate while camping, and Cabot made her watch a couple of YouTube channels about how to prepare everything from an omelet to pineapple upside-down cake over a camp stove. Then it was, "How will I ever carry all of my things?" Cabot rolled his eyes and pointed to her new backpack in the corner of his apartment. "What if there's a rattlesnake? What if I get lost? What if...?"

Cabot gently handled her questions one by one. He dismissed each one of her worries and concerns but not without challenging her. "Why are you holding yourself back?" he asked, stunning her to silence.

Why? Why did she keep getting in her own way and for what purpose? She had placed blame on not having the means, a lack of connections, and on Terese at times. But those were just excuses. The truth was, she was limiting herself and she'd intentionally kept herself, her dreams, and her experiences small for a long time... far too long.

Staying small meant she could remain unseen. If she didn't try, then she couldn't fail. If she kept her expectations low, then she couldn't be disappointed and she wouldn't disappoint others. By keeping ideas as dreams, not realities, she could experience them without failure. But they were only ever dreams and, as good as dreams could be, they were nothing when compared to reality.

Admitting she'd held herself back meant she would have to accept that she was the only one responsible for her fate, her happiness. It would mean understanding that she had withheld joy and only she could decide to change that. It was a big responsibility being accountable for your own successes and failures.

But here she was, living fully and enjoying the highs and lows of life. She wasn't scared anymore. She had taken a chance and succeeded. She was stronger and more powerful than she had allowed herself to believe before. She'd finally left Maine and flown across the country by herself. Even though she had been filled with nervous energy and doubt, she nevertheless took the plunge and hiked to the very bottom of the Grand Canyon. And when she was hurt, she still persevered. She'd tackled the demons that had long shamed her into silence and released herself in the process. She'd talked openly about who she was, fully embracing her scars, her past self, and her successes. She'd risen to every challenge and connected with the wonders around her. She'd taken a risk, but the rewards and the experience were more than she could have ever dreamt.

She wasn't the same woman who'd left Maine, the woman who had lost herself when her abusive girlfriend walked out. Staring up into the starry sky, Mae was most grateful that she would never be that person again. Over the course of a few days, she'd made new friends, found herself, and finally kissed her longtime crush.

Damn, she'd kissed Kes! A huge smile crept across Mae's face, and a warmth crashed over her entire body as the memory of their kiss filled her mind. If anyone looked up from their sleeping pads and over in her general direction, she was sure they'd be able to see her face glowing even in the dark. She couldn't help it. Every cell in her body was electrified at the thought of Kes's sweet lips. "It was far better than any dream," Mae whispered to herself.

Since they'd met, Mae had spent many hours dreaming about kissing Kes. She would never have considered being unfaithful to Terese and she'd scold herself whenever she woke up after one of the lovely dreams involving Kes. Still, she found her mind disobeyed and frequently returned to thoughts of Kes. In the darkest moments, when she was lost in the confusion and pain of being in an unloving relationship, it was the memory of Kes's arms around her that made Mae feel safe and loved. Kes was warm, accepting, and exciting. When Kes ran her fingers down Mae's spine, Mae had felt the first stirrings of desire. It was a simple gesture, so soft and gentle. But it only accentuated the attraction Mae felt for Kes, even if she wouldn't acknowledge her feelings. She'd agreed to Terese's terms to cut off all contact after the wedding because she felt guilty about what she had experienced in those moments. But her subconscious wasn't ready to give up the feeling, once it'd started.

In her dreams, she reimagined Sara's rehearsal dinner a hundred different ways, but the result was always Kes grabbing her and kissing her senseless. Sometimes she dreamt she asked Kes to meet her down by the beach, and they walked along the waves' edge, watching their steps illuminated by bioluminescent algae. Other times, she felt Kes reach over for her hand under the table during dinner and squeeze it. Then Kes would stand and make her way to the bathroom, shooting a look back at Mae to follow. The minute they were alone in the bathroom, Kes would push

Mae against the door and kiss her. Once, Mae imagined Kes arriving at her apartment door, standing in the rain, professing her undying love for her. After that one, Mae stopped watching sappy romance movies just before bed.

But this kiss wasn't anything like those dreams, and not just because Mae was the one to initiate it. This first kiss wasn't simply lust. It was sweet, meaningful, powerful, electrifying, warm, passionate, and kept her entire body soaring, not just her hormones. When Mae slipped her hand into Kes's she felt like she fit there, and the same held true for their kisses. They fit together. When Kes kissed her back, Mae was pretty sure the world spun faster on its axis. Everything around her faded out, and every doubt and worry in her mind was gone. Filling all the corners and crevices was excitement and peace. Mae couldn't wait to kiss and touch Kes again. "I'll see her tomorrow," she whispered with a smile. Tomorrow seemed forever away.

Shit, tomorrow was her last night in the canyon. How did this trip fly by so quickly? Mae wondered what would happen after tomorrow. Mae couldn't imagine flying back to Maine now. She wasn't the same person who left and she wasn't sure she fit there anymore. What was waiting in Maine? Not much. No job and no job prospects. No apartment. A toxic ex-girlfriend and her new wife. These thoughts didn't cause Mae any stress and didn't throw her into a panic like they once would have. Instead, they were just facts, just statements. They held no power and no inherent value, positive or negative.

There was nothing in Maine but Cabot. Mae smiled thinking about her best friend's face, imagining the look he'd give her when she told him about kissing Kes. She laughed, imagining him fluctuating between excitement, disbelief, and pride. Though Cabot was amazing, his presence there wasn't enough to keep her in Maine.

So, what then? Where would she go and what could she do? Possibilities flooded Mae's mind, all filled with hope and newness. She wasn't sure where to go, and for someone who had never left Maine before, it was exciting! She had only a little in her savings account, but if she picked up a few editing jobs and lived frugally, she could survive until she found something long-term. And if she got some online editing jobs... well, then she could be anywhere!

Mae couldn't help but smile at that prospect. She was living the adventurous life she'd always wanted. The world was open to her and the possibilities were endless. She wanted to feel the Pacific Ocean lap at her toes. She wanted to sleep under the open stars, her body bone-tired from a day well-used. She wanted to see all of the places she'd only seen on the backs of postcards. She wanted to document her explorations in words and sketches. She wanted to live fully, unbound, and unafraid. She felt empowered and inspired. She could go anywhere. She would be happy to pursue her dreams alone, to wander like a vagabond, exploring all life had to offer. But, if she had her choice, she would love to share the adventure, to explore every day and come home each night to one person: Kes.

How very lesbian of me, she laughed to herself. *I kiss a woman and suddenly I'm renting a U-Haul and imagining our life together.* She shook her head and rolled her eyes, but she couldn't deny the truth of her feelings. She wanted to be with Kes, to experience all life had to offer with Kes by her side. That point wasn't in question. But what would Kes want?

Mae smiled remembering every tender moment in Kes's presence over the last few days. She knew what she felt and how deeply she cared for Kes. Whether or not this relationship continued, nothing would diminish nor detract from the realness and importance of what she felt. With a deep breath, Mae sent a silent thank you out to the stars, the universe, and herself for coming here.

Chapter 21

Crackling bacon and fresh-brewed coffee. Kes was positive there wasn't any better way to wake up. She could smell the deliciousness even before she opened her eyes. Rolling out of bed, she stumbled into the shared kitchen to find Trudy in all her glory yet again. Kes marveled at Trudy's ability to always squeeze in a spot of baking between her duties. With their busy schedules, it seemed the only time the two rangers spent together was in the kitchen, preparing for their shift or returning from a long day.

"Mornin'," Kes mumbled sleepily to Trudy's back.

Trudy spun around, a huge smile across her face. "So... how was Ribbon Falls?" she asked, placing special emphasis on the waterfall's name as if she knew something had happened.

A smile crept across Kes's face almost immediately, and Trudy nearly jumped in the air with joy. "I knew it! What happened?! Tell me all about it," she said as she dashed to pull out a stool and pour a steaming cup of coffee. Kes sat as instructed and took a long, luxurious sip of coffee. She wanted a moment or two more with her memories of the kiss under the waterfall before she shared it with Trudy.

Kes grinned inwardly, remembering the tenderness of Mae's kiss, the caramel still lingering on their tongues, the way the kiss had intensified. Her heart pounded in her chest and throughout her body as she remembered the rush of emotions in that moment. She'd wanted to kiss Mae for years, and the desire had been building since the moment she first saw her resting in the creek. Yesterday's kiss only stoked the fire even more, and she couldn't wait for Mae to return to Phantom that afternoon. *Oh, the things I'd like to do*, Kes thought.

"You're killing me…. Spill!!" Trudy barked, shaking Kes from her naughty daydreams. Kes blushed, realizing where her mind had wandered, took another sip of coffee, and then met Trudy's gaze.

"We had a nice hike. It was beautiful out and Mae loved the waterfall," Kes said simply, an impish grin barely contained on her face.

"Aaaand…?" Trudy asked exaggeratedly.

"And… we shared my chocolate," Kes said, dragging out Trudy's agony.

"Aaaand… I mean, you sharing food is a big step, but please tell me that's not all that happened," Trudy begged.

Kes couldn't help but laugh. Trudy seemed desperate to hear more, and Kes loved how supportive and excited she was.

"And… Mae kissed me," Kes said, her voice dropping off at the end. Kes's heart fluttered saying those words aloud. *Mae kissed me*, she thought. And it was a damn good kiss.

"Eeee!!" Trudy exclaimed, leaping into the air! "I knew it! I knew she liked you. Eeee!!" It was a funny sight, seeing this strong, badass ranger with her duty arm strapped around her waist, jumping for delight in the kitchen. Kes loved Trudy's heart and sappy side, and internally, she was jumping for joy in the same way, even if she didn't bounce around the kitchen. She chuckled and looked shyly down at her coffee.

Trudy bounded around the island and threw her arms around Kes from behind, squeezing her tight. Kes smiled and placed her hands on Trudy's arms. She was grateful for Trudy's friendship and support. Internally, she chided herself for keeping everyone at a distance for so long. She was loved, and at that moment, she realized just how not alone she was.

"This calls for a feast! Bacon, eggs, and banana bread, sound good?" Trudy asked, whirling around the kitchen. "It'll be ready in a few!" she continued, without waiting for a response from Kes.

Kes beamed as she sipped her coffee and watched Trudy bounce from the frying pan to the oven to the microwave, efficiently preparing breakfast. While Trudy moved around her with the energy of a tornado, Kes's mind wandered off thinking about what Mae was doing right then. She imagined Mae slowly waking up, stretching in the early hour, her warm, still sleepy body snuggled deep in her sleeping bag. She imagined the adorable way her curls were probably a mess and the glow of the early morning light reflecting off her sweet face. She imagined Mae's soft lips smiling broadly as she looked up at the canyon walls.

Kes couldn't wait for those sweet lips to be close enough to kiss again. She glanced at the clock and did a quick mental calculation. Five hours. If Mae was just waking up, she should arrive back at Phantom in about five hours. Kes smiled, knowing she'd be a little distracted carrying out her duties today, awaiting Mae's arrival.

For a moment, Kes's breath caught in her chest. This feeling was new, and it filled every bit of her senses. It was a mix of desire, joy, openness, adoration, want, lust, and... peace. The self-imposed numbness she'd blanketed herself in for the past few months was gone, leaving her especially sensitive to these emotions. She relished in feeling again, experiencing the world fully.

"Stand by for the morning report," the radio in the corner crackled to life, and both she and Trudy turned to face it.

"Be advised. A flash flood warning is in effect for the inner canyon today. Heavy monsoons are expected on the North Rim. Avoid narrow side canyons and creeks."

The voice on the radio continued with other news while Kes and Trudy sprang into action. There was never a dull moment in the canyon. After stuffing a few bites of breakfast in their mouths, Trudy pulled Kes into one more hug before dashing out the door.

Kes headed toward the campground and river while Trudy hiked up to the cabins and the canteen. The plan was to warn everyone of the dangers and start moving items away from the creek to higher ground. Kes shuddered, thinking about what happened the last time Bright Angel Creek flashed.

It had been a summer day, just like this one, not a cloud

in the sky. There had been reports of monsoons, though it didn't look like there would be much of a threat. But by the end of the day, half of the picnic tables, most of the campground, and two of the bridges had been washed away into the Colorado River, never to resurface. It had taken years before everything was repaired. Kes prayed no one would be hurt this time.

Making her way through the campground, Kes stopped at each campsite. Even in the early hour, everyone was welcoming and pleasant, wishing her a good morning and often offering her breakfast or coffee. In the heart of the canyon, everyone was open, giving, and worked to help each other without fail. Some of the campers packed up early, taking the warning seriously, and hit the trail to avoid the flash. Nearly everyone else offered to assist in preparations. Within short order, Kes had a line of people efficiently moving sandbags from storage to the low spots along the pathway that could wash out, blocking their escape to higher ground. With a clear path established, the team moved on to the next task: caching drinkable water.

It took a little coaxing, elbow grease, and a few choice cuss words to bring the old system to life, but soon the rusty pipes sputtered and spit until clear water flowed steadily out of the pump. Every available bottle, bladder, bucket, canteen, and container was filled with crisp, cool water. Fresh water in the inner canyon was supplied by a pipe that paralleled Bright Angel Creek for the majority of the way. If the creek flashed, tumbling boulders and downed trees were likely to damage the ancient water line, and repairs could take days, if not weeks.

Kes removed her cap and wiped the sweat out of her eyes. She was surprised it was so hot early in the day until she looked down at her watch and found it was well after noon, the morning eaten up by preparations. She stretched and cooled herself by pouring a full bottle of chilly spring water down her back. With a moment to breathe, she looked around and took in the scene.

"We're as ready as we're going to be," said Kes, dismissing her helpers. The overnight campers started their hike up to the plateau to hang out for the day and wait out the worst of the storm. Although the typically brilliant blue skies were completely blocked out by heavy rain clouds, not a drop had fallen in the inner canyon. The deceiving safety of the inner canyon; rain may not fall here today, but that didn't lessen the danger. Up on the rims of the canyon, over a mile above Phantom, rain was likely already falling. Those waters would inevitably tumble over the edge, cascading down side canyons and amassing substantial power along the way.

Kes looked around the campground. *Mae should be here by now*, Kes thought, worry building in her gut. As the last of the campers packed and headed up the trail to spend the day out of danger, Kes saw Mae's friend walking toward her.

"It's Frankie, right?" Kes asked. Frankie nodded.

"Lookin' for Mae?" Frankie asked, reading the concern laced in Kes's brows. "She's not back yet."

The knot in Kes's stomach grew. Something wasn't right. She thanked Frankie, grabbed her pack, and jogged up the North Kaibab Trail, running into Trudy along the way.

"I'm going to head up the trail and warn hikers along the way," Kes blurted, out of breath, her brow furrowed in concern.

"Kes, what is it? What's wrong?" Trudy asked, stopping Kes from running off.

"Mae didn't make it back yet. I've got to go look for her," Kes said.

Trudy knew there was no point in arguing. She couldn't have made Kes stay at the ranch even if she handcuffed her to the mule corral.

"Be careful. I expect radio updates every 20 minutes, and do not put yourself in harm's way. Promise me that," Trudy said, not breaking eye contact.

Kes nodded before dashing off. As she headed up the trail she kept an eye on the creek, checking for any change in color. The first signs of mud or debris in the water would indicate flooding was already happening upstream, and she would be wise to turn around. For the first few miles of the hike, there was no high ground to escape to, just steep, unscalable canyon walls on either side of her. She couldn't risk getting trapped without an escape, and she broke into a steady jog. So far the water was still clear.

Crossing over the second bridge, Kes spotted something out of place along the side of the trail and hurried to check it out. It was a bright red backpack with an "I <3 Maine" patch sewn on top. "Mae," Kes said, looking up the trail, searching for any sign of Mae. Why would she have left her pack next to the trail?

"Ranger Wylde, Ranger Thatcher," Kes's radio crackled on her hip, and she unclipped it to respond.

"Ranger Wylde. What's up, Trudy?"

"You okay?"

"I'm good so far. I just found Mae's pack, but no sign of Mae," she responded.

"Where are you?" Trudy's voice popped through the radio.

"Just after the second bridge, by the mouth of Phantom Creek." As she said those words, her stomach dropped out and she felt the blood drain from her face. She heard her own words just over 24 hours earlier, encouraging Mae to check out Phantom Creek sometime. She wouldn't have known about the possible flash floods. She wouldn't have known not to hike up the narrow side canyon.

"Trudy, she went up Phantom Creek. Fu—" she released the radio button before she finished cursing. Dispatch didn't need to hear that.

She didn't wait for Trudy's response. "I'm headed up Phantom Creek. I won't have any signal for a bit, but I'll check in as soon as I can."

For a moment there was silence on the radio. "I copy. Please, be careful," Trudy responded. Since there was usually only one ranger at the station at any given time, it wasn't unusual for them to go off on a rescue by themselves. Still, Kes felt nervous as she reclipped her radio and dropped her backpack on the ground beside her. Opening Mae's pack she grabbed a few warm layers of clothing and a thin sleeping bag. From her own pack, she removed a waterproof sack and stuffed everything she could into it.

Kes debated finding a way to fit her radio into the drybag. If it got wet she'd lose all communications with Trudy and rescue, but it was already full and she figured it would be better to keep the radio somewhere she could hear it. She tucked it into the very top of her pack. She needed to hurry. Every wasted minute meant she was putting herself and Mae at greater risk of being in the path of a flood.

Securing her pack to her back, she checked the water again. Still clear. Maybe, just maybe she could find Mae before the floods began.

Please, Sara. I can't lose her too.

Chapter 22

Stepping into the creek, Kes felt the cold water seep into her shoes and over her socks. The air temperature had dropped significantly over the last hour, and although it was still in the low nineties, Kes felt the chill travel up her spine. A rock of worry sat heavily in her gut. The fear deep within her core spread throughout her body. She took a deep breath and cleared her mind. She listened to her heart and Sara's voice in her mind. Mae had to be up Phantom Creek. She would find her.

Slowly, Kes sloshed across Bright Angel Creek to get to the mouth of Phantom Canyon, the water slowly rising as she made her way to the center of the creek. At the deepest point, the creek lapped the hem of her shorts, but quickly she rose out of the water again. *Hopefully it doesn't get much deeper*, she thought. She knew the pitfalls of being soaked to the bone during a monsoon. Temperatures would likely continue to drop, and being wet only amplified the dangers.

As she entered the side canyon, she methodically looked for any sign of Mae. She imagined Mae seeing the first waterfalls in their picturesque glory. Clear water cascaded over the rock face, crashing and rippling downstream. Even now they provided no hint of the real danger they could quickly become. Kes looked over the banks of the creek, hoping to find Mae's smiling face beaming at her. But all of the banks were empty. She looked at the surrounding rock faces, but again, no sign of Mae. Kes tried calling Mae's name, but her voice was immediately drowned out by the rushing water. The cold weight in her stomach grew heavier, but she pushed it away and found the path to continue upstream.

The side canyon trail wasn't listed in any guidebooks or on any park maps because it wasn't really a trail; more of a "choose-your-own-adventure" scramble. Sometimes the trail was a well-worn narrow path weaving alongside the creek, and at other times the trail was the creek itself. As Kes made her way up the canyon, she kept an eye out for a quick egress to higher ground the moment the water turned muddy. But most of the time the trail was surrounded by high, tight canyon walls. Bighorn sheep could scale them with ease with their agile hooves. *A sheep, I am not*, Kes thought to herself.

Somewhere in the distance, she heard the low rumble of thunder rising over the roaring creek. Kes looked up to find nearly all of the sun's light was choked out by heavy clouds filling the skies. Kes moved quickly upstream, knowing her time was short. If she didn't find Mae soon they might both be caught in a flood. Kes waded mid-waist deep through the creek, desperately searching for some escape from the rising waters. Her eyes narrowed on a small game trail, just a few hundred feet away. Suddenly, she lost her footing, slipping on a loose rock, and came crashing forward onto her hands and knees, taking in a face full of cold creek water in the process. She felt her lungs involuntarily tighten, the cold water contracting every muscle. Gasping, she stood, her clothes fully soaked through, and looked down at the creek shocked. It took her a minute to refocus, but when she did, she noticed she couldn't see her feet. The cold water was no longer running clear, but instead, it was a rusty mud color. The deep rumbling thunder continued. And continued. Rolling on and on. Quickly, Kes sprang to action, moving toward the game trail. "Fuck, fuck, fuck..." she repeated to herself, with every step. The low rumble grew louder and louder, increasing in volume and proximity.

She made it to the game trail and, without looking back, she started up the precarious path. The route was only a foot wide and so steep she had to climb it on all fours. With every step, small rocks came loose and tumbled down, clattering onto the ground below her. Her heart pounded in her ears, and she stayed focused on the ground in front of her. The thundering noise of the flashing flood was growing closer and closer, and if she didn't get out of harm's way in the next few seconds she'd be swept away. Sneaking a peek behind her, Kes saw the wall of mud crashing down the canyon upstream. She tasted the bitter adrenaline in the back of her mouth and haphazardly scrambled higher. The path petered out and she found herself standing at the base of a sheer wall. The wall topped out a few feet above her head into what looked like a small alcove. Stretching to reach as high as she could, she grabbed onto a scraggly juniper trunk growing out of the wall with her right hand.

It seemed sturdy enough, and she prayed it would hold her weight. After a little bit of searching, she found a decent hold in the granite wall for her left hand. Her hands secured, she placed her feet on the wall. With a quick movement, she pulled herself up, using her feet as a counterweight to push her higher. Suddenly her feet gave way, and she slammed hard into the wall, knocking the wind out of her lungs. With the weight of her body hanging solely from her hands, it took her a moment to regain her breath and reposition her feet. Behind her, the thunder was deafening, but she couldn't risk any delay to turn and look at the oncoming wall of water. Taking another deep breath, she tapped into all of her reserves of strength and hauled herself up over the wall, finding hold after hold, until she crested the top, dragging herself up across her stomach onto the ledge.

Facedown on the ledge she hugged the ground, thankful to be alive. She took a deep breath in and inventoried the sensations coursing through her body. Her heart raced, her knees felt raw, and there was a warm pain throbbing and seeping from her left hand. A strange sensation pricked her exposed calves, like tiny, cold pins. She felt the rock face below her vibrate and rumble. Taking a deep breath, Kes pushed herself up off the rock, slowly rising to her feet. Tentatively, she gazed out over the canyon ledge. Phantom Canyon was completely unrecognizable. Muddy water filled every crevice and corner. Boulders the size of small cars tumbled and crashed into the walls and each other. Nondescript branches, trunks, and entire root systems of trees joined the fray, along with dirt and every manner of debris. The sheer magnitude of the flood destroyed everything in its path: plants, rocks, and creatures. No one could survive the flood if they were unfortunate to be caught in its path.

Tears pricked at the corners of Kes's eyes, and her stomach dropped. She collapsed to her knees as if the puppeteer had abruptly released her strings. As she crashed down, her shoulders rolled forward, and she felt cold seeping over her back and course through her entire body. The joy she'd felt in the morning was nothing but a lovely dream as the darkness came crashing in again.

"No. Please no..." Kes cried out. Her heart ached and she felt the pain fill her every cell. Tears streamed down her face and dropped onto her open palms, the flash flood drowning out any noise she made. Tears blurred her vision, all the colors around her blending like an impressionist painting. Her mind turned to Mae's sweet face until it was all she could see. Kes felt her heart warm, despite the ache, and the love she felt for Mae filled her every fiber. Blinking hard, she cleared the tears from her eyes.

Something was nagging her, begging for attention, but she couldn't quite place it. She closed her eyes and took a deep breath in. She needed to take control of the situation, get to safety, and update Trudy. I'm sure she's crazy with worry. With a slightly clearer mind, she reached for her pack to fish out her radio. As she pulled it open a pain seared through her left hand. Immediately, she withdrew her hand and cradled it to her chest. Turning it over, Kes blanched at the sight of a jagged cut that spanned the entire length of her palm. She must have sliced it on the granite in her attempt to get out of the flood's path.

"Clean, inspect, disinfect, bandage," Kes whispered to

herself. Instinctively, she set to work relying on years of experience. Within minutes, a bright white bandage encased
her hand, and she returned her medical supplies to the dry
bag. With her hand taken care of, for now, she fished in her
pack for her radio. Everything around the radio was damp,
and Kes remembered the last fateful face full of water. With
a deep breath, she turned the dial on the radio, willing it to
life. Slowly the red power light glowed. The radio remained
silent but appeared to be working. Depressing the micro-
phone button, she hoped her voice would cut through despite the cacophony dominating nearby.

"Ranger Thatcher, Ranger Wylde." Kes closed her eyes
and pressed the radio to her ear, praying she'd hear Trudy's voice come through. She needed the familiarity of her
friend's voice. She needed some grounding. She'd always
been self-sufficient and usually alone. She explored remote
areas of the canyon by herself, camping out under the stars
for nights on end, without an issue. "Independent to a
fault," her grandmother had said, kindness and pride in her
eyes. She'd never needed anyone before. But right now…
right now any voice crackling over the radio would be a
welcomed response. "Please…"

But there was no response; only static. She tried again.
"Ranger Thatcher, Ranger Wylde."

Again, nothing but silence.

She looked up at the canyon walls and felt completely
insignificant. She was alone, hurt, and had no contact with
anyone. "RANGER THATCHER, RANGER WYLDE," she
shouted into the radio, her voice cracking. Stress built up in
her chest, and she felt tears prick the back of her eyes again.

Pull yourself together, Wylde. You can do this. She cleared her throat, wiped away her tears, and clipped her radio to her belt. Returning everything to her pack, she shrugged the shoulder straps on. Looking out over the canyon she took a minute to survey the area. Usually, she could estimate approximately what time it was, but with the dark storm clouds overhead, it was hard to tell. It could very well be mid-afternoon, or perhaps almost dusk. She only knew it was after six o'clock thanks to the waterproof watch on her wrist. She had a few hours of daylight left, as dim as it was.

From what she could tell, Kes was on top of a plateau that stretched out as far as she could see. Below, the waters ravaged on. Even if she waited for the waters to recede, it was likely the entire course of Phantom Creek Canyon would be changed, and possibly be impassable. No, that wasn't a path she could use. There must be another way back down to the ranch... she just had to find it and preferably before it was too dark to see her way.

Chapter 23

"Ranger Wylde, this is Ranger Thatcher. Do you copy?" Static.

Trudy let out a huge sigh. "One more time," she said in a small voice.

"Ranger Wylde,… Kes, are you there?"

Ever since Kes took off up Phantom Creek Canyon, Trudy hadn't had a break. She'd run across every square inch of the inner canyon. She informed arriving hikers of the danger and got them to safety. She kept Dispatch in the loop every 20 minutes. She helped the mule wranglers pack and saddle up the stock to send them on their way. In her frantic rush, she ran into Frankie, who quickly offered to help. Over the last few hours, the two moved efficiently, and Trudy was incredibly grateful for the tiny spitfire next to her. With the storm moving in, the pair returned to the ranger station to warm up and wait for Kes to return.

When Trudy first heard Kes's voice crackling over the radio she breathed a deep sigh of relief and felt an invisible weight lift from her shoulders. Frankie beamed at the sound too, and the pair exchanged a brief hug. But it had been almost an hour since then, and although Trudy used the more powerful base radio in the ranger station, she was still unable to raise Kes on the radio.

The silence troubled Trudy. According to the radar, it looked like the storm would continue for another hour or so. Depending on where Kes was, it was pretty likely she wouldn't be able to return to the station tonight. Next to the ranger station, Bright Angel Creek roared and filled its banks with muddy water, boulders, and debris. Thankfully, at least for now, the waters weren't threatening the ranch or ranger station, but Trudy was sure parts of the campground were gone.

"We know she's alive. I'm sure she's trying to find Mae," Frankie said reassuringly and placed a hand on Trudy's back.

Frankie was right. Worrying wouldn't get them any- where, and anyway, there was no one better equipped to survive in the canyon than Kes. In any case, there was noth- ing Trudy could do. All helicopters were grounded because of the storm, and a crew on foot wouldn't be able to make it down to Phantom to start a search until at least dawn any- way. Trudy knew Kes could take care of herself in the back- country no matter what she faced, and Trudy needed to stay at her post in case any of the campers or guests of the ranch needed her help. Still, Trudy worried out of habit, and in an effort to ease her mind, she vowed to try to reach Kes on the radio at least once an hour.

Chapter 24

The canyon below was completely unrecognizable, but the surrounding plateau seemed familiar. Best Kes could estimate, she was about a mile down canyon from the junction of Phantom Creek and the Utah Flats trail, though perhaps calling it a trail was a bit generous. Utah Flats was more of a rough, unmaintained, unmarked route, well-known but not well-used.

Even in the best conditions, finding a hint of the Utah Flats route would be difficult or even impossible, depending on what part of the trail she stumbled upon. It wasn't so much whether or not she'd cross the route but rather if she would recognize she had. For most of the way, the path was only a footstep and a half wide, and the only indication it was a path of any sort was the near-total lack of vegetation. Kes had hiked the route many times, but approaching from this angle, with the ever-darkening skies, she felt disoriented. Her body shook slightly, shivering against the wind rolling over the landscape.

Keeping Phantom Canyon on her right side, Kes picked

her way along the edge of the plateau. Progress was slow and involved a fair bit of backtracking. She followed game trails as they carved a clear path around the desert vegetation, avoiding the fine spines of the cholla cactus and the sharp spikes of the larger yucca plants. She made her way until one barrier or another blocked her path. Sometimes the trails petered out into nothing, and she was forced to turn back, retracing her steps until she found another. Other times the trails descended into the canyon, where she would not find a safe way back to the station through the torrential waters. The ground was soaked, and every few steps, she sank into the mud a half-inch or so, pulling her down and slowing her progress. With all of the backtracking and rerouting, she'd barely made it half of a mile in the last two hours.

As Kes stopped to survey the canyon, yet again, she felt the throbbing pain in her hand pierce through her focus and invade her consciousness. In the dim light, she could just make out the dark stain of blood seeping through the bandage. Kes needed to stop the bleeding. Dropping her pack to the ground, she fished out her medical kit again in search of something to apply pressure and hold the gauze firm against her wound. She felt as though she were in a fog, and struggled to keep her mind focused on the task literally at hand. Finding what she was looking for, she awkwardly wrapped an elastic bandage around her palm. It needed to be tight enough to add sufficient pressure to the wound but not so tight it cut off circulation to her fingers. As Kes donned her pack again, she tucked her hand under the shoulder strap, keeping it pinned against her chest. She hoped the bandage and the weight of her backpack would provide the necessary pressure and elevation to stop the bleeding.

Kes shivered as she stood motionless for the first time in a few hours and felt the chill of her still-wet uniform clinging to her skin. Goosebumps prickled and covered her skin. Usually, she purposefully got her clothes wet before a hike. Then, as she hiked her clothes would dry in the hot Arizona sun, cooling her off in the process. When temperatures were well over 100 degrees, that was desirable. But right now, she needed warmth, not to be chilled further. The humidity in the air was high enough from the monsoons that her clothes weren't drying and, under the star-filled skies, the temperatures continued to drop, both around her and within her core. She felt semi-numb all over, and her legs refused to cooperate as she tried to keep moving forward.

Light was getting scarce, but Kes didn't pull out her headlamp. Not yet. A headlamp would illuminate the area directly in front of her and likely save her from stumbling into a cactus or tripping over a rodent burrow, but having the bright light on would narrow her vision to only what was within the path of the beam. If she needed to turn the light off, it would take her eyes a few minutes to adjust, leaving her blind and vulnerable. Almost all sound was deafened by the tumultuous flow below, and she didn't want to lose her night vision, too.

Ah right… all about the night vision. Nothing to do with bat kisses? Kes chuckled to herself hearing Sara's voice in her mind.

"What can I say, bats love me," she responded.

Kes remembered the night she and Sara were hiking out of the canyon, the sky pitch black, no moon to be found. They both wore their headlamps and hiked mostly in silence, exhausted from a long day. Kes, in the lead, trudged on, one slow step after another, focused only on the small circle of light on the ground in front of her. Suddenly, a bat swooped down into the light in an attempt to feast on the delectable insects swarming the beam, narrowly missing Kes's face. The shrill scream that escaped Kes's mouth left Sara doubled over in laughter for a solid ten minutes, tears streaming down her face. After the shock wore off, Kes joined in on the laughing but refused to turn her headlamp back on or take the lead again. From that point on, anytime they saw a bat, Sara imitated the shriek, causing them both to laugh until their sides hurt, much to the bewilderment of anyone else nearby, visitors and coworkers alike. The memory warmed her heart, and she felt a little less alone.

"Sar, I miss you," Kes mumbled.

"I know you do. I'm still here."

Kes let out a deep breath. She could see Sara standing beside her. Sara looked healthy and strong, not exhausted and worn thin like Kes felt. Sara stood in her uniform with her thumbs tucked under the straps of her backpack near her collarbone to pull some of the weight of the pack off of her shoulders. Her uniform was slightly askew like it often was. Her smile was brilliant and her expression warm and understanding. She put a warm hand on Kes's uninjured arm, and Kes could feel the heat radiating down her limb. It was good to feel Sara's presence again. Kes didn't feel so scared and alone. So much had happened since Sara passed, and Kes wanted to tell her everything.

"You love her," Sara said, a knowing smile on her face. She uncovered the words Kes secreted away deep in her heart, too scared to let them out. Sara had a way of cutting through Kes's fear, picking out the most important parts and bringing them to light. This time was no different. Under the cover of darkness, Kes felt the light inside of her burn brighter. She didn't want to ignore her feelings or hide them any longer. "I do," Kes whispered.

Kes felt the marbles in her mouth and struggled to get out her next thought. "She's probably dead, Sar. Everyone leaves," Kes said, her voice trailing off as her eyes fluttered closed. She felt drunk, not in control of her words or her body. "I love her... but she's gone."

"You'll still get your chance, I bet. Your love story isn't a tragic one, I promise you, my dear Kes," she heard Sara's voice reassure her.

Kes felt sheer exhaustion roll over her body. The weight of the day was dragging her down, and she longed to fall into a warm, soft bed and sleep without end. She didn't feel cold anymore, just a feeling of vague numbness in all of her extremities. She tripped over the uneven ground and stumbled to gain her footing. Fumbling with her pack, Kes struggled to undo the buckle of her hip belt and cursed as she mistakenly used her injured hand to release the clasp. She let the pack fall off her back and crash into the ground behind her. She needed to stop and rest. She needed to close her eyes and let sleep overcome her. Without looking, she sank down next to her pack, unable to continue. If she could just rest her eyes for a little bit, she'd be ready to keep going.

"You can't stop now, Kes. You need to keep moving," Sara's voice begged as it faded away.

"Leb me lone," Kes babbled, unable to put in any energy to argue with Sara.

She was lost but unafraid as she focused on finding safety. She turned her face upward praying for some heavenly intervention to help point the way and was rewarded with a brilliant star-studded blanket enveloping every corner of the sky. The last of the storm clouds dissipated to the north, and in their wake, she saw the celestial heavens more clearly than ever before. With a deep breath, she turned her focus back on the narrow trail in front of her, hoping it would lead her wherever she needed to go to get back down to safety.

Glancing to her left, the canyon next to her was merely a dark, noisy abyss. It was terrifying, but the rushing water seemed quieter, if only just slightly. Out of the corner of her eye, she caught a glimpse of a red light. She whipped her head back toward the trail to search for the light. There it was again; ever so faint and tiny but definitely real. It was dim, and if she stared at it directly, it faded into the midnight darkness around it.

Her heart leaped in her chest. With a burst of adrenaline, she started to jog toward the light. It was difficult to estimate how far away it was, but with every pounding step it grew stronger and bigger. As it grew, so did the hope in her chest, fueling her tired legs. She was free without a pack to hold her back. She regretted leaving it behind and assumed it had been lost in the flood. She longed for a warm layer or two tucked inside, but she could move much faster over the landscape without it. She needed to reach that red beacon in the distance. It called to her.

Please, she thought, *please guide me back to her*.

Chapter 25

Within minutes, she could make the faint outline of a person a couple of hundred yards ahead. The figure was huddled into a ball, barely illuminated by the tiny red light glowing on something on the ground in front of them. She sprinted the rest of the way, crossing the remaining distance. Winded, she stopped a few yards away, bending over to place her hands on her knees and catch her breath.

Mae was paralyzed for a moment. The figure had yet to move or notice her appearance. Though her lungs burned, she held her breath for a moment, not willing to reveal her presence yet. From what Mae could tell, they were alone in the canyon, just like she was. Mae felt a deep affinity for whoever this was, venturing into the wild solo. She didn't want to frighten whoever this was as she came out of the darkness, somewhere unknown in the canyon, without a pack, a headlamp, or any supplies. She needed to find her way back down to Phantom Ranch. She was sure her absence was noticed. She hated to think of Kes, Frankie, or Trudy worrying about her, and she wanted to let them know she was okay.

A shiver coursed through her body, shaking her out of her thoughts. She'd started her hike in shorts and a t-shirt and had felt the delicious heat of the inner canyon. She longed for that now, but the temperature had dropped over the course of the storm, and the sun had long since set. The cold night air seeped through her clothes, chilling her to her core.

Cautiously, she moved forward, one step at a time. The figure before her seemed frozen in place. As Mae circled around to the front of them, they remained statue-like without looking up. They sat with their legs tucked into their chest, shrinking into themselves. Their arms were folded on top of their knees, and they had their head face down on their arms.

They must be frozen, Mae thought, noticing the woman's clothing looked wet as it clung against her back and legs. Mae squatted down, took a deep breath in, and placed her hand on the woman's icy cold arm. For a moment, nothing happened. Mae rubbed the arm gently. "Are you okay?" she asked.

Slowly, the woman stirred, lifting her tear-and-dirt-stained face from her arms. Immediately, the breath Mae was holding escaped with a heavy sigh. "Kes…" Mae said with a deep smile. She felt like her heart was going to burst as she threw her arms around Kes's frozen figure. She felt her heart pound a little stronger. Mae tried to transfer the depth of her feelings to Kes via their hug, hoping she was communicating just how happy she was.

"M-m-m… Mae?" she heard Kes whisper. Kes's voice

was small, timid, childlike, and confused. Mae sat back on her heels and took Kes's face in her hands. Kes's skin was icy-cold and clammy against Mae's palms. "I'm here."

Kes's eyes were unfocused, and for a few minutes, she struggled to keep them open. Her head bobbed a few times before she was able to look up and find Mae's eyes again. She seemed as though she were in a deep fog, and Mae struggled to reach her. "Where...?" Kes asked, unable to finish her question before her forehead dropped again.

Mae shook her gently, "Where what, my love?" For a moment, Kes didn't move and Mae wondered if she fell asleep. She was probably exhausted after whatever ordeal she had faced. Gently, she rubbed Kes's back, feeling the cold dampness of her uniform.

Finally, Kes stirred again and looked at Mae briefly. A look of confusion lingered on Kes's face. She seemed surprised to see Mae in front of her. "Mae? I was looking for you. Where are you?" Kes's words were slurred, tumbling out of her mouth without the effort to shape them into their proper form.

Mae's stomach dropped out as the realization set in. Kes wasn't okay. She sprang to her feet to retrieve Kes's pack, hopeful there would be something in there to help. Nearby the red beacon that had led her to Kes was still glowing, and Mae bent down to retrieve it. Kes's radio! Perfect! If she called Trudy on the radio, help would surely be on the way shortly. Mae pressed the button on the side, lifted it to her mouth, and started to speak. "Trudy, I'm with Kes, she's—" Out of the corner of her eye, Mae noticed the red light on the top of the radio start to dim. Slowly it faded to complete black, taking with it any hope of a quick rescue. Mae desperately tried turning the knobs on the radio, hopeful she could bring it back to life. But nothing she did worked.

Okay, Mae thought, *no one is coming. Take a deep breath. You can do this.* Clipping the radio to the elastic waistband of her shorts so she wouldn't lose it in the dark, Mae set Kes's pack down beside her. *First, I need to check Kes for any injuries*, Mae thought as she remembered a basic first aid class from years ago. She dug a headlamp out of Kes's pack and turned it on, illuminating everything around her. A quick inspection of Kes's head and neck dismissed the possibility of a head injury. Other than a few bumps and bruises, the only noticeable trauma Mae could find was under the bandage on Kes's hand. She gently peeled back the edge of the gauze, but since the wound wasn't actively bleeding, Mae decided that the injury would have to wait. Kes seemed in relatively fine form physically.

What worried Mae more was how cold and confused Kes was. Kes's uniform was soaked, and the chill Mae had felt on Kes's arms and face permeated every part of her body. Summer nights in the canyon weren't known for being dangerously cold, but it wouldn't take long for hypothermia to set in if Mae didn't get Kes dry and warmed up. Mae was no stranger to the dangers of hypothermia. She'd seen countless young lobstermen come into harbor barely upright, soaked to the bone after a wicked wave attempted to topple them over the side rail during the winter storms. Kes's symptoms matched: confusion, mumbling, drowsiness, and she was absolutely freezing. Mae worked quickly, withdrawing anything warm she could find from Kes's pack.

She pulled out a few layers of dry clothing, a fleece blanket, and a soft, down sleeping bag she recognized. Kes faded in and out of consciousness as Mae hurried. Mae wasn't sure if Kes would understand or remember what was happening; nevertheless, she talked to her throughout the process.

"Kes, stay with me. Please."

"I've got to get you undressed and warmed up. I promise you'll feel better soon."

Carefully, she unbuttoned Kes's uniform and spread it out over a nearby rock to help it dry. Nervously she lifted Kes's arms over her head, peeling her wet sports bra off of her skin. It would have been a hard enough feat to accomplish had she been dry, but of course, the wet stretchy material clung and suctioned itself to Kes's skin. As soon as the blasted garment was removed, Mae wrapped a fleece blanket around Kes's shoulders. Mae rubbed Kes's arms vigorously, encouraging blood to flow into her extremities and warm her up. She untied and removed Kes's muddy boots, sliding them off as gently as she could. She carefully peeled off Kes's soaked socks and finally wiggled her out of her shorts and underwear.

With surprising ease, Mae lifted Kes's dozing form and set her down gently on top of the open sleeping bag she'd arranged nearby. Quickly Mae zipped it up and used her warm hands to rub Kes's back. Throughout the entire procedure, Kes's eyes remained closed and she mumbled nonsensically. Mae hushed her, "Get some sleep. It's okay. I'm here."

"So c-c-c-cold. Please." Kes's voice was weak, and it broke Mae's heart to see her like this. Without a second thought,

Mae stripped off her own clothes and slipped into the small sleeping bag next to Kes. Wrapping an arm around Kes's waist, Mae pulled the shaking form tight against her body. She felt the chill of Kes's cold skin against her own and she imagined her body heat pouring out and flowing over Kes's body. She hoped it would be enough.

After a few minutes, Kes's shivers quieted and her breathing fell into an easy rhythm. Mae kissed Kes's shoulder, nestling her face into the bare skin.

Mae let out a deep sigh. She had her love in her arms and for now, Kes seemed stable. If Mae could keep her warm and let her sleep, they'd make it through the night. By the position of the Milky Way overhead, she estimated they still had several hours before there would be any light, warmth, or hope for help.

Mae fought her own exhaustion, wanting to watch over Kes's dozing form. But the stress and physical beating of the day caught up to her, and within a few moments, she drifted off to join Kes in dreamland.

Chapter 26

Warmth flooded her core and she felt embraced in love. Her love's arms were wrapped around her naked form, exploring every inch of her exposed skin. She felt soft lips on the back of her neck, and her love pressed her warm, curvaceous body against her back. She moaned at the pressure of a tongue against the tender skin on her neck and ground her hips back into her love's lap. The response was immediate, as a firm hand settled in on her hip bone and pulled her tight until there was no space between the two bodies. The desire she felt coursed through her cells, igniting her passion, causing a thrumming between her legs. She was tempted to guide the hand on her hip down where she was aching to be touched.

Nearby, the crescendoing din of predawn birds stirred Kes slightly. She groaned and closed her eyes tight, willing herself to fall back asleep so she could continue with that particular scenario. The dream was always the same; a sexy woman holding her from behind and waking her with tender kisses and touches. It set her sexual desires into overdrive every time, and inevitably she would awake just before the good stuff started. These dreams left her wanting, needing, and aching for this dream partner to release her.

In the years since they started, she'd never seen the face of her dream woman, but instinctively she knew who it was. Something in her heart recognized the presence.

She felt the lightest of kisses on her shoulder blade. It felt real, vivid, and electrifying. She felt a mix of excitement and intimacy fill her senses. The kiss's mark left a lingering sensation, cool as the wind blew over the spot, but deeply warming beneath the surface. She smiled to herself. A body stirred behind her and burrowed deeper into her back. She felt warm, smooth skin pressed against the length of her, and a warm arm pulled her closer.

Kes's eyes flew open. That kiss was real.

It was barely light out, and after a minute, she recognized the iconic walls of the canyon off in the distance. Cold pricked her skin around the edges of the sleeping bag. She was confused why she felt the silky material of the sleeping bag against more of her body than normal until it registered; she was absolutely naked.

For a moment she took in each sensation she was feeling. As far as she could tell, the body pressed against hers was naked as well. She knew logically she should be scared and confused as to how she ended up in this situation, but the same presence that existed in her dreams was here too. No one else spoke to her heart the way Mae did.

Kes snuggled in deeper, smiling to herself. She wasn't entirely sure how they ended up naked in a single sleeping bag, but she wasn't about to complain. Last night was a blur, as if she was trying to view it through a rain-streaked window. The last thing she remembered was feeling freezing cold and lost while she searched for Mae. She'd seen Sara next to her at one point, though she wondered if that had been just a dream. In the past, not being in control and not being fully cognizant of everything going on around her would have thrown her off-kilter and made her fight or flight response kick into overdrive. It was the same emotion that had overwhelmed her the morning after the wedding when she had woken up next to a sleeping Trudy. But she didn't feel that now. Instead, she felt comfortable, safe, and protected in Mae's arms.

A sweet, sleepy voice muttered in her ear. At first, it was just gibberish, without definition. More like babbling. Kes giggled to herself. She never pictured Mae as a sleep talker, but it was endearing and adorable. Mae continued, the words becoming ever clearer. Kes could make out every few words, though how they connected was anyone's guess. She lovingly stroked Mae's hand lying across her middle. Here in Mae's arms she was safe, cared for, and at home. Kes couldn't help but let her thoughts escape the barrier of her lips. "I love you, Mae."

The words were no more than a whisper, but they were enough to wake Mae from her dreams. For a moment, she lay perfectly still, unsure if she heard correctly. She didn't want to break the moment, afraid she'd fully wake up and find herself still lost and alone. But as she took a deep breath in, she felt the length of the warm and inviting body that she held tight. Smiling, she opened her eyes.

Feeling the flutter of Mae's eyelashes on her back, Kes

turned slightly to face her.

"Good morning," Mae's voice cracked. Kes's sleepy smile was intoxicating and inviting.

"We're naked," Kes said, immediately scolding herself. *That's the best you can come up with when the woman of your dreams wakes up next to you?* she thought to herself.

The simple statement of fact made Mae blush intensely. Until that moment she had temporarily forgotten they were both very much naked. The blush that spread across Mae's sheepish face made her all the more adorable, especially combined with the deep, heartfelt giggle that immediately started bubbling up. Mae didn't look at all apologetic for their condition and instead seemed to be enjoying it.

Mae's giggle was contagious, and soon Kes joined in. The two of them, laughing together in the predawn, happiness unbridled and overflowing. Mae felt Kes's joy radiate through her body, bubbling over and filling her heart with warmth. In the early morning light, Mae was awestruck at Kes's beauty; the softness of her features, the openness of her expressions. The real Kes was unhidden, peeking through, just like the first streams of light breaking over the canyon walls high above. She was gorgeous and fully present. The corners of Kes's eyes crinkled in joy, her laughter deep and all-encompassing, and there was a message of love traveling through her fingertips as they rested gently but firmly on Mae's arm. She didn't hold back.

Tears caught in the corners of Kes's eyes, as she felt her joy overwhelm her senses. It had been too long since she had laughed to the point of tears, but right now, there was nothing holding her back. She felt her happiness reach ridiculous levels inside, as if the sun itself had taken up residence in her heart. Fear didn't linger in the corners or threaten to douse her joy; it was banished from this realm. As tears streamed down her face, she felt cleansed. The pain and darkness that shadowed her view for the past few months were finally released. The last twenty-four hours had been difficult, but today was a new day, one that started with Mae safe beside her. And when it came down to it, Mae wasn't the one who had needed rescuing. Kes was forced to let someone save her for a change, and she found she liked it.

Kes looked at Mae's sweet face, only a few inches from her own. Mae's face radiated in the early morning light. Kes withdrew her hand from somewhere between their warm bodies and gently stroked down the side of Mae's face. Her fingertips traced their way over Mae's features, taking special care to remember every inch of her face. Leaning in, Kes captured Mae's lips with her own, drawing them in between hers. The kiss was firm and slow, their warm lips pressing against each other without hesitation. Kes opened her mouth to deepen the kiss and was immediately met by the tip of Mae's tongue. A fire coursed through her, electrifying the very tips of her being, and she pressed the kiss further. Wanting to feel more, she rolled Mae onto her back and laid the entire length of her body on top. She delighted in the quickening of their shared breaths and the delicious moans escaping Mae's throat. Easily, she slipped her knee in between Mae's legs and felt a pulsing against her thigh, echoing the one she felt at her own core.

The world faded away. There was nothing but an attempt to physically express all the unspoken words, the desire coursing through her system, the softness of Mae's skin on her own, each breath, heartbeat, and sensation. Nothing mattered but this moment. She felt Mae's hands run gently over her sides, up over her shoulders, and back down her spine. She felt Mae's tongue press against her own, causing hormones to flood her senses. God, that woman could kiss. Kes wanted to stay in this moment forever.

"Fuck," Kes said, wincing in pain. In an attempt to shift her weight and get closer to Mae, she'd tried to balance on her left hand, forgetting the deep cut across her palm.

Immediately, Mae's expression changed, concern clearly etched on her face. Without a word, she rolled Kes gently onto her side and sat up, slipping out of the sleeping bag. She lifted Kes's hand to inspect her wound, delicately unwrapping the bloodied gauze, strip by strip. Kes inspected Mae's face and was overwhelmed by the care and kindness she saw there. The worry evident in her expression was endearing. "We've got to get this taken care of," Mae said, her eyes never moving from Kes's hand. Kes wanted to kiss her again, sweetly, thanking her, but instead, she just watched Mae's face as she set to her task. Mae looked so serious and mission-driven; it was adorable. Kes was pretty sure Mae wasn't aware of Kes's gaze, giving Kes permission to continue admiring her. Backlit by the rising sun, Mae was stunning. The sun glowed against her skin, highlighting every curve. It was difficult not to stare at the soft contour of her breasts, with their deliciously pink nipples hardened against the morning chill. How Kes longed to take them between her lips and break them down with her tongue. She licked her lips just thinking about it.

"We ought to head back to the station so we can get this cleaned out properly," Mae said, breaking Kes's concentration.

"I'm guessing you'll want to put on a shirt before we do that? We wouldn't want you to end up with sunburn on your delicate places... though I wouldn't mind liberally administering burn cream if you did." Kes smirked and bit her lower lip, holding back a giggle. The look on Mae's face was priceless when she looked down and realized she was completely topless, exposed to the entire canyon. Her laugh bubbled up and filled the air as she quickly crossed her arms in front of her chest and shot Kes a look. "Naughty!"

Kes laughed and sat up. "You are absolutely beautiful," she whispered, and she gently kissed Mae. She could feel Mae smile against her lips, and it made her want to draw her in even closer. It didn't take long for the kissing to turn urgent again, leaving them both out of breath.

"Okay, okay, okay... we should get going before it gets hot," Kes said, pulling away to catch her breath.

"I'd say it's already pretty hot," Mae said, lust dripping in her gaze. It was Kes's turn to blush.

The sun rose quickly, filling the canyon with warmth as the last vestiges of the storm clung to every surface. The canyon felt alive, plants suddenly rejuvenated, vibrant sage and green dotting the landscape. The distinct smells of creosote, petrichor, and fresh earth filled the air, bringing with it the excitement of new life.

Kes smiled, hearing Mae's voice excitedly point out a bird flitting across the path. For the last hour, the two hiked along, equally in conversation and silence. When the width of the trail allowed it, they walked side by side, fingers intertwined. Kes wasn't scared anymore. All of the guards she'd hidden behind were gone, leaving their posts abandoned. She had no reason to keep herself at a distance; there was nothing to fear here.

Kes learned about Mae's hike up Phantom Canyon and delighted in hearing her joy as she talked about all she saw. She shuddered hearing Mae's fear when she'd just made it out of the canyon only to see the flash flood heading downstream. She laughed at Mae's description of the flood as a "rocky road milkshake." She loved seeing the canyon through Mae's eyes. It was awe-inspiring and magical. She looked around at the canyon walls, admiring their majesty and sheer size.

"There's something about standing at the bottom of the Grand Canyon that leaves me feeling humbled," Mae said. "It is huge here, in every aspect. The massive rims rising above you, the open skies, the sheer power of the water carving the canyon walls... it's all at a scale beyond compare. But more than the massive size of everything that is here, there's the vast expanse of nothingness. The openness. Here, there's nothing between you and the world. We are left in space, in the void. You can't shrink from the universe or hide behind the trappings of society. We're not less in this space, we are more because we are a part of it. I am not lost here."

Feeling Kes's hand squeeze her own, Mae blushed, realizing she verbalized the wanderings of her mind. She hadn't meant to share her musings, but with Kes, it was easy. She didn't feel the need to customize her character based on what she thought Kes would like. She felt bolder, stronger, more in tune with the person she truly was. She could share and knew instinctively that the only person Kes wanted her to be was herself. And that's all Mae wanted too; to be herself fully.

"This is home for me. The rocks, the walls, the openness have always been a place to find myself. Sometimes it was my sanctuary, my school, my playground. But lately, it felt more like my fortress, my keep, my facade." Kes opened up to Mae, looking out over the view.

"I've defined myself by the canyon and felt it was my one constant when everything changed. I feel strongest here, or at least I had. But last night I felt the weakest I've ever felt."

Mae turned to face Kes and placed her free hand on Kes's forearm. Kes's eyes pricked with tears, and she took a deep breath, pushing herself on.

"Last night I was reminded of what it felt like to fear losing someone, and I couldn't stand it. I don't think I would have survived if it hadn't been for Sara."

Mae remained quiet, hoping Kes would go on. All morning, Kes had seemed open to her in a way she hadn't over the last few days. They had shared deep conversations, but somehow it still felt like she was holding back. Mae had seen Kes collapse out of exhaustion, and although she may have been vulnerable in those moments, Kes hadn't opened her heart to Mae then.

"I was convinced I had lost you before I had a chance… before I could…" Kes's voice cracked as she lost her words. "I couldn't bear the pain, and I didn't know what I would do." Kes smiled sadly, remembering the darkness that enveloped her. "That's when I heard Sara's voice. She didn't let me give up hope and lose myself to the depths of the canyon. I believe it was thanks to her that you found me."

Kes's eyes finally met Mae's, and all she saw was love. Not fear, not worry, not expectation. Just love.

"Love. That's what she reminded me of…love," Kes said, quietly, in a voice barely above a whisper.

"I had been so afraid to open my heart again. Losing Sara meant losing a huge part of myself, and I wasn't sure I was willing to open up to the possibility of that pain again. I thought if I kept everyone at a distance, I would be okay. If I didn't let them in fully, I couldn't lose myself again."

Mae knew that feeling well. After Terese broke her heart, she lost almost all semblance of an identity for a while. Loving fully meant accepting you could experience pain and loss.

"But keeping myself closed off meant keeping love and beauty out and killing a big part of my heart. I don't want to do that anymore. I don't want to keep myself from loving. I don't want to keep myself from you." Kes's smile and words touched Mae's heart deeply. Mae felt her heart bursting at the deep affection in those words. Perhaps it was possible Mae hadn't been dreaming this morning when she thought she heard three sweet words slip out of Kes's mouth. Mae's heartbeat quickened as she remembered Kes's soft voice.

For a moment, the two just looked at each other, the magnetism between them growing stronger by the minute. Mae leaned forward and lightly kissed Kes, sealing the unspoken between them. It was sweet, innocent, and only lasted a couple of seconds, but it was exactly what Kes desired at that moment. She longed to express the depths of her feelings for Mae, even if she couldn't do so in words just yet.

Pressing their foreheads together, the two shared a few breaths, letting their feelings course through their bodies and fill the space between them. In the stillness of the moment, a low rumble grew between them. Mae looked up in alarm, scanning the horizon wildly.

"Another flash?" She asked, looking bewildered toward the sunny skies and the nearby cliffside, terrified to see if another muddy wall of water was headed their way.

Kes burst into laughter, unable to contain her embarrassment and sudden joy. "This time it was my stomach." She could barely get the words out between her laughs. She hadn't realized how hungry she was until her stomach decided to voice its opinion on the dawdling pace of their hike. After a beat of shock, Mae quickly joined in laughing. "We better get a move on! I wouldn't want you fading away to nothing."

Mae moved to lead them on the trail but was stopped by Kes's hand in hers, spinning her around. She found herself in Kes's arms, looking deep into those electric eyes. Before she could even raise her eyebrows to ask a question, Kes leaned forward and kissed her, deeply, passionately, lighting a spark deep within her core. This kiss was steeped in desire and need, a different kind of hunger. When the kiss broke, Mae's head spun wildly.

"Listen here, Ranger Wylde. That's not getting us any closer to food. Or to a bed, for that matter. So, we're going to hike now... because I really need to get you fed." Mae's voice was low, rumbling in her throat, and Kes knew she didn't just mean food.

"Yes ma'am. I'll follow you anywhere."

Chapter 27

The creek was utterly changed. The water that had once run crystal clear was now a muddy swamp of silt and pebbles as the last of the storm waters drained down toward the Colorado River. Large boulders had reshaped the course of the creek, destroying the banks and swimming areas where Mae had lounged just days earlier. Tree trunks stuck out of the creek at weird angles, the skeletons of branches destroyed. Kes was wide-eyed as she surveyed the campground. From what she could see, the damage was relatively minimal, thankfully. A few campsites were half eroded by the powerful waters, and repairing them would take months of work. But knowing the power of the water, Kes felt a sense of relief knowing the damage could have been much worse.

Kes was grateful they hadn't been caught up in the flood, and from the looks of it, no one else had been either. It was early enough in the day that there still ought to be some campers lingering in the area, but the campground was completely empty. No one had risked camping there overnight.

Crossing the still-intact footbridge over the creek, Kes saw the outlines of at least twenty tents crowded into an old unused mule corral in the distance. She smiled to herself. *Good ol' Trudy*, Kes thought gratefully. She knew her coworker would have made sure everyone was protected and cared for. *I wouldn't be surprised if they were all enjoying some of Trudy's famous cinnamon rolls at this very moment.* Kes laughed at that thought. Grateful to see everyone was safe and dry, Kes turned toward the ranger station with Mae a few steps behind.

Just as the pair walked up the steps to the station, the door burst open and a warm figure lunged at them, wrapping them both in a bear hug.

"Trudy. It's okay. We're okay," Kes said, laughing. But when Trudy didn't let go, Kes relented and returned the hug, feeling Mae's hand already wrapped around her friend.

For a moment, the three of them stood there in a cuddle pile until a soft voice from the doorway said, "Maybe y'all would like to come in and get some grub?" Kes opened her eyes to see Frankie standing in the doorway, donning an apron and beckoning them in. Kes laughed at the flour on Frankie's cheek and gave them a quick hug as she stepped across the threshold. Her stomach rumbled again as the smell of cinnamon, sugar, warm bread, and a million other delicious scents filled her senses. Quickly, Kes threw off her pack and walked as fast as she could into the kitchen, her jaw dropping. Every available space was covered in some form of fresh-baked goods. There were cakes, cinnamon rolls, pies, various pastries, and a few items she couldn't identify. She guessed correctly that Trudy would make delicious treats for the campers, but Kes never imagined the sheer number of marvelous delicacies that awaited her in the kitchen.

Trudy's voice rose shyly behind her. "I was just a little worried."

Mae's laughter filled the room, and soon Frankie and Kes joined in. Kes turned and pulled Trudy into her arms, tears stinging her eyes. "Thank you."

Trudy held her tight as she whispered, "I knew you would be okay. You just had to be. Thank you for being okay." The two pulled back from their embrace, each with tears in their eyes.

"Now, who wants something to eat?" Trudy said, happily pulling open the oven door to reveal yet another fresh-baked delight waiting to be devoured.

There was something absolutely indescribable about the feeling of hot water streaming over sore, dirt-encrusted muscles. As the water poured over her scalp, she ran her palm over her face, feeling the salt crystals washing away. She hadn't realized how sore she was from yesterday's adventure, but standing here, she felt every ache and pain radiate.

"You'd better not be getting your bandage wet," Mae's voice called out from behind the shower curtain. Hot water was at a premium in the station, and Mae was patiently waiting her turn, having insisted Kes go first.

"Well, that makes it pretty difficult to wash up," Kes re-
torted, pulling back the shower curtain and shooting Mae a
devious look. Mae stood completely naked, an arm wrapped
around her chest with the other covering the space where
her legs met. She looked incredibly sexy, and Kes ached to
touch her. "Maybe you could come in and give me a hand?"
Kes said, her voice equal parts flirtatious and hopeful. Without hesitation, Mae pulled the curtain back and happily
stepped into the tub. She still had her arm across her chest,
which made Kes grin devilishly.

Kes reached for Mae's waist and pulled her against her
body, laying a wet kiss right on Mae's surprised lips. Within
seconds the innocent kiss deepened, with Mae running her
tongue over Kes's lips, asking them to open. Mae's kisses
moved from Kes's mouth to her neck, firmly running her
tongue from Kes's collarbone to her ear. Mae could feel
Kes's pulse quicken under her touch, and she loved the reaction she was getting.

Drawing Kes even closer, Mae ran her hands down over
Kes's body, delighting in the complement of curves and defined muscles. Moving her mouth down Kes's body, she enjoyed the path the water flowed. First, she stopped at Kes's
collarbone and was captivated by the tender sensations she
could produce there. Moving farther down, she took her
time exploring the fullness of Kes's breasts, moving lazily
from one nipple to the other. She lightly licked each nipple,
feeling it harden under her touch. Then she sucked it in between her lips and broke it back down with the flat of her
tongue. Kes moaned loudly at that sensation, intertwining

her fingers in Mae's hair and pulling slightly. The tension caused Mae to moan and pull back from Kes's body. Looking up, she saw the need in Kes's eyes, which only served to heighten her own desire. She ached to press Kes against the shower wall and fulfill their needs.

A sudden blast of cold water stopped them both in their tracks, and they pulled apart as if they'd just been caught. As the warm water returned, they looked at each other and laughed, sheepish grins crossing both of their faces.

"I think that's our warning that we'd better finish up here before we only have cold water," Kes stated, the hormonal fog still lingering heavily in the air. With a grin, Mae placed a sweet and innocent kiss on Kes's lips. "Well, hand me the soap, and let's get clean, dirty ranger." At that, Kes laughed outright.

The spread was incredible. In the short time they'd been in the shower, Trudy had managed to cook up scrambled eggs with cheese, bacon, ham, hash browns, and pancakes. The small slice of cake they'd eaten before their shower was long since forgotten, and Mae and Kes piled their plates high with food as if they had never eaten before.

While they ate, Trudy filled them in on what had happened at the ranch while they were on their adventure.

"No one has been reported injured or lost; now that you two are safe. Some hikers didn't have tents or rain gear. Others had their food supplies destroyed in the rain. But everyone came together. Frankie had the great idea to set up a group campsite in the mule corral, and everyone brought what they could. Strangers shared tents, dry clothing, and anything they could. It was amazing. We had a potluck last night, and I'm not sure I've ever seen the heart of the true Grand Canyon experience shine more brightly," Trudy told Kes and Mae, her eyes shining.

"I was really worried about both of you and was nearly out of my mind with fear. I heard you call in, Kes, and I tried to respond, but I couldn't reach you." Trudy's voice was filled with the earnest concern she'd felt all night.

"About that... my radio may or may not have taken a swim in the creek." The sheepish look on Kes's face made Trudy smile and helped Trudy release the worry she felt.

"I was just glad to know you were alive. A couple of hours later, when I heard Mae's voice over the radio, I knew you were together, but her voice cut off before I could hear where you were or what was going on. I was sure one of you had broken your leg, had gotten trapped under a boulder, or was lying hurt somewhere. I was planning on sending out a search party if I hadn't heard from you by this afternoon," Trudy continued.

Kes reached over and squeezed Trudy's hand, taking in the gravity of what she had gone through. She couldn't imagine how she would have handled being in Trudy's position if their roles had been reversed.

"I'm sorry, Tru," Kes said softly. "I didn't mean to make you worry. To be honest, I don't think I would have made it back here if it hadn't been for Mae."

Kes turned to look at Mae gratefully. Mae beamed back

at Kes and allowed herself to feel proud. She had survived the flash flood, navigated the dangers of the canyon alone, and had come to Kes's rescue. Between bites, Kes and Mae filled their friends in on most of what had happened after the flash flood, of course, leaving out any of the salacious details from their sleeping bag make-out session.

"Well, thank goodness for Mae! Perhaps we ought to make you an honorary ranger," Trudy suggested.

"It's a dream come true!" Mae said as a huge smile filled her face.

"I believe Frankie should also receive their own honorary ranger designation. I really don't think I would have made it through yesterday and last night without you, Frankie. You were incredible, and you kept me calm through all of the mayhem and stress." Trudy shot Frankie a kind and thankful smile.

"It was my pleasure, ma'am. I have one serious question first. Do I get a badge?"

"Ooo I want one too!" piped up Mae.

"I think that can be arranged," Kes said with a smile. "I believe we have a couple of junior ranger badges lying around here somewhere."

Kes reached for Mae's hand and gave it a quick squeeze. Mae smiled her way, making the world disappear around them. She was beautiful, and Kes could feel Mae's love radiating out through her eyes. Kes couldn't help but smile, glowing in the light of Mae's gaze. She admired Mae's sincerity and joy, her strength, and heart. She remembered what it felt like waking up with Mae's arms wrapped around her. It was glorious, and without reservation, she felt the depths of the love she had for the woman before her. For a moment, she let herself think *What would it be like to wake up every day wrapped up with this amazing woman? Heavenly,* she decided.

Trudy observed her friend from outside the lover's gaze Kes shared with Mae. She noticed just how at peace Kes seemed and how open as well. Kes was there, fully with Mae. Trudy saw how Kes treated Mae, how she spoke about her, the way she looked at Mae with love in her eyes. Trudy was touched. In all the years she'd known and worked with Kes, she'd never seen her fully let down her guard. There had always been remnants of her protective armor lurking in her demeanor, keeping her from letting anyone too close. But not now. She was beautifully exposed and present. The sight brought tears to Trudy's eyes, and she wiped them away before Kes noticed.

Frankie was the one to break the moment. "Well, I ought to hit the trail if I have any hope of topping out before dinner," she said, catching Trudy's eyes.

"You'll keep in touch?" Trudy asked, standing to embrace Frankie.

"I will, I promise."

"Wait, what is today?" Mae said. With everything that had happened over her trip, it wasn't surprising she had lost track of the days. Deep in the canyon, everything was measured by the rising and setting of the sun. Individual days of the week blurred together.

"It's Monday," Frankie responded.

"Shoot, my flight is tonight," Mae laughed. She would need to get going if she was going to cover the almost ten miles of trail that lay between her and her rental car, drive the 90 minutes down to Flagstaff, and catch her red-eye flight. Strategically, she sorted through everything that needed to happen. She didn't feel panicked or fearful as she once would have when plans changed last minute. She felt focused and capable, determined to solve the problem at hand. Still, there was a lot to do, and she stood frozen in place as she evaluated what to tackle first.

Kes placed her hand on Mae's arm, interrupting Mae's thoughts. "How about we call and change your flight?" Kes asked.

"I'm going to insist you spend another night down here before you hike out, anyway," Trudy piped up. "You need a good night's sleep and more food before you trudge out of here. You can stay in Kes's room with her. I'll make sure you have a full breakfast, and then we'll get you out of here."

"I was able to grab your backpack before the waters rose," Frankie said, retrieving a pack from a corner of the room, just out of sight. "I think everything is in here, but you can borrow some of my extra clothes if you need anything."

Mae looked around the room at the amazing friends surrounding her. In her adult life, she'd only ever felt this level of kinship and love with Cabot and Marie. But here she was, in the depths of a huge crevasse surrounded by people who cared for her and genuinely wanted to support her. She was grateful for each one of these incredible human beings.

"You don't have to twist my arm to stay another night," Mae said, leaning into Kes's open arms. Kes beamed at her and placed a tender kiss on her cheek. Being wrapped up in Kes's arms, Mae felt at home.

"Just promise me you two won't go wandering up any side canyons in the next twenty-four hours? After that, you're someone else's problem," Trudy said, with mock reproach on her face.

The sound of Kes's hearty laugh vibrating in response brought a smile to Trudy's face. She loved seeing her friend in love.

Chapter 28

"Where are you? Wait, don't tell me; some hot ranger picked you up, you're having wild, dirty sex, and you missed your flight," Cabot said upon hearing Mae's voice on the phone.

"Well, yeah, kinda," Mae responded, a smile in her voice.

"Wait, what?! Mae Ridley Mack, you tell me everything right this instant!" Cabot's voice echoed through the phone, causing laughter to erupt from Mae.

"Kes is here," Mae said.

"Kes? As in Dreamy McDreamster Kes? As in THE Kes? That Kes?" Cabot asked.

"That's the one," Mae said, a goofy smile plastered on her face.

"What is she doing there? Did you talk to her? What's happening? Woman, give me the details!" Cabot said, exasperated.

"I promise to fill you in fully when I'm back from the canyon," Mae said

"Wait, is that a euphemism? Mae, you naughty, naughty

girl!" Cabot said.

Mae couldn't help but laugh. Cabot's excitement only reflected the joy bubbling inside her. She loved her friend and loved how supportive he was. "You dirty man. I'm still at Phantom Ranch. It's a long story, which I promise to tell you in excruciating detail. The short version: Kes is a park ranger. There was a flash flood. Kes almost had hypothermia, but I saved her. We're both safe now. Oh, and also, we kissed. Like a lot," Mae said, her smile deep and touching her heart.

"Ahhhhh! Mae!" Cabot screamed into the phone. Mae could hear a loud crashing noise and picture Cabot jumping around the room. "What does this mean? Are you two a couple now? Are you together? Do you love her? Does she love you?" Cabot asked in quick succession.

Mae paused for a moment and pondered those questions. She wasn't sure what it meant and if they were together, or where it would go after tomorrow. But those questions didn't cause any anxiety or worry. Something deep within trusted this moment and made her believe that no matter what came after tomorrow, she would be happy and strong. But one answer to Cabot's questions rang loud and clear in her heart, *Yes, I love Kes.*

Mae finally got Cabot off the phone by claiming she ought to leave the line clear in case there was an emergency. She promised to call him as soon as she was safely out of the canyon and returned to the land of cell service. Replacing the phone in its cradle, she looked across Kes's desk at the collage of photos Kes had taped to the walls. There was one of Kes and Sara, sitting at a point overlooking the canyon, their arms around each other, laughing. There was a black and white photo of a woman who looked exactly like Kes, though with significantly longer hair. There was a twinkle in her eyes as if the photographer had caught her just before she started laughing. The woman's ranger uniform looked different too. Mae surmised it was likely Kes's grandmother. There were a few others of people she assumed were friends or family. Mae smiled seeing all of the people Kes loved in plain view of where she worked every day. It touched her heart that Kes kept this collection nearby. Moving her fingers over the photos, she looked at each face, at each person Kes cared about.

As she moved, one photo came loose and tumbled to the ground. Bending to pick it up, Mae noticed a small note on the back. It read "K, Love wholeheartedly. Like this. - Sar." Flipping the picture over, Mae felt her heart catch in her throat.

Kes was the main focus of the photo, her profile highlighted by the setting sun on a very familiar beach. Mae recognized Kes's outfit from Sara's wedding. Kes seemed unaware her photo was being taken. Without knowing the context, it would be clear to anyone looking at the photo the depth of love Kes had for the person she's looking at. It was unmistakable and radiated off the paper. The smile the photographer had captured was genuine and secret, as if Kes was in a private moment, oblivious to how evident her feelings were to anyone who saw her. The look in Kes's eyes alone would be enough to make any person believe in love. But that wasn't the reason why Mae's eyes filled with tears and her heart pounded.

The woman of Kes's affection was standing only a few feet away, lost in laughter with someone not captured in the frame. Mae recognized the woman in an instant. It was the same one that looked back at her in the mirror every morning.

Mae was sure Sara had written the note on the back to Kes, but what did it mean? Did Kes love Mae, even then, when they'd first met?

Mae wasn't sure, though she felt the beginnings of hope building in her chest. Replacing the photo, Mae made her way to Kes's bedroom, suddenly aching to be by Kes's side. She longed to kiss Kes tenderly. Quietly, she opened the door to find Kes sprawled out on the bed as if she had fallen asleep in the middle of creating a snow angel. For a moment, Mae stood in the doorway and watched. Kes's breaths were regular and even, and a soft smile graced her beautiful face. Not wanting to disturb her, but wanting to be close, Mae quietly removed her shoes and climbed in next to Kes, laying her head on Kes's shoulder and draping an arm across Kes's chest. Taking a deep breath in, Mae closed her eyes and enjoyed the pleasant exhaustion that took over her body.

Chapter 29

Kes woke up, feeling Mae's body against hers. She turned her head slightly and placed a light kiss on Mae's forehead. She loved how right this felt, having the woman she loved lying in her arms. Usually, at the point in any relationship where she started to develop feelings, an overwhelming sense of panic would override any affection she might have, and she'd run for the hills, or the canyon to be more accurate. There she'd hide until the person she had been seeing got bored and left. Was it the most mature way to handle emotions? No, absolutely not, as Sara was often quick to point out. But she always felt something was off. To most of the women she dated, she was whatever they wanted her to be: a hot park ranger, or very butch, or the outdoorsy type. She felt like with everyone else she was only ever a simplified, characterized version of her true self. No one really saw the whole picture; the person who carved because she loved feeling wood metamorphize under her fingers, the person who loved making up new stories about the stars, because it was how her grandmother calmed her after she had nightmares. She was the person who could sit still for hours watching for birds but also who ran regularly to expend built-up energy. She was more than her uniform and more than any one moment or impression.

But with Mae, she felt wholly seen. Those damn piercing eyes saw past her armor and genuinely welcomed every diverse facet of Kes's heart. Mae never demanded or required anything from Kes and always accepted her just as she was. Kes never felt she had to be any less or more than her true self. Mae had seen her in the moments when she could no longer be strong and had cared for her in the hardest times.

There was no panic, no desire to run, no fear of being hurt. There was no anticipation of pain, no anxiety building, no armor standing in the wings ready to hide her again. In this moment, she felt nothing but love. Mae was here… in her arms and her heart.

Looking down at Mae's face, Kes saw two deviously twinkling eyes looking up at her.

"Hey, sleepyhead," Kes said, placing another gentle kiss on Mae's forehead.

"Hi," Mae said with a sleepy smile. She craned her neck up to place a kiss on Kes's lips. It was sweet, gentle, innocent—at least to start. Kes ran her hand down the side of Mae's face, feeling her warm skin and pulling her face closer for another kiss. Mae responded by pressing herself up to get closer to Kes. It didn't take long for the kiss to deepen, their tongues finding each other, playing, swirling, pressing, communicating their needs. Mae pushed herself up higher, swinging one leg over Kes's body until she found herself straddling Kes's waist. For a moment, they broke their kiss, and Kes held Mae's face, just taking in the beautiful woman on top of her.

"I want you," Mae said, taking the words right out of Kes's mind. Kes wasn't sure her heart could handle the anticipation building between her legs, but she was excited to find out.

Mae leaned forward and kissed Kes, trying desperately to communicate the depth of her desire without words. Kes responded in kind, making Mae's head spin. Mae felt Kes's hands at the hem of her shirt, slowly raising it to expose more of her skin. Mae sat up planning to quickly remove the offending garment but was stopped. Kes rose to meet her and placed a loving kiss on her lips and then her neck. Slowly, Kes slipped her hands under Mae's shirt and gently traced her fingers up Mae's sides. Mae moaned at the feeling of Kes's light touch and pulled Kes's head back to kiss her again, silently begging her to hurry up and remove the shirt. With a devilish grin, Kes lifted the shirt and deftly unhooked Mae's bra. Completely topless, Mae watched Kes's eyes survey her body. Any fear or self-consciousness she might have felt was quickly wiped away the moment Kes looked up with a look of pure desire filling her eyes.

With a quick soft kiss, Mae returned the favor, releasing Kes from her top. Mae pulled Kes close and sighed deeply, feeling Kes's nakedness pressed against hers. She audibly sighed at the sensation. Kes buried her face in the crook of Mae's neck and traced her fingers down Mae's back. Pulling her face back, Kes started a trail of kisses down Mae's exposed torso, stopping along the way at every spot that elicited a response.

Mae delighted in the sensation of Kes's warm lips and tongue on her collarbone. She felt the anticipation build in her chest as Kes moved closer and closer to her very sensitive nipples. From her perch, Mae admired Kes's sweet attention to her body. Every nerve ending was alive, and even the lightest touch sent a thrill aimed directly at her core, causing her head to spin. Mae closed her eyes and took a deep breath to steady herself. But with the visual cues blacked out, the experience was all the more exhilarating. Arching her back, she silently encouraged Kes to continue exploring her body, her nipples hard in aching anticipation. When the sudden sensation of Kes's warm mouth on her nipple hit, she felt the pulsing in between her legs intensify to near breaking.

She needed more, wanted more, desperately craved more. Her eyes fiery with desire, Mae intertwined her fingers in Kes's hair, pulling slightly to release her nipple from the delicious tortures of Kes's tongue. As soon as Kes's still agape mouth was free, Mae leaned in and drew a deep moan from Kes's chest as she ran her tongue over Kes's bottom lip and pulled it in between her teeth. Having the upper hand, and a very willing partner, Mae pushed Kes down onto the bed and quickly followed. Wanting to lead, Mae lifted Kes's arms above her head and, with a quick press, communicated she wanted Kes to keep her arms there.

Shifting her weight, Mae slipped her knee in between Kes's legs and delighted in the moan the new pressure elicited. With her tongue she drew a path down Kes's body, paying special attention to every spot that made Kes writhe with pleasure. Mae enjoyed the way Kes's hips bucked slightly when she sucked Kes's nipple between her lips and flicked it lightly with her tongue. She smiled against Kes's skin, adoring every part of Kes's exposed torso. Moving lower still, Mae admired Kes's hip bones, peeking out above the line of her shorts. Gently, she pulled slightly at the fabric to expose a little more before she drew the flat of her tongue against the sensitive skin stretched tight against the elegant ridge. Kes's back arched as she drew a ragged breath in. Mae loved this feeling; bringing pleasure, communicating her deepest desires. She looked up at Kes's beautiful face, a question evident on her face with one hand on the button. Kes nodded with a sweet smile, and, given permission, Mae released Kes from all remaining garments. Unceremoniously, she slipped out of her own shorts, wanting there to be nothing standing between them. With an arm tucked behind her head, Kes grinned at Mae in her adorable and sexy way that drove Mae wild. Mae longed to capture those delectable lips with her own and quickly crossed the distance to do just that.

Kes reached up to run her hand through Mae's hair and draw her in closer. As she did, she slipped her knee up between Mae's legs, her need becoming amplified by the sensation of wetness that welcomed her. Kes pressed her hips up and, in a single fluid motion, flipped Mae onto her back and followed right behind. The suddenness of the role reversal caused a laugh to bubble up in Mae's throat, the sound of which reminded Kes of a beautiful song written for her heart. She smiled down at the stunning woman beneath her. She fought competing desires within. Kes ached to take her time and draw out Mae's desire, slowly bringing her closer and closer to the edge. Equally, she didn't want to hold back but instead wanted to ravage Mae's body, the friction building to absolute ecstasy.

Running her thumb along Mae's lower lip, she quickly followed it with her mouth, tracing the same path with her tongue. She wanted to stay in this moment when the world didn't exist outside of her bed, when everything she wanted in the world was literally within her arms. She wanted to show Mae the depth of her desire, put action to the feelings she ached to express. As she kissed Mae, she lightly pressed her leg into the wetness. Mae responded by grinding harder into Kes's thigh. With her uninjured hand, Kes traced Mae's curves, making her way down to the places she ached to experience. Mae's grinding intensified with every inch she moved closer. When Kes reached Mae's hip, she stopped and pulled back from her kiss. As much as she longed to continue, she wanted more to know she wasn't alone in that desire first. Mae's eyes were filled with lust as she opened her heavy eyelids to meet Kes's gaze. "May I?" Kes asked simply, her voice not much more than a whisper.

"God yes, please fuck me," Mae moaned in a voice dripping with want. It sent a shiver up Kes's spine, her own desire ignited all the more with those words.

Kes moved her hand down between their bodies, moaning slightly at the contact with Mae's desire. She lightly traced a line around and then between Mae's folds. The reaction from Mae was intoxicating; she pushed down against Kes's hand, increasing contact. Without hesitation, Kes slipped two fingers in and delighted as Mae arched and threw her head back. Capturing Mae's lips between her own,

Kes curled her fingers, placing light pressure on the bumpy, swollen section of the front wall. Immediately, Mae tightened, causing Kes to smile devilishly. Gently, she moved the tips of her fingers back and forth over this sensitive spot, increasing pressure as she went. Mae, lost in the all-encompassing swell of pleasure, ground harder into the palm of Kes's hand. Taking it as a request for more, Kes moved her thumb to apply light pressure on Mae's clit. The response from Mae was immediate, as a moan escaped the depths of her delight and sang to Kes's ears. Kes captured Mae's lips, feeling the thrilling vibrations radiate through her. As Mae writhed underneath her, Kes struggled to maintain contact, but the movement was erotic and drove Kes's body closer to climax. She ached to be touched by Mae.

As if she could read Kes's mind, Mae slipped her hand between their bodies and wickedly slid in exactly where Kes most longed to feel her. For a moment, Kes lost the world as Mae deftly entered her and simultaneously pressed her palm against the swollen nub protruding out of Kes's upper lips. Instinctively, Kes pressed harder inside Mae and immediately felt the same pressure applied deep within. Mae rubbed the heel of her palm against Kes's clit, and as Kes tightened, she mirrored the movement, eliciting a delicious, throaty, moan. Together they moved as one, delighting in the sensations coursing through their bodies with every firm pump of their joined hearts. Kes opened her eyes to find Mae's beautiful eyes staring back at her. Tenderly, she leaned down to kiss Mae and fully connect their bodies. As they kissed, Kes increased the pressure and speed of her fingers gliding in and out of Mae. Mae matched her pace, their breathing becoming more and more labored. Kes tightened around Mae's fingers, her climax quickly approaching. Mae's body was alive below her, desperately close. Pressing hard against Mae's G-spot, Kes gasped on the brink of ecstasy. "I'm going to come," Kes heard Mae moan beneath her, her raspy voice sending an electric thrill directly to her core.

"Please."

Kes wasn't sure if she or Mae had spoken that word, but it was all the permission either of them needed. With a flood of pleasure filling every fiber of her being, she felt the crash hit, the euphoric high, the electricity sparking behind her closed eyes, her pleasure screaming through her core, stretching every muscle in her body to hold on as the sensation blinded her. The waves pulsed through her, pleasure causing convulsions around Mae's fingers, as she opened her eyes. Mae's face was still scrunched up in rapture, her climax still firing every neuron in her brain. She was stunning, beautiful, real, vulnerable, and beyond compare, Kes thought. Her lips were parted gasping for air, her nipples were hard, her stomach tense, her legs squeezing Kes's hand in a vise grip. Kes admired Mae. Gently she kissed Mae's neck and felt the pulse there pounding strongly against her lips. Slowly, Mae's body relaxed, little by little, moving down her body in streams. First, her face relaxed, then her arms and torso, and finally her legs. Inside, she still felt tense, her walls sucking in Kes's fingers, threatening not to let them go. Kes had no complaints and wouldn't mind remaining a willing prisoner to their delights.

Mae's breathing slowed, gradually returning to normal. As she opened her eyes, Kes noted tears clinging to the corners, but from the look on Mae's face, she did not assume they were the result of sadness. Gently, Kes wiped away Mae's tears, following each swipe of her thumb with the lightest of kisses. She adored this woman and ached to express the depths of her affection. With Mae's eyes locked on her own, she felt cherished. She had found her place and wanted nothing more than to stay right in this moment. She loved Mae's laughter, her heart, her smile, her kindness, her gumption, her pleasure, her mind, her adventurous spirit, her vulnerability, her scars. She felt her heart open to all that lay, quite literally, before her, and deep within, words bubbled up, escaping before she could attempt to stop them.

"I love you, Mae," Kes said, her voice raw and rumbling.

Shock spread through Kes's entire body, and her jaw dropped as she rambled on, panic and nervous energy hitting full tilt. "I'm sorry. I shouldn't have said that. I didn't mean to. I mean, I do love you, but I didn't mean to tell you yet. And it's not just sex brain. I mean I love you even when you've not just fucked me senseless. Wow, that was crass. That came out wrong. I mean…"

Kes's lips were silenced by Mae's, and she felt the breath drawn from her lungs. Mae kissed her passionately, quieting the worry in her brain, allowing her to release the building panic. Pulling back, Mae cupped Kes's face in her hand and placed a gentle kiss on her forehead before looking deep into Kes's eyes. "I love you too, Kes. I always have."

The smile that spread across Kes's face was strong enough to light the darkest night with the power of a billion brilliant stars. She was absolutely radiant, the joy inside filling every inch of her body. She loved Mae, with all of her heart, and Mae returned that love.

Kes kissed Mae, this time slowly lingering, expressing her heart's truest vows. With a sigh, she removed her fingers and repositioned herself so that her head lay on Mae's shoulder, the bridge of her nose nestled up against the side of Mae's neck. Lazily, Mae stroked Kes's hair and placed a kiss on Kes's forehead. Physically and emotionally drained, in the best sense, Kes closed her eyes and surrendered to her exhaustion in the arms of her love.

Chapter 30

Groggily, Mae stirred. She begrudgingly opened her eyes and for a moment saw nothing but darkness. Safely somewhere in the limbo between night and day, she closed her eyes again. She wasn't certain if she'd been asleep for a few moments, a few hours, or a few days. Soreness clung to every muscle as she stretched and yawned. Her calves screamed as she pointed her toes and willed her body awake. Her shoulders groaned at every movement. The ache in her abs convinced her she probably had a six-pack, considering how tight they were. Her glutes felt as if she'd attempted to complete the entire "Buns o' Steel," as Cabot called it, box set in a single day. She'd slept peacefully and deeply, only waking once when Kes's hand teased her nipple awake, electrifying her core and sending the two of them wrestling in want yet again. She didn't remember a single dream. But she remembered every intoxicating moment in Kes's embrace and every reason why she might be sore. Kes's eyes, as she begged for release, her whole body clenching as she came hard against Mae's hand, the shape of her mouth as she whispered, "I love you." All of it was etched in Mae's mind as clearly as if she were right there.

Mae rolled onto her side, feeling new aches along the way. She blindly reached for Kes's sleeping form, longing to pull her close and bury her face in Kes's neck. Careful not to wake Kes, Mae reached gently at first, pawing the bed for her love. When her hands made no contact, she opened her eyes and found the spot next to her in the bed empty and cold.

Mae sat up, reached for the light, and looked around the room. Kes was nowhere to be found. Just as Mae reached to check the clock, the door opened quietly and Kes's sweet face peeked through. Her eyes were alit with cute impishness.

Kes entered the room, never taking her eyes off Mae, her smile growing ever bigger with every step. It wasn't until she was right next to the bed that Mae noticed Kes's hands were full, carrying two mugs, each balancing a napkin-covered plate on top. Mae relieved Kes of the plates and set them on the table next to the bed. Kes handed Mae a fresh cup of coffee, the scent wiping away the last of the sleep webs entangling Mae's mind. Removing the napkins, Kes revealed two fresh cinnamon rolls. As if on cue, Mae's stomach growled, the night's acrobatics catching up with her need for sustenance.

"Good morning to you too," Kes giggled, looking at Mae's noisy abdomen. "Eat up. You'll need your energy to hike out."

Mae took one of the plates and, with her mouth salivating, bit into the still-hot cinnamon roll. Mae smiled as sadness lingered in the back of her mind. Mae wasn't ready to go. She didn't want to leave. She'd fallen in love, and it wasn't just with the sexy woman who delivered hot and fresh postcoital cinnamon rolls. Mae had fallen in love with the canyon, with the freedom in adventure, and with the wildness of the wilderness. Most importantly, she had fallen in love with herself. She felt more alive and more in tune with the unfiltered and uninhibited version of her identity. She was inspired by the world around her again, brave in the face of danger, and awake to the life she wanted. She'd proven to herself that she was more than the pain of her past, more than the judgments of the narcissists she'd been drained by, and more than any fears or anxieties that had forced her to remain small. She wanted to explore the re-awakened parts of her person and pursue some of her long-time dreams that she'd like to turn into realities.

One of those dreams-turned-realities included Kes. Although they hadn't talked about it, Mae felt the realness of their budding relationship. This was much more than a fling or a one-night stand. She wasn't sure what Kes was looking for, but Mae had faith that no matter what happened between them, it would be alright. If she had learned anything over the past week, it was that sometimes, you had to let go and just trust.

Mae felt Kes's eyes on her, and she turned to meet her love's gaze. Without a word, Kes sat down on the bed and leaned over to place a sweet, frosting-laced kiss on her lips. Mae smiled into the kiss, her heart light in her chest. Kes pulled back and stroked Mae's face. "Well, we'd better get dressed and packed up if we're going to make it out of here before it's too hot," Kes said, rising to her feet.

Mae moved to get out of bed and find some clothing. She was halfway through packing her bag when Kes's words finally hit. "We?" she turned to Kes with a question on her face.

Kes beamed at her, the impish grin returning to her sparkling eyes. "Well, it's my hike-out day, too. I thought maybe I could keep you company and make sure you get out of the canyon without any further injury," Kes said, joy lilting in her voice, hopefulness lingering on every word.

The broad smile that spanned Mae's face caused Kes to giggle. Quickly, Mae crossed the space between them and wrapped her arms around Kes's waist, pulling her close. "I think it's the other way around, dear ranger. I'm the one who needs to keep an eye on you," Mae said with a smile. "I'll keep you safe if you keep me safe," Kes said with a smile as she pulled Mae into a hug and buried her face in Mae's neck. "It's a deal."

Although it had been hours since they left the ranger station, time flew by. As they hiked up the Bright Angel Trail, Kes pointed out different rock features and fauna along the way, telling tales about each. She told Mae about the time a boy at school called her "a little schist" and how she went running home to her grandmother in tears, certain it was a swear word rather than a rock. That made Mae laugh to the point of tears, and Kes wiped them away with a light kiss.

There was the time in high school when she had a crush on a seasonal biologist and spent every free moment studying the names of the plants of the canyon, hoping to impress the young woman, to no avail.

For the first part of their hike, Mae and Kes were mostly alone on the trail. Only a very small percentage of the visitors who came to the park every year ever hiked into the canyon, and those who did tended to stay on the upper mile-and-a-half section of the trail. The closer Mae and Kes got to the rim of the canyon, the more visitors choked the trail. Kes's uniform made her easy to identify, and they had to stop often so Kes could perform her duties. She answered questions, posed for several photos, and moved people safely off to the side of the trail when the mule train came plodding by. She was at ease and handled every single question that came her way with ease. Everyone they met seemed genuinely excited to be hiking and experiencing the majesty of the canyon, despite the heat. Mae giggled hearing all of Kes's silly and incredibly quick responses whenever visitors asked about the bandage on her hand. They varied from "I zip-lined down to Phantom and all I got was this nasty rope burn," to "I tried to high-five a yucca," to Mae's personal favorite "Don't feed the condors, they bite." Mae loved seeing Kes in her element. She was brilliant, beautiful, and wonderfully herself.

Mae's legs burned and her breathing became more labored with every step. Kes found a shady spot on the corner of a switchback in the trail and stepped into it. Mae willingly joined and felt immediately cooler. Kes waited until her breathing slowed enough to take a long drink of water.

"The elevation gets me every time. We're not far from the top now, so you've climbed nearly a mile in elevation over the last nine miles of trail." Mae's breathing slowly came back to normal as she looked out over the view. From here, you couldn't even see the innermost section of the canyon. It was completely hidden deep within.

Mae took in the view and was astounded by the sense of accomplishment she felt. She was fortified by her hike, stronger in body but even more so in mind. She believed that no matter what came her way or what she chose to pursue, she would be okay. She was no longer stuck in the small and cheap imitation of herself, but instead, she fully embodied her strength and power.

"Do you have plans tonight?" Mae heard Kes ask. "I was wondering if you might want to have dinner with me."

"I would love to," Mae said. She smiled brightly and leaned in to kiss Kes quickly while they weren't surrounded by visitors. "If it isn't too forward to ask, may I stay with you tonight? I just realized I don't have a hotel reservation and I'm guessing all of the hotels are fully booked."

Mae was rewarded with a brilliant smile that spread across Kes's face in a millisecond. "Absolutely. Maybe you'd like to stay for more than just tonight?"

"What did you have in mind?" Mae asked, with a twinkle in her eyes.

Epilogue

Water lapped at her toes as she sunk a little deeper into the sand with every wave. The rhythmic crashing spoke to her soul like a familiar meditation. The first fire-flies of the evening blinked to life, dancing into view. She took a deep breath in, filling her lungs with the salty air. A peaceful smile played on her lips as she felt two arms wrap around her waist and pull her close. A warm face snuggled at the back of her neck, covering her exposed neck in a few tender kisses.

Kes sighed and relaxed into Mae's embrace. She adored this feeling; being wrapped up in the arms of the woman she loved. Over the last month and a half, every night she wasn't on duty deep in the canyon, Kes had fallen asleep in Mae's arms and woke the next morning surprised and grateful to love and be loved by this incredible woman.

On her "hike-in" days, Mae often joined Kes on the trail until they reached the halfway point. Then after a long kiss (sometimes Kes pulled Mae around to a hidden make-out corner just off the trail), they parted ways. Kes would continue on her hike. Mae would find a place to sit and sketch in the shade while she waited out the heat of the day before she started the long hike back to the top. With each trip into the canyon, Mae grew stronger, more confident, and bolder.

Mae filled her days with time in nature, and she always had her sketch pad with her. She cataloged all of the incredible sights she saw and adventures she had in colored pencil and lead. She'd leave Kes's home before sunrise and often not return until sunset. She documented the canyon in words as well as images, describing the trails, the changing character of the canyon over the course of a day, and the experience of being alone in the vastness.

One evening, a week ago, Mae asked Kes, "What if this was every day?"

"What do you mean, my love?" Kes asked.

"What if I stayed? Other than a few belongings and seeing Cabot, I don't really have a reason to go back to Maine. I've submitted a few articles to the local newspaper and they liked them. They've offered me a part-time position. It's not much, but between that and the canyon sketches I've been selling through the gift shop, I can get by," Mae said, excitedly. "If it's too much or you want your own space, I can find a place to rent, and we can take this slow."

Kes laughed heartily as tears sprang to her eyes. "I think we're past the point of taking it slowly. We've pretty much been living together since our first official date." Kes's laugh tickled Mae to her core, and Mae leaned in and kissed Kes, her excitement renewed. "My dearest love, this is your home, too. Please stay."

Flying to Maine, Mae was filled with nerves. As ready

as she was to officially start her life out West, she was unsure what coming back to her hometown would feel like. As
they walked through security, hand in hand, Kes nudged
Mae and looked off into the airport with a nod, silently
guiding Mae to look up. There stood the larger-than-life
Cabot, holding a huge sign that read, "I LOVE YOU, MAE."
Next to him stood a short, warm lady holding a second sign
saying "AND YOU, TOO, KES." Within seconds, Cabot had
spanned the distance between them and wrapped both Mae
and Kes up in a warm hug. Mae's heart burst open, flooded with gratitude and surrounded by love. When Cabot released them, the smile on his face said all the words that
were running through Mae's heart. Pulling Mae into another hug, Kes was left admiring the friendship between the
pair. Feeling a hand on her arm, she turned to find Rose
with tears in her eyes. Rose opened her arms wide and
pulled Kes into a genuine and loving hug, squeezing her
tight. "I'm so glad she found you," Rose whispered, giving
her another squeeze. Kes smiled, thinking exactly the same
thing. She looked over at Mae and again felt the flood of
joy wash over her entire being. For not the first time since
they'd met, Kes was found.

Mae nibbled on Kes's earlobe, stirring her from her
memories. She felt Mae smile into her neck. "This is where
we first met," Kes said, looking out over Sand Beach. She
felt Mae pull her a little closer. "It was. It's where I first start-

ed to fall in love with you," Mae said, honestly. She hadn't been ready to admit it at the time, but she knew in those first moments what she felt for Kes, truly. Kes smiled, her feelings very much the same.

"Will you miss it?" Kes asked, for the first time worried Mae might not want to leave. She felt Mae turn her slightly until they faced each other. "I'll miss the mountains and the fresh salt air. I'll miss picking fresh blueberries along the trail. I'll miss seeing Cabot every day," Mae answered honestly. "I will miss it but I am excited for our new adventure. I can miss it here without longing to be here," Mae continued, placing a light kiss on Kes's lips.

"We can always come for a visit," Kes pointed out.

Mae smiled. "I was hoping you'd say that. I was thinking this might be a nice place to make a promise to you," Mae said, unable to hide her impish grin.

"Oh? What did you have in mind?" Kes asked, her heart pounding in her chest.

"Forever?" Mae asked.

Kes smiled widely and replied, "Forever would be nice."

Acknowledgments

This was a long process and I am ever so grateful for the love, encouragement, and support I received from friends and family throughout.

Karen, thank you for your incredible support over the years and encouraging me when I felt overwhelmed by the process (and by life). You were my first beta reader and you helped me see that writing a novel was actually a possibility.

Tori, I don't have words to describe what your friendship has meant to me. Thank you for always being down for movie nights, Kava, candy runs, sleepovers, endless memes, and deep conversations.

Sara, thank you for consistently being the sass and sunshine I need in my life. You help push me past my grief, help me figure out if people are flirting with me (since I never know), and always find a way to make me laugh.

Cate, thanks for being my twinsin (not that either of us had a choice in that), for reviewing this book when it was still quite rough, and for pointing out the parts that weren't quite fully fleshed out so I could see past the story in my head to what had or had not translated to the page.

Rachel, I'm ever so glad our paths crossed and we became friends, bonding over BOTW, and taking some pretty epic road trips together. Thank you for your detailed edits, helping with my comma usage (I like commas and I cannot lie), and for fixing my unintentional anagram.

To all of you, Kes and Mae's story never would have made it to the page without all of your help. I will be forever grateful for each of you for helping me make my dream a reality.

About the Author

Kris Rugg (they / them) is a contemporary queer romance novelist. Kris has lived and worked in national parks across the country for more than a decade. They've rafted the lower 200 miles of the Colorado River through the Grand Canyon, hiked every trail in Acadia, biked across Prince Edward Island, eaten glacial ice  while sitting in a kayak in Kenai Fjords, helped release baby sea turtles at Cape Hatteras, and one night escaped the clutches of a rattlesnake by leaping onto a picnic table in Joshua Tree. It turned out to be a mouse running through bladder sage, but let's just pretend their lightning-quick reaction was warranted. More often than not

Kris is somewhere in nature with a love story brewing in their mind.

Kris is queer, deaf, non-binary, and neurodiverse. They are an advocate for full access to wild spaces for all people. Kris hopes their books help accurately represent the diversity of people who enjoy outdoor adventures and who find romance along the way.

"In a Flash" is Kris's debut novel. Their writing was also featured in "On Foot: Grand Canyon Backpacking Stories." To learn more, visit: www.krisrugg.com

www.ingramcontent.com/pod-product-compliance
Lightning Source LLC
Chambersburg PA
CBHW020435030726
47495CB00006B/1809